CHARLIE NEXT DOOR

Debashish Irengbam is a Mumbai-based scriptwriter by profession – and now a novelist as well. He has written episodes for TV crime thrillers and youth-based shows like *Dil Dosti Dance*, *Adaalat*, *Aahat*, *Webbed* and *Gumrah*.

Charlie Next Door is his second novel with HarperCollins *Publishers* India, following *Me, Mia, Multiple*, which was published in 2015.

You can find out more about him on
www.debashishirengbam.com

CHARLIE NEXT DOOR

DEBASHISH IRENGBAM

HarperCollins *Publishers* India

First published in India by
HarperCollins Publishers in 2017
A-75, Sector 57, Noida, Uttar Pradesh 201301, India
www.harpercollins.co.in

2 4 6 8 10 9 7 5 3 1

P-ISBN: 978-93-5277-443-2
E-ISBN: 978-93-5277-444-9

Typeset in 11/14.5 Minion Pro by
R. Ajith Kumar

Printed and bound at
Thomson Press (India) Ltd.

For my family.
For my friends.
For S.

1

The details flitted past her gaze in a stream of inviting stats.

Age: 27

Height: 179 cm

Build: Athletic

Body hair: Goatee/ Mostly smooth

Size: L.

Rate: Rs 8,000 for—

A click and the next stud's profile popped up on screen. This one had a rather muscular torso and boasted a size XL. It had taken Anupama a while to figure out that these were not shirt measurements.

The man's face was hidden, as always. Renu had warned her it would be so. The escort – or 'adult friendship', as they preferred to term it – agency's thriving success amongst its niche clientele in the city was mostly due to its emphasis on discretion, both for its customers as well as its staff. The only way you could unlock the pictures and see the men's faces was by signing up for a permanent membership by paying and providing your personal details to the website. Not that she ever would. Heavens. God knows what a stupendous amount of time and courage it had taken her just to create a faceless, temporary profile and sign in – if only to see what all the hype was about.

She had intended to take a quick peek at the site and then delete her account immediately.

That was five months ago.

And as her profile counter so kindly informed her, she had made almost two hundred and fifty visits to the site so far. The guilt had stopped a long time ago, those little residual pricks of conscience vanishing every time she deleted her browser's history cache. She used her own laptop, but she preferred not to take any chances, especially with two teenage kids in the house who had grown old enough to accept their own sexuality, but not quite their mother's.

It wasn't wrong really – she would remind herself every now and then whenever the need arose. It was human to have instincts, just as long as she didn't act on them, unlike those women who had actually posted detailed reviews of their experiences with the various samples on display. She half-admired, half-baulked at the nonchalance with which they had put up profile pictures of themselves too, pictures in which they were smiling with smug satisfaction, just in case the message wasn't clear enough. Many of them appeared to be married, mothers even, like her. She shook her head in dismay.

This was why she loved moral pedestals. As long as you had someone below you, things seemed fine.

Besides, it was just harmless curiosity, an act that was barely even sexual, having become more like a casual part of her routine. Wake up, pack lunch boxes, bid children goodbye, shower, read newspaper, have tea, have breakfast, watch TV, soak dal, chop vegetables, log on, check out the physiques and stats on display, log off, clear history, make lunch, wait for kids to return … and so on and so forth. Just a sensible spender, window-shopping around the mall – glancing in, appreciating, and then exiting without any loss of dignity. And since when was mere appreciation a crime?

Her inbox beeped with a message. She muted it hurriedly, even though she was alone. Her heart skipped a beat every time she heard that ping, even though she knew what it would be. Another reminder mail from the site to upgrade her membership if she wanted to enjoy the unlimited and uncensored privileges available to paying customers. Check. Delete. Inbox: 0.

The nagging itch at the back of her neck returned, and as she scratched it, her eyes glimpsed the pallid greyness peeking in through her windows.

The drizzle outside had turned into a shower, heavy drops spattering ominously onto the gravel and dirt and plastic sheets and pigeons perched bravely atop streetlight poles. The world had turned ashen, with a distant boom of thunder for added effect. Anupama strolled over to the windows and inhaled that heady, lingering smell of freshly wet earth. It was interesting how predictable the monsoons could be, yet how they never failed to get an audience every single time. Something reassuring about that.

In a couple of minutes the fragrance was gone, and all that lingered was that delicious chill in the air which made you forget where you were and induced cravings for masala chai and cream biscuits. How long had it been since she had a cream biscuit?

A flutter of warning rose within her, but it was too late.

One year and nine months, she recalled, as her heart recoiled with that familiar, cruel pang.

Tea and cream biscuits at 5.30 p.m.

It was one of the few shared habits in her married life that had survived and cemented itself into a routine. The biscuits would always be arranged in a full circle, and the flavour would always be vanilla, because that's how Rajeev liked it. He could be pretty meticulous when it came to such details, and that was one of the things she had liked about him when they first met. It was also one of the first things she had realized she couldn't stand about him, but that was another story, for another time.

How casually she had taken that evening for granted, expecting it to go the way that all the previous evenings had gone ... She had never bought a single packet of cream biscuits after that.

A sinking heaviness crept upon Anupama; the kind that made her aware of her knees supporting her entire body. She closed the windows and turned around. Her laptop was glaring back at her, its obscene images of faceless, semi-naked men popping out of the screen. She strode over and shut down all the profiles one by one, before logging out and clearing her history. Her cheeks and ears had gone warm, as if she had a fever, and the back of her neck was itching worse than ever.

It was barely one in the afternoon, yet the room had already turned dark. In an hour or so, both Misha and Nimit would be home. But for now, she was alone, and she had a few minutes to spare before the kitchen summoned her, so she hurried to her bedroom. Time was of the essence.

Opening her cupboard, she fetched the dark brown bottle of cough syrup surreptitiously hidden between her clothes and opened it, filling the lid to the brim before swallowing it in one go. Two capfuls later, her breathing began to steady, and a warm, fuzzy feeling spread through her insides, calming her down. She considered having another capful, but that would be too risky, especially with the kids coming in soon. In a world where going to the local liquor store would have raised too many eyebrows and every clinical sedative required a prescription, little blessings like this OTC medication were what kept disturbed souls like her afloat. She thanked herself for having had this brainwave months ago – a secret shared only between her and her closet.

Enjoying the rising sense of numbness within her, Anupama sauntered over to the berber carpet in the centre of the living room and lay down on her side, curling up into a foetal ball, legs folded into her arms, knees pressed against her chest. She shut her eyes tight, and had just begun to enjoy the little tinning sound in the back of her ears when the abrupt, shrill ring of her mobile jarred her back to her senses. She picked it up without opening her eyes.

'Hello?'

'Hey,' chirped Renu. 'Got to go check on Kay's loo at six. He's freaking out over the tile shades. Again.'

'All right.'

'Everything okay?'

'I'm fine.'

'Where are you?'

'Home.'

'Living room?'

'Yes.'

'Floor or sofa?'

'Sofa.'

'Don't bullshit me.'

Anupama sighed. 'I'm just tired.'

'So get your ass up and make yourself a coffee like a normal person. Or better yet, meet me for lunch in twenty minutes. I know this—'

'I'm too tired to travel.'

'I'll come over.'

'I'm too tired to host.'

'You know you're going to kill yourself at this rate.'

'Don't worry. I'm too tired to die. I'll see you at six.'

She hung up and opened her eyes. The nether region of her sofa was gaping at her like a forbidden cave. Within, a single, solitary hair lay beside one of the sofa legs, amidst faint residues of dust – abandoned and forgotten. Was it Rajeev's? The thought made her uneasy. Could it be – after all this time – there was still a trace of him left behind? How ironic would that be? He was always petrified of losing his hair, and now his hair was all that was left of him. Was that poetic, or simply a bad punch line? Misha would know. She had a knack for these things.

She brought her attention back to the lifeless strand, which suddenly didn't seem so lifeless anymore.

How long did it take for hair to decompose? She would have to tell the maid to sweep it away in the evening. No more souvenirs. The memories were enough.

The tinning sound was back in her ears, and she was grateful for that. She closed her eyes again, welcoming the blackness.

———

Anupama woke up with a jolt and checked her watch. Her head was splitting. She had dozed off, and now it was only twenty minutes before for her kids returned from school. The dal hadn't even been boiled yet!

All philosophical musings of loneliness forgotten, she hurried to the kitchen and dumped the soaked pulses into the pressure-cooker. As soon as that was done, she set about chopping the onions and chillies. Her mother would have been appalled at the sheer girth of her onion pieces. *Annu, chop the onions, don't slaughter them* – she had chastised her every time her mincing skills fell below the mark. Anupama smiled joylessly at the memory and chopped the onions into even thicker pieces, enjoying the private pleasure of an unacknowledged defiance.

Three pressure-cooker whistles later, she retrieved the dough from her fridge and set about shaping them into balls. She had barely made two when her doorbell rang.

She checked the time. It was still too early for the children to be back.

The bell rang again.

Who could it be? The replacement gas cylinder had arrived a week ago, the cable and newspaper bills had been paid, no one had ordered anything online, the neighbours knew better than to disturb them during the afternoon, and she rarely got any visits anyway.

The pressure-cooker whistled again.

The bell rang a third time.

She wiped her hands in dismay and ran to the door. The bell rang a fourth miserable time before she unlocked the door and swung it open to see a stranger outside, drenched to the bone. A young man, probably in his mid-twenties. The wet locks of his hair were plastered all over his forehead like a careless painting, and when he swept them away, she saw a pair of greyish-green eyes that couldn't possibly be real. His face reminded her of those European models she had seen in passing on glossy magazine covers – triangular, lean and heavily dotted with stubble in all the right places.

Of course, all of these musings and reflections took place in her head within a fraction of an instant, by which time the stranger had cleared his throat and said, 'Hello, I am Charlie. I only just shifted next door. C-704.'

'704?' she asked, surprised. The apartment had been empty for almost two years now.

'Yep.'

'Didn't they tell you about the pipe leakage problem there?'

'Yeah, I Sellotaped it.'

She stared at him. 'You Sellotaped it?'

'Yeah, I just Sellotaped the shit out of it.'

She nearly asked him what he would do once the tape dampened out, or why he hadn't taken any of the other two empty flats on their floor, before realizing it was none of her business.

'This was the only flat available,' he said, almost as if reading her thoughts. 'The other two aren't for bachelors. Anyway, I was wondering if you had a spare umbrella,' he went on, 'because it's raining like crazy outside, and I still have a couple of boxes to carry in from the truck. There's this scary lady outside. Mrs Gobi-raita-something…'

'Mrs Govindikar. She's the society chairperson.'

'Yeah, so she's not letting the truck come in 'cause it's a society rule or something, 'cause children play inside the compound. And I was like, who's going to play in this weather? And she was like, rules are rules. So I was like—'

'Sorry, I don't have an umbrella right now,' Anupama cut in. 'My daughter's taken the spare one, and my son has the other.' Why did she have to mention her children to a complete stranger?

'Oh, okay…'

'I have some plastic bags that you could perhaps use.'

'That could work. But I would need really big ones.'

'I do have big ones.'

He burst into a loud guffaw, startling her.

'Sorry, very sorry, I have a sick sense of humour,' he said. 'I should go.'

'Do you want the bags or not?' she asked irritably, not quite getting what he was so apologetic about.

'Er, yes, please.'

Anupama fastened the door-chain in place before hurrying back to the kitchen. She pulled out the cardboard box containing the larger polythene bags, only to realize she didn't know how many he needed. She hadn't asked, and why couldn't the fool have told her? She huffily carried the whole box to the door and unchained it.

'I just need four,' said Charlie.

'Just take them,' she said, thrusting them into his arms. 'And return them when you're done.'

'Okay. Thank you ...' he leaned back, checking the name plate outside her door. 'Mrs Arora.'

'Bye-bye,' she said, closing the door.

She peered out the eyehole and waited until he was gone before softly knocking her forehead on the wood.

'*Bye-bye*?' What was she – six?

Her heart stopped. How many times had the pressure-cooker whistled so far? She bustled into the kitchen. Just as she was reaching for the stove, she noticed that the lights of the kitchen window opposite hers were on for the first time in years, giving her a clear view of the unfurnished space inside.

Charlie's kitchen window.

The thought that henceforth, they would both be visible to each other from their respective kitchens discomfited her for a moment, before the pressure-cooker's whistle tore through her eardrums. How many whistles had it blown by now? She cursed herself and turned off the gas hurriedly.

———

'What's wrong with the dal?' asked Nimit, as Anupama spooned the viscous yellow gel onto his plate.

'It's just a bit overcooked.'

'I can't even see the pulses. It's like soup.'

'There are worse things in life. How was school?'

Nimit shrugged. 'Teachers taught. We studied. Gaurav got

a nosebleed during chemistry practicals. Prashant joked it was AIDS and got sent to the principal.'

'I hope you're not hanging out with those boys.'

'I'm not.'

He was lying. His recent Facebook photos showed him at the school football ground with those two and a bunch of other ruffians – ties loosened, arms flung over each other's shoulders, sporting grins and gestures that belonged to baddies of a bygone era. Of course she knew who Gaurav and Prashant were, but experience had taught her that it was only by feigning ignorance that she could pry out the really juicy details from her kids. It was for this reason that she had never told him or Misha about how she was on both their Facebook friends' lists under fake aliases. The whole process had been unexpectedly simple too. With Renu's help, she had created two fictitious alumni profiles from both Nimit's school and Misha's college, put in a comic-book character as a profile picture, added a few details and interests, and sent out multiple friend requests to a horde of students from their institutes, just to avoid suspicion. And quite frankly, it was alarming how many of them had accepted her as a friend (her own kids included) without even verifying her identity.

'I'm serious, Nimit. This is a very crucial time of your life. You don't want to be making any wrong decisions now.'

Nimit rolled his eyes. 'Mamma, it's eleventh class. Half the guys don't even bother coming in anymore.'

'Well, my son isn't going to be in that half.'

'How come you only call me your son when you're warning me about something?'

His mobile beeped.

'Di's going to be late by another half hour,' he said, checking it.

'Why didn't she message me?'

'You don't have WhatsApp.'

'Where is she?'

'She didn't say.'

'Can you ask her?'

'Why?'

The doorbell rang.

'Just do it,' she instructed Nimit as she rose and went to the door.

It was Charlie, back with the box. He smiled cheerily as she opened the door, revealing a dimple on his left cheek that Anupama hadn't noticed before. He had changed into a fresh shirt too, the top two buttons of which were undone, revealing a few stray tendrils of chest hair which—

'Smells nice.'

Anupama snapped back to focus. 'Sorry?'

'Chana dal, right?'

'Yes,' she said, surprised.

'It's on your fingers.'

Anupama immediately lowered her right hand, embarrassed. 'Sorry, I—we were eating.'

'Not at all. I love chana dal, actually.'

'You can take this if you want,' called Nimit from behind. 'We will order some—'

'Nimit,' snapped Anupama, before turning back to Charlie.

'So, do you want me to bring this inside or—'

'No, that's okay. Just leave it here,' she said, moving aside to let him in.

Charlie shuffled in and set the box down beside the door. Anupama noticed that he had those fleshy veins popping out of his forearms, like a criss-crossing circuit of thick greenish wires just beneath the skin. How did men get those?

Behind her, Nimit's mobile beeped with a message.

'Di says she has left the country with her French boyfriend and two illegitimate children,' he announced, reading from his phone.

Mortified to the bone, Anupama glanced back at Charlie. 'Kids,' she said, with a weak smile.

He mirrored her grin. 'Sorry for disturbing your lunch. And thanks again,' he said. Anupama smiled in acknowledgment and shut the door with as much cordiality as she could muster. 'Bye-bye.' *Damn it!*

'Who was that?' asked Nimit.

'Charlie. Our new neighbour.'

'We have a neighbour named Charlie?'

'Something wrong with that?'

'He didn't look like a Charlie. And since when did you start saying "bye-bye"?'

———

After lunch, Anupama carried the box of plastic bags back to the kitchen and set it back in its original place. She was about to straighten up when her eyes glimpsed something gleaming inside, and when she gave it a closer look, a cold shiver ran down her spine.

It was a packet of cream biscuits.

Why?

Had he forgotten it? Or was it a gesture of gratitude? But why would he gift someone like her a packet of cream biscuits of all things? Was it a sign? Was the universe playing some kind of cruel joke on her?

She gingerly picked it up and turned it over in her hand, as if the answer lay in its packaging.

Chocolate. Not vanilla. Lots of people ate cream biscuits. It was just a silly coincidence and here she was making so much of it.

In a swift series of movements, she swung on her heel, pedalled open her dustbin and dumped the offending packet inside. On second thought, she decided to get the broom and sweep under the sofa too. No point waiting for the maid. For some reason, that damn strand of hair had really started to bother her.

2

Gone were the days when yellow was just yellow.

A discreet glance at her watch told her that they had been staring at those three sample tiles for almost fifteen minutes now. And the worst part was that they were all ... bloody ... *yellow*. Granted, there were miniscule shades of difference between them, but, come on, how much attention did one pay to these details while urinating? It was the futility of it all that got to her. Fifteen minutes of her day lost just because the prissy little client standing between her and Renu couldn't make up his mind about which shade of yellow would be the best choice for the rear wall of his bathroom.

She knew she should be grateful, in a way. Had it not been for this job, she would have spent most of her days curled up on the living room floor, drunk on cough syrup, brooding over memories that were too pointless to think about anymore. However, try as she might, she couldn't shake off the tiny suspicion that her part-time employment as a vaastu consultant at Renu's agency had little to do with her knowledge of vaastu and Feng Shui and more to do with an old college friend's sympathy, in spite of her fervent denials.

She didn't mind the salary of course, notwithstanding being on the payroll for a job that barely required her to step out of her home more than four or five times a month.

The argument finally ended with Anupama resorting to her last defense and declaring that as per the energies of the house, the middle yellow shade was the most conducive option to go with. What these "energies" were and how they communicated with her, no one questioned, as long as she kept the mystic look on her face intact. There was a time when she felt guilty about it, until she realized that it wasn't wrong, technically. Vaastu really didn't give a crap about whether the shade of yellow you were selecting was mellow or royal. Yellow was yellow. Period.

The client, Kay, seemed happy enough, as he sashayed out to get some refreshments.

'So what was up with you this afternoon?' asked Renu. 'You sounded drunk. And depressed.'

Anupama kept her eyes on the tiles. 'Just one of those days, you know.'

'Went to that site again, huh?'

'Which site?'

'Bitch, please. You haven't looked me in the eye since we met. I know you logged onto JD's and checked out the guys.'

'Shh!'

'I just don't get what you're so embarrassed about. We're not in the fifth grade anymore. You can have a sex drive. It's legal, I swear.'

'Renu, I swear I'll flush you down this toilet if you don't shut up!'

'Get a permanent membership, at least. If you want, I can

even sponsor your first session. Baaki it's up to you whether you want to continue screwing the same guy or no—'

'Shhh!' hissed Anupama, as Kay entered carrying a tray with three iced teas.

'I heard screw,' he said. 'What's cooking, ladies?'

'I was trying to get her to sign up on JD's site.'

Anupama stared at Renu, aghast.

'Oh yeah, they are the best,' he said casually.

Anupama stared at Kay now, aghast. 'You have hired their services too?'

He nodded, taking a sip. 'They have a gay segment on their site as well.'

'It's almost the same as the straight segment,' explained Renu, 'but with more abs and less body hair.'

'Can we please get back to the tiles?'

'The tiles are done and stop changing the topic. You need this.'

'No, I don't. You think I'd actually hire a whore—'

A duet of horrified gasps from Renu and Kay.

'Honey, I should douse your mouth with soap water!' he cried, clutching his chest.

'Never, *ever*, demean JD's boys by calling them whores again,' warned Renu. 'You never know which one of their clients might jump out of the crowd and tear your hair out.'

'So what are they then?'

'Sanctums of healing intimacy,' chimed in Kay, 'where beauty, charm and wit are fused in delicately balanced doses to cure the urban aliena—'

'They are studs you can fuck as well as talk to,' cut in Renu. 'Sex is just part of the deal. The point is that they are really,

really good company, and that's why they are so much in demand. Picture a perfect date where you meet this charming young guy who happens to be besotted by you. He talks to you with all his heart, listens to everything you have to say, understands you, supports you, makes you feel like you are the most beautiful woman—'

'or man'

'*person* in the world, and then rounds it off with a passionate bout of lovemaking that would make you believe in miracles all over again.'

'And what if someone catches you?'

'Big deal. Just say he is Misha's friend or something.'

'Ugh. Please! You think I'd ever hook up with someone my daughter's age?'

'I don't think you have a choice there, sweetie,' said Kay. 'You won't find a single forty-plus in JD's profiles, I assure you.'

'And who said I am forty-plus?' asked Anupama.

The bathroom became as quiet as a cemetery. Kay looked at Renu. Renu looked at the wall.

'I think my croissants are done. Excuse me,' he mumbled, shuffling out hurriedly.

Anupama turned her eyes back on Renu, who was still pretending to concentrate on the wall. 'I really love the pattern we have here, you know. Very contemporary and experimental …' She took a few deliberate moments to notice her. 'What?'

Anupama stomped out without a word.

Her sullen mood persisted throughout the drive back home. Renu pretended not to notice it, even though she knew that Anupama had noticed that she had noticed it, so Anupama pretended not to notice she had noticed either, which Renu noticed. Soul sisterhood could get rather complicated that way.

'Anu, I have had a really long day,' said Renu, wearily. 'So if you have a problem, just do me a favour and get it out of your system instead of giving me these zombie vibes.'

No response. Renu sighed.

'If you don't want to call JD's, then don't. I was just trying to help—'

'No, Renu, you were trying to *fix* me, just like everyone else,' hissed Anupama through pursed lips.

'Fix you? What, are you broken or something?'

'I don't know. You tell me.'

'I repeat, I've had a really long day—'

'Just … be … a … friend, Renu. Can you do that? Don't be my therapist. Don't try to give solutions like everyone else. And for God's sake, don't feel sorry for me. Just let me be. Do you think that's possible?'

Renu stared at her for a moment or so, before turning her eyes ahead.

'Fine,' she said brusquely.

'Thank you.'

'You're welcome.'

She turned off the ignition. Only the sound of raindrops on metal could be heard about them now.

The silence dragged on. Renu began a slow tap on her steering wheel with her index fingers, in sync with the symphony of the drops overhead.

Anupama glanced over at Renu, who had switched to her cool and detached stance – the one she had perfected in college to serve the dual purpose of warding off any unwanted creeps, and keeping her dear ones at bay when she was too pissed off to speak.

'Oh, so now you're mad at me.'

'I'm … just … being … a … friend,' she said, drumming on the steering wheel idly.

'Let it out, Renu.'

'What? It's not like I am your therapist or anything.'

'You have two minutes of ceasefire.'

'I am just so fucking sick of it!' she burst out. 'You don't want to do anything, you don't want to go anywhere, and you don't want to meet anyone. All you want to do is mope around and feel sorry for yourself and expect the rest of us to just ignore it. Tough-love time, honey. You know I'm sorry about Rajeev, but it's been almost two years now. *And* with all due respect, the guy was an asshole. What are you punishing yourself for, then?'

It just took an instant, and Anupama felt that familiar flush of pure, unbridled rage rising within her. Her heart was beating loudly, and she could feel the heat waves creeping up her neck. She was reaching a dangerous point of no return, so she quickly closed her eyes and took a few deep breaths, blocking Renu out. This was crucial. She couldn't afford losing another friend to a meltdown. So she waited for the anger to abate, and when it didn't, she opened her door and stepped out into the flooded street, the slushy water swallowing her legs almost up to her knees, drenching her sandals and salwar. She could feel the rain splattering her hair and shoulders. She could hear Renu yelling out to her from behind. But she kept on walking until her feet carried her over to the other side of the road, where she flagged down a cab and got in. She didn't even know where she was going. All she knew was that she wanted to get away.

Her mobile rang with an incoming call from Renu. She cut it and switched off her phone. Her heart was still thumping wildly, almost as if she were having a nervous breakdown. Unfortunately, the taxi she had chosen turned out to be one of those dhinchak ones with multi-coloured rice-lights blinking all around her and a Bhojpuri number blasting off the bass speakers behind her head. She wanted to ask him to stop it, but her voice didn't come out. Her throat was still too tight. At times like these, she felt she would never be able to breathe again. However, she had always pulled through, just like she knew she would pull through again. People like her, they couldn't go so easily. Their very existence was a karmic penance that had to be served out in its entirety.

'Where to, madam?' asked the driver.

She took a moment to catch her breath. 'CST station.'

The driver dithered. 'Oho, that's quite far...'

'Do you want me to drive?'

He promptly slid the car into gear.

———

The rain was still bucketing down when she reached home. Anupama held her handbag over her head and ran in through the gates, taking care not to slip over the tiles. The old, withered watchman – now an heirloom of the building more than its guardian – was dozing as usual in his cabin, the uniform hanging off his bones, his thick glasses hanging off his nose tip, dithering on the edge. His glass of tea was still half-full with a weak layer of malai floating on the surface – the sole remnant of its youthful prime. The open visitor's book on his desk was blurred and blotted with streaks of water running across the pages, until you couldn't make out whether the person who had visited Mrs Desai at 1.00 p.m. was a Patel or a Palkar – stuff which could tear a marriage apart in the wrong hands.

As she passed by the old chap, Anupama felt a twinge of sympathy tinged with contempt.

Anupama reached the lobby just as the outer grilled door of the elevator was slammed. She called out just in time to stop the second from shutting, and scurried over. To her discomfort, she found Charlie inside, wearing a transparent raincoat with little daisies printed on the outside. She hoped he wasn't in a chatty mood again. The last thing she wanted now was a conversation.

'Hello, Mrs Arora,' he said, beaming. His smile reminded her of those vintage toothpaste ads she had adored in her teens, and found herself despising him for it. No one had a right to look this happy and this good in this weather.

'Hello, Charlie.'

A dim yet distinct awareness of her own train-wreck appearance struck her mind. She wanted to take the stairs now, but knew it would look ridiculous. Charlie slid open the door and waited as she walked in and pressed the button for the seventh floor. With two hard slams of metal on metal, they were on their way.

'You look angry,' he remarked.

'Hm?'

'You have that tightened look in your eyes.'

'It's just the weather.'

'You still don't have an umbrella?'

'My friend picked me up.'

'And she didn't drop you back?'

Anupama glared at him. 'No, Charlie. She didn't.'

'Sorry. It's just that I don't like closed spaces, especially elevators. So I end up talking to whoever is inside just to take my mind off it.'

'What do you do when you're alone?' she asked, hoping he would take the hint.

'I sing.'

Anupama looked up at him in disbelief.

'Just to myself,' he clarified. 'To divert my attention. If you don't mind, I could do that. This lift is quite slow.'

Anupama looked straight ahead. She should have taken the stairs.

A moment later, she heard Charlie's low, quivering voice beside her:

'*O re khevaiya ... paar lagaa more saiyaan ko ... tarse re ankhiyaan...*'

It was all she could do to keep a straight face. She cast a sideways glance at him to see if he was joking, but his left leg was fidgeting as if out of control. He was actually anxious. Of all the people she could have shared an elevator ride with on this day...

Charlie's phone rang.

'Oh, thank God,' he mumbled, picking it up. 'Yes, Mrs Saini ... yes, the charges vary, of course. Depends on what you're looking for … well, you could start by sending me your pictures, just so I could have a mental image, you know … Helps me prepare myself beforehand…'

Anupama's ears pricked up.

'…that depends on how much time you have … I've got two ladies right before you, so I will obviously need a break, but I assure you I won't let you leave until you're fully satisfied…'

Her trepidation turned into full-on alarm. Beside her, Charlie broke into a chuckle. 'Of course, I understand … so what time does your husband leave?'

They had reached the seventh floor. Anupama quickly shoved the doors aside and scuttled out.

'See you, Mrs Arora,' she heard Charlie call out from behind her.

'Bye-bye.'

She felt like slapping herself. *Bye-bye*? *Again*? The words had slipped out her mouth before she could stop them. What was wrong with her?

Trying hard not to break into a trot, Anupama crossed the hallway and rang her doorbell, taking care not to glance behind. She heard Charlie unlock his door and get in, and was relieved when the door closed again. What was happening to the world? Was everyone a horny bugger these days? She would have to warn her kids against fraternizing with this one.

She pressed the bell again, impatiently. After a few more seconds, Nimit opened the door. She already knew the excuses, so she didn't bother complaining. He must have been in the washroom, and Misha must have been on the phone inside her bedroom. Lately, both these activities had increased in duration and frequency – something that worried her. Whoever came up with the genius suggestion of letting teenagers have their own space should have also provided a back-up manual of precautions against your children becoming sex maniacs. Or escorts.

Her thoughts meandered to Charlie's mother. She felt sorry for the poor, unknown woman, picturing her in the middle of a family dinner, boasting to her relatives about how her son had managed to survive the big, bad city through sheer grit, honesty and talent. How traumatized would she be if she had overheard him on the phone just now, shamelessly discussing his hourly rates with random strangers? Where was this generation headed?

She knocked on Misha's door and waited until it opened to reveal her daughter, still dressed in her college clothes, with her phone glued to her ear.

'One sec, I'll call you back,' she said to the caller, before hanging up and turning to face her. 'Hi.'

'What time did you get back?'

'I don't know … seven or something.'

'So you missed lunch again.'

'I ate out.'

'With whom? Your French boyfriend and illegitimate children?'

'Oho, I was just kidding around.'

'Misha, who were you with?'

'Friends. Who else?'

'Was Tarun there?'

'He's dead.'

'What?'

Misha rolled her eyes. 'I mean, he's dead to me. I haven't spoken to him in like forever.'

She had just posted a selfie on Facebook two days ago of her and Tarun inside an auto, with him licking her earlobe as she grinned widely into the camera. It had more than fifty Likes by the time Anupama saw it, with comments ranging from 'Awwww' to 'Twue luv wonly' (sic).

'What?' asked Misha, staring back at her.

Anupama softened her stance. 'Beta, I just want you to know that you are now at an age where we can be frank with each other. As friends.'

'Right.'

'And I trust you completely.'

'Great.'

'And I hope that you trust me too.'

'Sure.'

'You are a big girl now.'

'I know.'

'Show me your phone.'

'What?'

'Give me your phone. I want to know who you were talking to.'

'I thought you trusted me!'

'I do. And I trust you have nothing to hide right now, which is why you will give it to me.'

Misha shook her head in disbelief. 'Unbelievable...'

She fished out her phone and keyed in her code. The moment it was unlocked, Anupama snatched it from her hand and went to the call records. The last call was to an unsaved number. Her suspicions heightened. She glanced up to see Misha's face was blank, giving away nothing. Her suspicions wavered for an instant, before she took a decision and dialled the number.

'What are you doing?' asked Misha uneasily, just as the call was answered.

'What you wearing now, babes?' drawled Tarun's voice.

'This is Misha's mother here.'

'Oh fu—Namaste, ji! How are you?'

'Better than you will be when your wife gets a call from me. Didn't I warn you not to get in touch with her?'

'Arey, it's nothing like that, Anu ji—'

'To hell with your "ji"! And consider this your last warning.'

She hung up to see Misha gawking at her. 'Could you *be* any more dramatic?'

'Could you *be* any more reckless? The man's married, Misha! *And* he's old enough to be your father!'

'Who cares? And he promised me he's leaving his wife!'

'I can't do this again,' murmured Anupama, walking away.

'This is so unfair,' screamed Misha.

As the door slammed hard behind her, Anupama began the familiar chant inside her head.

Shut it away, she hummed to herself, as the migraine in her head turned into a bongo drum chorus. *Shut it away, and then open it later.*

———

Gently and cautiously, Anupama squeezed out a tiny dollop of the 'miracle' anti-ageing cream that Renu had coaxed her into buying last week, and rubbed it over her cheeks and forehead, trying to cover as much surface area as she could with her fingers. Considering how much the little tube had cost her, she would have to ensure it lasted at least two months to fit within her budget. The makers had tried to justify the exorbitant pricing by claiming the product contained traces of gold, silver and copper peptides. Add in aluminium and zinc and she could, neck up, double up as a Periodic Table of Elements for a chemistry lab in her free time.

She brought her face close to the mirror – a daring act reserved only for when she was alone in her bedroom and mentally prepared to withstand the harshness of direct, overhead lighting. Was it her imagination, or had the laugh lines by her mouth deepened? How was that possible when she couldn't even remember the last time she had laughed? Another cruel joke of nature against women past forty, she supposed. Her forehead seemed fine – no better, no worse, thank God – but the bags under her eyes were a whole different story. The worst was her neck though – loose, sagging, and with creases that seemed to mark her age like the rings on a tree stump.

Slap on all the gold, phosphorus and platinum you want, honey. That neck will give away everything, the bitter voice inside her said. She wondered why the bitter voice inside her always sounded a bit like Kay.

She pulled back from the mirror and diverted her attention to the rest of herself. Her metabolism – a solitary blessing from her gene pool – ensured that she never grew overweight, although her waist had seen better days. She looked at her cleavage, revealed by the neckline of her nightgown. Time had been gentler in that area, at least. She cupped her breasts and pulled them up a bit. For a moment, she was in her early-thirties again. Then gravity took over, and she was back to being forty-two. Perhaps this is what Renu meant when she said that the right bra could change your whole personality. But how much of a change was deemed appropriate for her at this stage? And why now? For whom?

It hadn't even worked with Rajeev. She remembered the mix of anxiety and delight with which she had worn her first babydoll lingerie a couple of years into their marriage – three, four? The very notion had seemed controversial to her naïve mind at the time, and that had excited her even more. She had ensured that Misha went to bed early that night, and then the minutes seemed to tick by so slowly. She remembered the naughty thrill as she changed into that skimpy garment in front of the dressing table mirror, seeing an image of hers that had only been confined to her fantasies … the mounting anticipation as she waited for him in the bedroom, lying seductively in bed like she had seen those heroines do … the titillating range of possibilities that flew through her mind, arousing her further … the acceleration of her heartbeats at the sound of the door being unlocked, keys jingling and clattering as they landed on the dining table, the sound of his footsteps growing louder as he approached … the catch of her breath as he opened the door, switched on the lights and turned around – only to freeze in surprise when he saw her … their eyes locking … time had stood still…

And then, his reaction – a single, amused chuckle.

Like he had caught her in the middle of doing something childish.

That was it.

Her desires, confidence and self-worth – all swept away in one chilly wave of disillusionment. She had quickly yanked up the sheets to cover herself. She didn't want him to look at her body anymore.

Had he ever realized what he had lost that night with his sniggering? What the moment could have been? And what it had become? He had apologized later of course, claiming that he didn't need any such fancy tricks to feel attracted to her, but the damage had been done. She had never tried anything erotic with him after that.

With the passage of time, sex with Rajeev had gone on to acquire the same charm as her evening walks. She indulged in it every now and then to convince herself she was still putting in the effort, the movements were always the same and at the end of it all, she wondered what the point of all that exertion really was.

Anupama turned off the lights and crept into bed. The exhaustion of the day had begun to numb her muscles in that comforting manner that promised a good night's rest. She still slept on the left half of the bed, even though the entire queen-sized mattress was available to her. Perhaps out of sentiment, maybe out of habit, or possibly both. *Who cared*? She had stopped pondering over these things now.

She had barely shut her eyes when she realized she had forgotten to bring along her customary glass of water. With an irritable groan, she dragged herself out of bed and into the kitchen. She had turned around after extracting the bottle of water from the fridge, when she saw Charlie in his kitchen through her window. He was standing on a stool, scrubbing the top of his kitchen shelves, wearing a ganjee with abnormally deep armholes that stretched down almost all the way to his waist, exposing a rather significant amount of his torso in the process. Even from the distance and despite the obstruction of the grimy windowpanes of both their kitchens, she could make out that he had a rather athletic physique – the Olympic athlete kind with those bony, bumpy muscles. She had just begun to wonder whether it was a result of his genes or some hidden diet and workout formula, when his face tilted a bit to the side and she nearly had a heart attack at the thought of being caught ogling him in her nightgown. She scampered out with the bottle, leaving the glass behind, her heart thudding wildly at the close shave.

———

The next morning, she woke up early and glued sheets of newspaper over the panes of her kitchen window. It would diminish quite a bit of the daylight, no doubt, but anything was worth her privacy and dignity. Things were so much simpler when that Patel family lived next door. She just hoped the change wouldn't be too conspicuous to Charlie or her kids.

3

She checked the clock. 11.45 a.m.

She peered through the peephole of her main door. The corridor outside was empty. She pressed her ear against the door. There were no footsteps or voices or sounds of the elevator in motion. That was a good sign.

With a quick glance at the key-holder mirror to ensure that everything was in place, she slipped out with her purse and umbrella. She walked quickly to the elevator and pressed the elevator button, and then hurried back to her door to lock it in order to save time.

Over the months, Anupama had learnt that the art of dodging sympathetic and curious neighbours required, in addition to a generally asocial front, a precisely coordinated entry and exit timing. And of course, luck. Navigating seven floors without bumping into anyone on the way was a blind risk she still had to take. The men and kids were fine, since they hardly ever bothered to chat. But the ladies...

It wasn't so much their individual characteristics as the

homogeneity of their identities that really disturbed her. As far as her opinion was concerned, you could cut and paste one's face on another, and there would still be no noticeable difference in personality. It had been almost two years now, yet the questions and dialogues remained the same: 'How are things?', 'Kids coping well?', 'Let us know if you need anything, no?', 'Nimit's grown so tall so soon, no?', 'Let's catch up sometime over tea, no?', 'Saw the *Jhalak Dikhla Jaa* episode last night? So-and-so is really talented, no?', 'Have you lost weight? Get my cook to help along, no?' The expressions were always the same – the tight-lipped, uncertain smile hovering between encouragement and pity, the solemn softening of the eyes (followed by a gradual glazing if she spoke beyond the thirty-second mark), the automated nods of understanding no matter what or how she replied.

Her tragedy had bestowed upon her a spotlight of public sympathy from which there seemed to be no escape. Add to that the responsibility of raising two children on her own, coupled with the sexless decades looming ahead on the horizon, and it wasn't long before Anupama became the local poster girl for all that could go wrong in one's life if the stars weren't aligned right. Any new updates about her presumed state of melancholy became the CSR (Collective Social Responsibility) initiative of the entire housing society, with neighbours often ringing her doorbell to pass on little offerings of solace like a bowl of sweet curd, or some homemade dhoklas, or Baby's first baked chocolate cake ('she made it using honey instead of sugar. So health-smart, no?') And of course, they always made sure that the gifts were strictly non-marital in nature, lest it seem like they were waving their better fortunes in her face.

Like a recalcitrant pet, the elevator rose up and hailed her with a metallic thump. She got in and shut the doors, with a silent prayer to get through the outer gates without the pressure of having to look a single neighbour in the eye. The moment she saw the top of a head appear below the fifth-floor landing though, she knew it wasn't her day. And what joy to behold that the head – and subsequent neck, shoulders, torso, and limbs – belonged to none other than Mrs Govindikar, the Queen Bee of the lot. The residential iron lady with a heart of gold. Her sheer presence evoked respect and awe from those who knew her, and perhaps this was the key factor behind her uncontested reign as the Society Chairperson for the past seven years on the trot since her son left for the United States. Anupama instinctively took a step back as the lift halted. Mrs Govindikar pushed open the doors and strode in.

'Hello, Anupama.'

'Hello, Mrs Govindikar.'

'All well with the kids?'

'Yes, thank you.'

She shoved the doors shut and stood in that erect, dignified manner as befit a lady of her stature. To an inexperienced onlooker, Mrs Govindikar could appear almost grandmotherly, with her mehendi-streaked hair greying at the roots, petite frame and those large librarian glasses that almost seemed to hang off her nose. However, as any flat-owner, tenant, broker, newspaper boy, garbage-collector and departmental store worker connected to the A, B and C blocks of Atharva Hari

Cooperative Housing Society would tell you, that assumption was just about as true as Santa's existence at the North Pole. For within that tiny, willowy frame of a retired school principal existed an iron-fisted leader with an uncompromising set of principles and steely grit that dared anyone to challenge her autocracy.

'There's a new tenant on your floor, I believe,' said Mrs Govindikar.

'Yes. Charlie.'

'You've met him?'

Anupama nodded. 'He wanted some plastic bags.'

'Let me know if he causes any trouble, and try to keep a watch on your children as well. Never know with these people. God knows what he does.'

Anupama nodded again. A few seconds passed in silence.

'I hope you are planning to join us this Saturday?'

'Sorry?'

'The mini-marathon? Till Inorbit?'

Anupama stared at her blankly.

'Didn't you read the circular on the notice board?'

'No, I must have missed it...'

'It's been there for a week now, Anupama,' she said, with a hint of admonishment in her voice. 'We are all participating in a mini-marathon this Saturday, the proceeds of which will be donated towards the cause of protecting our mangroves from extinction. I am one of the key organizers.'

Of course she was.

'Sounds great, Mrs Govindikar, but I'm not much of a runner—'

'Well, none of us are going to be *running*, obviously. We don't want to make a spectacle of ourselves. The point is to be a part of the movement. There will be coverage in all the local papers, so it's important to have a good turnout. You can walk with us if you want.'

Anupama gave a non-committal nod, racking her brains to rake up a suitable excuse. Almost as if she were reading her mind, Mrs Govindikar remarked, 'It would be nice for you to step out more and socialize, dear. Living in a shell – it only makes things worse, trust me.'

Anupama gave another vague nod, wondering why the elevator was moving so damn slowly.

'I will send Gopal up with the circular. You can hand him the registration fees and sign up. It's at eleven a.m. sharp.'

The zombie nod again. The cursed lift finally reached the ground floor. Anupama pulled the doors aside and stepped out, grateful to be free when she realized that Mrs Govindikar was keeping in step with her, and marched alongside, not having been done yet.

'Try to get your children to participate too,' she insisted. 'I never see Nimit in the playground with the other boys.'

'Yes, he is more of the indoors type.'

'Why? What does he do all day?'

Play Xbox and watch porn in all probability. 'Research mostly. And he is also working on his grades. Eleventh class, you know.'

'That's fine, but one needs to be balanced in all aspects, Anupama. A little nudge every now and then, that's all that's needed. Or else next thing you know…' she lowered her voice to a whisper, 'he will end up like that Mrs Kaushik's son from A-Wing. Boy took up some literature course after twelfth. Literature! Can you imagine the poor woman's plight? Here she was harbouring dreams of her son becoming a neurosurgeon in the US like my Kunal, and now...'

With a heavy sigh, she lowered her eyes. Anupama had a petrifying premonition of the day when Nimit's board results would become public. Having full knowledge of her son's academic capabilities and track record, she had no doubt that he was hurtling towards a life in the humanities disciplines as well.

'Well, children *are* experimenting with newer fields these days, Mrs Govindikar.'

'To what end? When was the last time you heard someone say, "I hope my daughter grows up to marry an English lecturer one day"? Might as well be homo, God forbid.'

It was stupendous just how many offensive slurs and stereotypes Mrs Govindikar could subsume in a single sentence. The grim mood was abruptly shattered by a strident honk. Anupama glanced ahead to see Renu waiting in an Uber outside the building gates, much to her relief.

'Is that your friend?' asked Mrs Govindikar coldly.

'Yes.'

'The unmarried one?'

'Yes. See you, Mrs Govindikar.'

Anupama practically ran the remaining distance to the car, thanking her guardian angels for their impeccable timing.

'You are a life-saver!' she exclaimed, getting in.

Without a word, Renu shifted aside, keeping her eyes

ahead. From the tart look on her face, Anupama could tell she wasn't over the events of yesterday.

'Renu, I am sorry about yesterday,' she said. 'I just wanted to avoid a scene.'

'Anu, next time, just do me a favour and make a scene. *Anything* would be better than that zombie phase you slip into.'

Anupama nodded. Renu leaned forward and asked the driver to turn on the radio – a clear harbinger of peace. The RJ on air was chirping on about the joys of the monsoons with such enthusiasm you would think she came from a line of paddy farmers.

'How come you came by Uber today?' asked Anupama.

'I don't drink and drive.'

'We are drinking?'

'Anu, please. I don't have time for such superfluous questions.'

'It's not even one.'

'So? You got a lecture to attend after this or what?'

Anupama looked out her window uneasily, promising herself she would only have half a glass of wine. Her low tolerance for alcohol had been a favorite party joke for years, and she didn't intend to revive that tradition. Good thing she hadn't had her daily shot of cough syrup.

'By the way, Neena's getting a friend along too,' said Renu conversationally.

'Who?'

'No idea. She just bumped into him on the way, and he was going the same way, so you know.'

Anupama narrowed her eyes. 'Let me guess. Is he single?'

'Divorced. Ex wife turned out to be a psycho. You know how it is. Anyway, how does it matter?'

'Renu, if this turns out to be another pathetic blind date attempt by you guys to—'

'Oh, I love this song!' cried Renu, asking the driver to turn the volume all the way up.

———

The moment she saw the hot hostess at the restaurant door, Anupama decided she would let Renu pick up the tab. Any place that could afford a stunning maître de was deemed unaffordable by her, especially when the bombshell happened to be wearing a pair of shoes that were three times the price of her sandals. Her apprehensions were further confirmed when they entered the grand buffet hall, at the centre of which lay a huge, gushing fountain, with spotless white-sheeted tables placed strategically around it in a semi-circle. Platinum card holders like Renu noted the ambience and appreciated its nuances. Debit card holders like Anupama quickly totted up the resulting surcharges they would have to pay as tribute to all the sho-sha, and debated whether to order mineral water or regular water.

Neena was seated at one of the window-side tables, talking to a man who was seated with his back to them. Against her will, Anupama found her heartbeats pace up as they approached the duo. Neena was the first one to spot them.

'Hey, you two!' she trilled, as the man stood up and turned to face them with a smile; a smile that quickly dripped off when he spotted Anupama. Anupama froze too, staring back at him.

'This is my friend, Dr Satish Kumar. He's a—'

'Gynaecologist,' murmured Anupama.

'Why, yes!' cried Neena, surprised. 'But how did you…'

Now it was her and Renu's turn to freeze. A condensed cloud of realization and embarrassment swept over the table.

'Oh,' said Renu.

Anupama counted the days since her last appointment with him as she sat down, mortified to the bone.

'Nice to see you again, Mrs Arora,' said Dr Kumar, his face almost as reddish-pink as the roses on the table.

'Likewise.'

'You said you lived in Bandra,' said Neena to Dr Kumar in an almost accusatory tone.

'Yes, but my clinic's in Malad.'

The waiter strolled by. 'Would you like to order some drinks, ma'am?'

'Oh, yes,' said Anupama. 'Wine. Red. Glass. No, make that a pint, actually.'

The waiter nodded and turned to Renu, while Anupama and Dr Kumar struggled to look each other in the eye and smile at the same time.

'So,' he said brightly, 'how's that, er, balm working out for you?'

Anupama turned back to the waiter. 'You know what? Just make it a full bottle.'

It was so funny, the way the raindrops danced across the window pane at night, and everything looked so spotty and blurry and wet. Puddles of yellow light and white light and black spots – all flirting with each other as they rushed past her. The windshield wipers swinging left and right, left and right, almost like they were doing a Mexican wave at her. A poster of an underwear model on a huge banner, with a smiley drawn in the middle of his crotch by some miscreant flashed by. A dog lay limply beneath a sidewalk store awning, eyes closed, one ear cocked; oblivious to the cat perched on a low wall right beside him. A light-skinned actor on a billboard for a men's fairness cream. A local party chief being wished 'Haardik Shubhkaamnayein' on a giant hoarding with tigers and hawks and wrestlers photoshopped behind him. Was she drunk, or was the world always this hilarious?

By the time they reached her place, the rain had slowed down to a barely existent drizzle, so Anupama half-walked, half-trotted up to her block, throwing an affectionate smile to the sleeping watchman in his cabin en-route. Her merry mood carried on unabated inside the elevator, as she hummed a tune to herself of a song whose lyrics she couldn't quite remember.

She had just reached the antara of her song when the lift halted at her floor. She stepped out, shut the doors and had just turned to her apartment door when she felt a draft of cool air on the back of her neck. That was odd. A second later, a rustle reached her ear, and she gasped as something prickly touched her foot. She whirled around to see – an empty wrapper of cream biscuits near her foot.

What in God's name?

Her eyes shot up, almost as if expecting to see a ghost. The corridor suddenly felt empty and eerie. She swayed a bit, scanning the hallway with bleary eyes. The faintest flicker of light, or the softest footstep, and she would have passed out in shock. She waited and watched and listened. Nothing happened. Only the sound of her own heart thudding in her chest. Then, the cool zephyr touched her again, this time in the face. Gooseflesh broke out across her body. Where was it from? What was happening?

She was on the verge of abandoning any semblance of having a spine and making a dash for cover in her apartment, when her eyes spotted the large plastic bag outside C-704. Charlie's door. It had been stuffed beyond its capacity, and the top had ripped open spewing bits of paper, plastic and other litter about, probably owing to the nightly visit by the neighbourhood cat. Furthermore, the bag was fluttering every now and then signalling that the source of the breeze was on the other side. The combination of curiosity, wine and the resulting courage lent Anupama the will to step up and investigate the mystery for herself.

Slowly and noiselessly, she crept up to Charlie's door and peeked beyond to see a tell-tale sliver of light on the staircase which led up to the terrace. Odd, because the terrace door was always supposed to be kept locked as per society rules. She softly stepped forward to take a closer look – the terrace door was ajar. Someone had broken in! Her heart leapt up for the second time, and she was on the verge of rushing off to summon the watchman when … a low humming reached her ears from above. A familiar, husky/sore-throat voice.

The little prick! After scaring the living daylights out of her with his irresponsible littering, he was up there having a good time! She stomped back to the corridor, scooped up the biscuit wrapper, and then marched up the stairs and on to the terrace.

Charlie was perched on the parapet wall, smoking, with one leg swinging lazily as he gazed out into the night. She cleared her throat. He stopped crooning and turned around to look at her with those – grey/green/hazel – eyes. Surprise crossed his face.

'Mrs Arora?' he called out, as his lips dispelled a scattered cloud of smoke.

'The very same,' she replied haughtily, as she held up the paper wrapper. 'Is this yours?'

'Er…'

'It's not a very complicated question, Charlie.'

'Depends on where you found it, I guess.'

'It was right outside your door, fluttering and flying about, along with the rest of your trash.'

'Crap, sorry about that,' he said. 'I'm buying a dust-bin first thing tomorrow.'

'My issue is not with your garbage or lack of dust-bin, Charlie. My issue is *this*,' she snapped, holding up the crumpled wrapper again. 'Do you know what this means to me?'

Charlie stared at the wrapper uncomprehendingly and then back at her. 'Not really, no.'

'And yet, you had the audacity to gift me a packet of cream

biscuits after our very first meeting? Who do you think you are?'

'I … just had a spare packet with me. So I thought you could give it to your kids or something.'

'Oh, you *thought*, did you? So here's something else to *think* about, *Charlie*. You don't know me, all right? None of you do, so stop *trying*. Now I don't care what *you* are, or what you do in your own space, whatever it is that you do, but I expect to be treated the same way and allowed my space.'

'I don't—'

'You don't gift cream biscuits to strangers without knowing their back stories!' she yelled. 'Understand?'

Charlie stared at her. 'Yes, Mrs Arora.'

'You better understand!' she snapped her fingers at him, like she had once seen a heroine do in a film, neither of which she could remember now. And with that, she turned on her heel to swagger away triumphantly, when…

'Mrs Arora.'

'What?' she snapped, turning to face him again.

'Your sandal.'

She glanced down to see her sandal lying a few feet away. Her right foot was bare. When had that happened?

With as much poise and grace as she could muster, Anupama hobbled over to the wayward footwear, slid her foot into it, and shuffled to the door, all the while taking care not to look at him again. That hadn't gone down so badly, she reflected. The moment was still hers, and she was proud of it, until—

'Bye-bye, Mrs Arora,' called Charlie from behind her.

'Bye-bye, Charlie,' she replied.

Damn it! The sly bastard!

She fled down the stairs, with the sound of his chuckle ringing in her ears.

4

Her eyelids slowly fluttered open to a blinding flash of white light. The curtains fluttered, and she caught a glimpse of the sun radiating broken beams of sunshine through the gap in the shades. She rose to draw the curtains, when suddenly the walls came to life and began swimming around her in a synchronized choreography. *Bad idea.* She crashed back into her pillow and groaned, clutching her head. Her mouth was dry, as was her throat, and her head was throbbing faster than her heart. Talk about a bad hangover. Damn Renu. And damn that sun. Why was it looking so unnaturally bright today?

And then it struck her. The sun *was* unnaturally bright. Her eyes flew wide open. With a rising sense of fear and urgency, she raised her alarm clock to eye level – 9.11 a.m.

Doom.

Nimit was supposed to leave for school at 7.30.

Way to go, Anupama. Way. To. Go.

Overnight she had transformed into a textbook cliché of a child psychology course – the drunken, neglectful mother who couldn't be bothered about whether her kids ate or bathed or went to school. Oh God, had they even woken up?

Forgetting all about her screwed-up depth perception and wobbly eye-limb coordination and splitting headache, Anupama stumbled out of her bedroom and into the corridor. Nimit's bedroom door was open. She peeked in. The bed was made and the room was empty. His bag was gone, as were his school shoes. A gigantic wave of relief and surprise washed over her. She heard a clinking sound in the kitchen.

And lo and behold, there was Misha slicing a peanut butter and tomato sandwich into two halves. The milk-stained glass and empty ready-to-eat noodles packet were a testament to her previous efforts in getting her younger brother ready for school.

Watching from the doorway, Anupama felt her heart swell with pride. There is that one golden, unforgettable moment in every mother's life when she gets the confidence that her children will survive the big, bad world. The confidence may not last, but the memory does. She had heard, many times, of others having had that epiphany, and today she had finally experienced her own. Perhaps, she hadn't done such a bad job after all.

Not wanting to disturb the moment, she gazed on at her daughter in silent admiration as she carefully laid out the sandwiches on her plate. A moment later, Misha turned, saw her, and gasped.

'What happened to you?'

'I know. Sorry I overslept.'

'No, I mean what happened to your face? Almost gave me a heart attack.'

And just like that, the moment which was climaxing towards a new high point in the mother-daughter relationship tanked abruptly. Why couldn't life be as predictable as fiction sometimes?

'I came in late last night,' said Anupama, feeling her old crankiness return. The headache was making its presence felt again.

Misha passed her a glass of orange juice. 'For the hangover.'

'I don't have—'

'Mamma, I'm not four.'

Anupama accepted the glass with bad grace and followed Misha to the dining table. As they were both about to sit down, Anupama espied a tiny reddish tinge on her daughter's neck, half hidden by her muffler. It was then that Anupama also realized that this was the first time in years that Misha had chosen to wear that muffler, even though it wasn't really cold outside. Foreboding crawled up her spine with cold, clammy fingers.

'What's that on your neck?'

'Hmm? Oh, it's just an allergy …' she mumbled, flicking her hair forward. She checked the time on her mobile, grabbed her sandwich and got up to leave.

'To what?' said Anupama, rising from her chair as well.

'How should I know?' said Misha, sidling towards the door.

'Let me see it,' said Anupama.

And with that, mother and daughter moved into the subtle predatory circling mode, with both sides trying to keep their movements casual and non-alarming as they approached the main door.

'Seriously, Mamma! Why do you have to make an issue of everything?'

'I just want to make sure it's not serious.'

'It's not.'

With three large and rapid strides, Misha reached the door and had just turned the knob when Anupama closed in on her, stretched her arm out like a midfielder reaching for a long catch, and displaced the muffler to reveal what was unmistakably a rather aggressive love bite, its vulgar redness out there for all to see.

Her breath caught in her throat. Her worst nightmare had come true. Her little girl had been defiled. She grabbed Misha's shoulders.

'Who did this to you?' She almost choked. 'Who?'

'God, Mamma, control yourself,' shrieked Misha, struggling to break free.

She wrenched open the door as soon as she was out of her mother's grasp.

'Don't you dare walk out—' hollered Anupama, but the door had already slammed shut. She had an overwhelming urge to run out into the hallway and drag her daughter kicking and screaming back into the house. But then, the thought of her neighbours overhearing – or worse, *witnessing* – their scuffle swiftly dampened her fires. The last thing she wanted was for this scandal to go public. Instead, she found herself praying that Misha would have the good sense to readjust her muffler now before anyone else noticed.

Slowly and shakily, she made her way back to the table and sat down. At this rate, she would soon become one of those mothers who got pillow-murdered in their sleep following a minor argument with their children. A statistic demonstrating the rising intolerance amongst the youth of today. An episode of *Crime Patrol*. Suddenly, that old-age insurance policy didn't seem like such a bad idea. She made a mental note to Google a list of all the decent retirement homes nearby as well, just in case the need arose sooner than anticipated.

Shut it away, she chanted to herself. *Shut it away, and then open it later...*

She took another sip of the over-sweetened orange juice and leaned back in her chair, moving her head from side to side to ease the strain in her neck. As she did so her eyes fell on the framed photograph of an upside-down Rajeev smiling back at her from the living room wall. Good ol' Rajeev, free of all guilt, hangovers, erratic behaviours and parental worries.

Perhaps it was just her imagination, but his smile seemed to grow broader with each passing day.

She straightened her head, gulped down her juice and cautiously got to her feet. The walls stayed where they were. That was a good start.

On her way through the corridor, she glimpsed a disturbing reflection in the wall mirror, making her pause and glance back. The woman staring back at her through the glass was barely recognizable. Her eyeliner was smudged all around her eyes, her foundation had developed blots and runny lines, and her hair resembled a crow's nest post a bitter domestic squabble. It was a wonder her daughter hadn't pepper-sprayed her at first sight. It was an act of divine kindness that her son had missed seeing her this morning.

She ran into her bathroom, not wanting to confront any more remnants of last night. Unfortunately, fate had other plans, for the first thing she saw upon entering the loo was the discarded wrapper of cream biscuits lying beside her toilet bowl. *Charlie's* discarded cream biscuits wrapper.

The concluding events of the previous night flashed through her memory with the force of a freak hurricane, washing away every ounce of hope she could have ever had for preserving her dignity. She tried to convince herself that it was a dream, a bad dream in which she had had no control over her actions, but the desperation of her attempts only served to dampen her spirits further.

Had she really given him a moral lecture on cream biscuits? How could she ever face him again? Why hadn't she just slipped and fallen down the stairs in the end? At least, she could have claimed amnesia from a blow to the head or something. Or did that excuse work only in the movies?

Moving like a zombie, she splashed her face with water at the wash basin – over and over again, and then again. When she looked up at the mirror, she didn't see a face anymore; just a clumsy black-and-white graffiti of shame and resignation.

Misha's question echoed through her mind: 'What happened to you?'

Seriously, what?

———

Mercifully, the ride down the elevator was uneventful, with no intrusions. However, almost as if to counteract the benefit of this small blessing, Anupama stepped out of the building gates just in time to get a call from Renu saying that she was stuck at Juhu circle and would take at least forty minutes to arrive here. But since the venue was midway between them, could she please take an auto-rickshaw immediately to the place? This was a new client they were meeting today, and she didn't want to bungle the first impression by being late.

Anupama looked around. As per the tradition of the Mumbai auto-rickshaws to mysteriously vanish into a black hole whenever most required, the roads were predictably empty. The clouds overhead loomed ominously grey, thereby adding to her worries. She was sure that arriving soaked to the bone would rank lower in terms of first impressions than arriving late, especially after the sample she had seen of herself this morning. Why did she always forget to buy an extra umbrella?

She peered out into the distance, hoping to see a mirage of public transport, if nothing else. She barely noticed the approaching rumble of a bike from the gates behind her until it stopped right beside her. A familiar voice reached her ears.

'Morning, Mrs Arora.'

Her blood ran cold. *No. God, no. Anything but this.*

'Mrs Arora?'

Pretend you haven't noticed him. Look at your watch. Look ahead. Pray that he gets the hint.

The bike inched forward until the helmeted figure of Charlie was wholly in her line of vision. His mouth wasn't visible, but she could tell from his eyes that he was smiling.

'Oh, hello, Charlie,' she mumbled, barely looking him in the eye.

'Going somewhere?'

'Yes.'

A second passed, then two.

'May I ask where?'

Why couldn't he let anything go?

'Oshiwara.'

'Oh, I'm headed in that direction. I can drop you off on the way.'

'No, thank you.'

'Is your friend coming to pick you up?'

'No, but I'll take an auto.'

Charlie shook his head. 'It's a bad day to wait for autos. See that lady over there?' He pointed to a glum woman waiting at the intersection ahead with her glummer kid. 'She was there when I came in … forty minutes ago.'

'I appreciate it, Charlie. But I'm not comfortable sitting on bikes.'

'Don't worry, I'm a careful rider. Besides, it's about to rain, and you don't have an umbrella.'

'Neither do you,' she retorted. A part of her knew she was being juvenile, but the thought of journeying with a guy who had witnessed her in one of her worst moments of insanity was too much to bear.

'I have a spare raincoat. Plus, I could get you there in fifteen-twenty minutes flat depending on the traffic.'

Anupama glowered at him. 'You don't know how to take no for an answer, do you?'

Charlie shrugged. 'It's a character flaw.'

And that was when it happened. A single, threatening drop of water fell on her neck, like a ransom note. She knew she had seconds to make a decision.

She gazed out at the road in a final, desperate plea. Not a sign of anything even remotely mobile. Even the glum waiting woman looked despairing now.

'Take out the raincoat,' she said.

Charlie removed his helmet, twisted around and opened

a small duffle bag attached to the backseat. The familiar transparent, flowery raincoat emerged from it, disappointing Anupama, who was hoping for a more opaque one lest someone she knew spotted them on the way. However, beggars can't be choosers, so she quickly donned the damn thing and climbed onto the pillion seat, only to sit waiting as Charlie carefully set and arranged his gelled hair using the rear-view mirror.

'Are you done?' she asked irritably.

'Oh, so now you are in a hurry,' he murmured, putting on his helmet.

The bike gave a sharp jerk as he started up and opened throttle, nearly dislodging Anupama who grabbed Charlie's shoulder so tightly he winced. She apologized, but decided to keep her hand on his shoulder anyway. Her initial plan had been to avoid any form of bodily contact, but it was one of those bikes with a narrow back seat, and anything was preferable to bouncing off into the air at the first speed breaker. Just a precautionary measure, nothing more. Try as she might though, she couldn't help but notice how hard his shoulder felt.

True to her prediction, within the span of half a minute, the clouds above burst open with a torrential vengeance. Her suit was fine, thanks to the raincoat, but her feet and sandals were soaked. She shuddered to think what her condition might have been if she had dug her heels in obstinately and refused Charlie's help. At the same time, she noticed that Charlie hadn't brought up the subject of last night at all, which doubled her appreciation. Perhaps she had been a tad hasty in her assessment of him.

'Thank you, Charlie,' she said.

'Not at all. I had to make up for the cream biscuits anyway—'

'Stop the bike.'

'Joking, joking! Wow, you're sensitive.'

Anupama resolutely kept her eyes on the road, her mind struggling to absorb the surrealism of her situation. Here she was, a forty-two-year-old mother of two, seated on a motorcycle behind her twenty-something neighbour in a plastic raincoat, feeling guilty about her inebriated rendezvous with him the previous night. Add to that the probability of the aforementioned neighbour being a commercial sex worker, and for the first time, she found herself feeling grateful that her mother wasn't around anymore. This was probably not how she had envisioned her daughter's domestic future. Someone had once told her that the rains were actually the tears of our ancestors' souls up in heaven. If that were true, she was certain her mother was seated in the front row right now, wringing out her handkerchief.

'You don't have to feel guilty, you know,' said Charlie, craning his head back a bit. 'You should see me when I'm drunk.'

'No, thank you,' she said tersely, adding, 'I think it's best if we forget about that incident. I am usually not like that. In fact, I am never like that.'

'So what happened yesterday?'

'Nothing. I just got together with some old friends...'

'Yeah, that's how it normally starts,' he chuckled.

'Can we just drop it?'

He shrugged again, his right shoulder bouncing her hand as he did so. 'So, you like the rains?'

Anupama sighed. God forbid she got five seconds of silence

with this guy. 'Not really. I like them when they begin, but then it becomes all slush and muck and filth.'

'And yet, we miss them once they are over, right?'

'Not necessarily.'

'So you're more of an indoors type that way.'

'During the monsoons, yes.'

'Pity,' said Charlie. 'You don't get a lot of folks who like to get wet in the rain anymore.'

'Well, maybe in your own age-group—'

'Oh, you'd be surprised. Girls these days, they panic over stuff like tanning and frizzing and God knows what not. Some of them don't even drink regular tea for fear of staining their teeth. It's just become all about the looks with them, right?'

'Maybe.'

'That's why I prefer the company of older women.'

Her fingers convulsively loosened over his shoulder. 'Excuse me?'

'A lot of my clients are in the above-forty bracket, and they are so much more fun to be around, you know. Maybe because they aren't really obsessed with themselves anymore – maturity with age and all that…'

Anupama was barely listening, her eyes scanning the road for any empty auto-rickshaws or taxis. She felt outraged. How dare he discuss such things with her openly? One night, the one solitary night in her otherwise normal existence, she meets him when she is a tad tipsy, and he dares to assume that they are tarred with the same brush? Things were spiralling way out of control, and once again, she only had herself to blame. This was a terrible mistake. All she wanted to do now was to get away from him by any means and as soon as possible.

She could see the screaming headlines in tomorrow's Metro section: '*Woman Leaps Off Moving Bike. Motive Unclear.*' And for an insane moment, she did consider the possibility of getting off at the first possible opportunity, but the risk of getting run over by the rush hour traffic held her back, and then the probable news by-line occurred to her too: '*Traces of alcohol found in victim's system. Police interrogating male escort neighbour accompanying her.*'

She put her hand back on Charlie's shoulder, resolving to cut off all ties with him as soon as she got dropped off safely. He couldn't try anything objectionable on an open bike anyway.

———

She was relieved when they finally reached their destination. Mumbling a quick thanks, she got off the bike and was walking away when she heard Charlie clear his throat.

'Is your friend going to drop you back?'

'Probably. Why?' she asked, suspicious.

'So ... can I have my raincoat back?'

It was only then, looking at his dripping T-shirt and soaked jeans, that Anupama realized that his decision to get wet in the rain was probably not a voluntary one.

'You don't have a spare raincoat, do you?'

Charlie smiled sheepishly.

'Then why did you say so?'

'Would you have taken it otherwise?'

She was speechless, and upset with herself for being so. Quietly, she removed the raincoat and handed it to him. It took her a moment to realize he was staring at her face.

'What?'

'There's …' he muttered, and then without warning, his hand shot up and touched the side of her forehead. She shied away violently in alarm, startling him.

'What the hell are you doing?' she spat out.

Charlie looked at her in puzzlement, and then slowly brought his hand forward to show a small grey-white feather. 'It was stuck in your hair.'

Her eyes shifted focus between the feather and his widened eyes. For some reason, her heart was pounding, and her breathing was erratic, as if she had just had a near-death experience. She didn't know what to say, so she turned without a word and walked away. She could sense him behind her, waiting, staring.

A small voice inside her told her she was being rude and weird, but she didn't care. Pleasantries were the furthest thing on her mind. She held her breath – and hoped – for the rumble of his bike to fill the air, and when it didn't, she just turned around the corner of the nearest building and blocked him from sight, resolving to lock this memory away for future remorse in due time. Right now, she had a client to handle.

Shut it away. Shut it away and then open it later…

5

She couldn't shut it away, though. Not this time.

The incident kept playing in her mind throughout the meeting like a broken tape, each time with a different and better ending. Why did the imagination worsen one's humiliation by displaying a million alternate possibilities that could have happened instead of the one that actually did happen, after it's too late for anything different to happen? She could have just laughed off the misunderstanding and walked away with poise. Or she could have apologized to him and thanked him for the lift anyway. Or she could have explained her situation coolly to him and got an apology – albeit a confused one – in return. She could have done many things, other than behaving like a woman possessed by a demon with intimacy issues. Mrs Govindikar wouldn't have lumbered away like that. Neither would have Renu. Or Neena. No, that special demented response was reserved exclusively for select souls like her.

She could barely focus on the new client, despite all her efforts, and was relieved when the meeting finally got over. She did recall smiling and nodding a lot, and prescribing metal wind chimes in the centre of the living room for some reason, but the client seemed happy enough. Renu had passed her an enquiring glance from time to time, but she had nodded and smiled at her as well.

On their way back now, they had stopped at a traffic signal, its red gleaming light the only spot of colour in a street where every other colour was bleached grey by the weather. Anupama looked out at a young couple on a bike ahead of them. Neither of them had a raincoat, but they didn't seem to mind getting wet. The girl had her arms wrapped tight around the guy, unmindful that the lacy outline of her bra was clearly visible through her soaked top. The epicentre of her mental stress shifted to her daughter now as she wondered, feared rather, if Misha was also sitting pillion on a bike – or scooter, God only knew that man's economic strata – like this, her arms wound tightly around that unfaithful apology of a man. What was it about the rains that made people so reckless and hormonal?

She blamed it on the movies. No one hooted or ogled at the drenched-girls-dancing-in-the-rain item numbers in movies unless the sequence demanded that the hero rescued her precipitately. The rains symbolized a period of fertility, of unabashed, unapologetic sexuality. It was the time when bold heroines consummated their relationship with bolder heroes in abandoned barns, while the gullible supporting actresses hooked up with the lascivious villains only to get pregnant and dumped later. Your honour and fate depended on the amount of footage decided for you. The problem was that in real life, every girl imagined that she was the heroine and no one wanted to believe otherwise, and that was where all the trouble began. At least, that was the theory that her mother had expounded to her. And boy, would the old woman be dancing with joy now at her plight. It was all karma, her mother would croon. History repeating itself. *La-dee-dah … what goes around comes around … dum-dee-dah…*

'Where are you lost?' Renu's voice cut in.

Anupama took a deep, shuddering breath. 'I saw a love bite on Misha's neck today.'

She skewed around in the passenger seat to see Renu sitting still, her eyes amused and lips pursed shut.

'Don't you dare laugh.'

'I'm not,' she squeaked. 'I mean, that's – um – that's disturbing. So, who was it?'

'Isn't it obvious?'

'Mehul, really?'

'No, Tarun,' said Anupama.

'Oh.'

'Who's Mehul?'

'Hm?'

'Who's Mehul?'

'Who's "who's Mehul"?'

'You just said his name.'

'Oh, no, no, that was some other Misha I was talking about. Right. Misha … Dhanjani.'

Anupama looked ahead to see a giant hoarding of Dhanjani Jewellers in front of them.

'Renu!'

'He's just some guy she is seeing.'

'Then what's Tarun?'

'He's … another guy she is seeing. That happens, right? You know how I was in college.'

The fact that her daughter was turning into a younger version of Renu was enough for Anupama to mull over the degree of her sins in past lives to deserve this fate. Mass genocides, at the very least.

'And she told you all this?' she asked Renu. Her daughter. Trusting an acquaintance over her mother.

Renu shrugged. 'She just wanted to have a woman-to-woman talk.'

'And what am I, a dinosaur?'

'Come on, it's no big deal. You know how we were with our mothers.'

The fact that she was turning into a replica of her own mother was all the confirmation Anupama needed to conclude that this life was indeed designed to be one of martyrdom and penance. With some luck, she would be long gone and decayed before one of her kids ended up writing a Mommy-issues based bestseller or rap song dedicated to her.

'Look on the bright side,' said Renu bracingly. 'At least the day can't get any worse, right?'

———

If only things were so simple.

A strange premonition gripped Anupama the instant she stepped out of the elevator on her floor – a foreboding that intensified with each step towards her apartment door. Her eyes picked up the muddy footprints on the tiles leading to her apartment – men's shoes, bigger in size than Nimit's. Her pulse accelerated with every second as she hurried up to the door and unlocked it, swinging it open and barging in to see Nimit watching TV, while Misha sat on the corner couch with Charlie crouched on his haunches on the floor in front of her – her left leg stretched out and on his knee; her foot nestled in his hands. His fingers were probing around a spot by her ankle. His skin touching hers. His Calvin Klein underwear label half-visible in the gap between his T-shirt and jeans. Her muffler still around her neck. His skin touching hers.

It was all she could do to not scream on the spot.

'What's going on?'

'I sprained my ankle downstairs. Charlie helped me up,' replied Misha.

Charlie swivelled his head around to look at her. 'Hello, Mrs Arora.'

Anupama stared at him.

'I've done a short-term course in physiotherapy,' he explained. 'So, I was just—'

'Out.'

Every single expression within that room froze in place – the befuddled one on Nimit's face, the horrified one on Misha's, the stupefied one on Charlie's, and finally, the enraged one on Anupama's.

'Out,' she repeated.

'Mamma!' cried Misha.

'It's fine. I had to – get dinner anyway. Late, you know,' mumbled Charlie, getting up. Using the longest arc route around Anupama, he shuffled and slunk away.

'What is wrong with you?' Misha shrieked at Anupama.

'What is wrong with you?' Anupama hollered at Nimit.

'What did I do?' he said blankly.

'Have you no concern for your sister? You just let anyone in with her?'

'But he's our neighbour—'

'*So what!* What do you know about him?'

A series of low rattling sounds distracted them. Anupama whipped around to see Charlie still there, fidgeting and fumbling with the door knob as he tried to open it. He looked at her with the eyes of a mouse trapped in a laboratory cage.

'Sorry. It's complicated—'

He stepped aside hurriedly as Anupama strode over and unlocked the mechanism before pushing the knob aside to click the door open.

'Oh okay, that way,' he murmured. 'Thank you. Goodnight.'

He was out before his sentence was complete.

Refastening the lock, Anupama turned to face her children – two pairs of bewildered eyes. She faced Misha first. 'Who is Mehul?'

The anger on her face dissipated into nothingness within a fraction of an instant. 'Just a friend. An acquaintance really.'

'Tarun knows about him?'

Misha's cheeks and neck reddened to a deep puce, almost in sync with the shade of the love-bite she had exhibited this morning. Dimly at the back of her mind, Anupama mused over how proud Kay would be of her colour-cognitive skills right now.

'You can't—what are you—I don't—'

The strident ring of the doorbell came to Misha's rescue; the moment Anupama turned to answer it, Misha limped away to the sanctuary of her bedroom, locking the door from inside.

Outside in the hallway, Gopal, the building superintendent, was waiting.

'Reminder, Madam. About the mini marathon tomorrow. Govindikar Madam asked me to inform everyone.'

Anupama groaned, inwardly praying for a brain haemorrhage to mark a fitting end to it all.

6

The kick-off of the Atharva Hari 'Save the Mangroves' mini marathon was delayed by half an hour owing to certain technical glitches – mostly related to the T-shirts for the participants that had been ordered. For one, instead of the dark green that Mrs Govindikar had specifically requisitioned, the suppliers had delivered some horrendous fluorescent shade that was certain to turn translucent when wet. Furthermore, all the T-shirts turned out to be of the same 'S' size, thereby leading to much discomfort as residents of varying body structures struggled to squeeze themselves into it. To make matters worse, the proportions of one's chest and abdomen determined the message displayed on one's T-shirt depending on how many letters were visible. So, while the petite ones boldly displayed 'SAVE THE MANGROVES', others ended up portraying variants like 'AVE THE ANGR', 'VE HE MAN', 'SAVE THE NGRO'.

This would simply not do.

Fortunately, Mrs Govindikar, as always, had a contingency plan in place comprising of last-minute rental raincoats that were distributed to the walkers, since it was impractical to carry umbrellas over such a long distance. The T-shirts were unceremoniously discarded with only one sample preserved and nailed by its collar to a placard to serve the dual purpose of highlighting the cause and sending out a grim message to the errant suppliers. It was decided that this placard would be relayed among the members as they walked on, with Mrs Govindikar its flag bearer for the first hundred metres, as that was the maximum distance up to which the press had agreed to trail them.

The aforementioned press had arrived too, in the form of two reporters and one weary photographer who clicked a group picture of the waterproofed marathoners at the start line. The watchman, awake for once, did the honours by blowing on his whistle with all the air his vintage lungs could muster.

And they were off – well, figuratively, at least.

Anupama had always pictured the idea of a marathon as a row of panting, muscular runners tearing their way through hunger, thirst, exhaustion, hurdles and their own inner demons to battle the seemingly insurmountable physical challenges and emerge victorious. Here, huddled on the sidewalk with a troupe of black raincoats waddling about her, she felt more like she was in a funeral procession of penguins. At this rate, they would probably take all day to reach Inorbit, provided they didn't dawdle or make pit stops for tea breaks.

She could see the regular joggers in the younger crowd itching to break into a sprint. However, Mrs Govindikar and the committee members had been explicit in their declaration that this was not a competition, and they didn't want to risk anyone suffering any injuries or low self-esteem along the way, which is why a uniformity of pace was crucial.

Hardly surprising, since that was the same discipline with which Mrs Govindikar conducted her evening walks too with the members of her entourage. The sight of eight ladies marching in step through the colony roads, fanning themselves with their handkerchiefs, was a daily occurrence for the locals of Sector 5. Their speed, individual body weights, topics of conversation, and even the number of rounds they made around the colony park remained unwaveringly constant as they orbited every evening from 6 to 6.30 p.m. across their familiar trajectory. And their rituals didn't just end there, for after the walks were concluded, they made it a point to sit at the juice centre near Fine Chemists and have five servings of pani puri each, as a reward for their mental and physical exertions.

The group used to comprise of nine ladies at one time, until Mrs Divya Chatterjee from C-Wing made the mistake of losing five inches around her waist during her summer break. This was too much of a radical change to be processed by the members of the Govindikar Walkers Association, and matters were worsened when Mrs Chatterjee refused to divulge the details of her dramatic transformation, claiming it was all due to yoga and a balanced diet (as if!). The final nail in her coffin had been her insistence to wear track pants now that she could carry them off, instead of the prevalent dress code of salwar-kurta and sports shoes. Recognizing the signs of a rising anarchy on the horizon, Mrs Govindikar had promptly and politely conveyed to Mrs Chatterjee the circumstances of her discontinuation with the group, and that had been the end of it all.

Now on rare evenings, if you were lucky, you could sometimes see the slim, solitary apparition of Mrs Chatterjee in a track suit, jogging all alone in the darker recesses of the children's park, like a rudderless ship cast adrift.

Incidentally, Mrs Chatterjee was rather conspicuous by her absence in the marathon today; an oddity for someone so fitness-oriented. Her husband had cited ill-health as the reason, but there were hushed murmurs of it being a subtle act of rebellion on her part against Mrs Govindikar's initiative. After all, as per Kamala bai's reports, madamji had looked hale and hearty enough this morning when she had gone there for her duties. Dark whispers had followed of the possibility of Mrs Chatterjee getting ousted from the Cultural Affairs Committee of the Society too at this rate, if her attitude didn't improve. There would be a vote, naturally, but then who could be expected to go against Mrs Govindikar's will for the sake of a woman who had drunk beer in front of everyone during the Holi celebrations last year?

Noticing a spot of slush on the sidewalk in front of her, Anupama made a small leap over it. Unfortunately, the tile on which she landed was a moss-ridden one. Her foot slipped and skidded out of control. She threw out her hands reflexively, and a hand grabbed her arm just in time. By some instinct, she knew who it was even before she saw his face.

'Careful,' said Charlie, holding on to her firmly as she steadied herself. He was wearing the same raincoat as the rest of the marathoners, but unlike the others, he looked as if he were modelling it. She cast a quick glance around to see if any of the others had noticed, but there was hardly any reaction. Everyone else was concentrating on watching their steps while simultaneously trying to shield themselves from the downpour.

'Thank you,' she said shakily.

He nodded, and walked on without another word or even a smile. Anupama felt a pang of guilt. Misha's ankle had really been sprained. She had physically examined it herself this morning when hunger and thirst had forced her daughter to abandon her self-imposed incarceration. She wondered whether it was too late for an apology, or if that would only make things worse. Perhaps she had managed to permanently scare him away. Perhaps it was all for the best. The only thing to do now was to let it be. No need to seek closure. She didn't care what he thought of her anyway. How did it matter? This was what she wanted to begin with, wasn't it? Good thing it had happened in such an effortless manner.

However, despite these mollifying thoughts whirling inside her head, her feet had somehow unconsciously carried her up to Charlie's level, and they were walking abreast now, each looking dead ahead. She didn't look at him. He didn't look at her. After a few steps, she glanced up at him, and then, he glanced at her. Then, they both looked resolutely ahead.

'Can I ask you something?' he said, keeping his eyes on the road.

'Yes?'

'Why don't you like me?'

'Who said so?'

'It's just that every time I meet you, I end up upsetting you so much, and I don't even know why.'

'No, nothing like that,' she said, trying hard to keep her

voice casual. 'It's just that things have been a bit tense lately so…'

'I am a nice guy, you know,' he added. 'I mean, I don't know what kind of an impression I've given you, but I just wanted to clarify that. You can ask Mrs Patil if you want.'

'Why would I ask Mrs Patil?'

'She knows me well. She's a client of mine. A regular, actually.'

She had almost forgotten about his 'profession'. And now, with this casual reference, she felt all her earlier misgivings flooding back into her mind. She turned around to catch a glimpse of the innocuous-looking Mrs Patil, clutching an umbrella (she was one of the few who had shunned the raincoats) as she chattered away with Mrs Saini. Who would have guessed? Even in the shock of the moment though, Anu couldn't help but notice the change in the woman's appearance, the centre of attraction being her hair – once long and tied back, her shoulder-length tresses now flowed freely, swoopy layers cascading down and framing her face perfectly. She looked five years younger, at least. JD's services were obviously suiting her.

She turned her eyes back to Charlie. 'Can I be honest with you?'

'Sure.'

'How can you be so open about these things?'

'What do you mean?'

'Aren't you worried about your reputation? What if someone finds out and reports you?'

'Reports me for what?'

'You know for what.'

'No, I think we are on two separate planes of understanding here.'

Anupama lowered her voice. 'You know what you do is illegal, right?'

He stared at her. 'It's illegal to be a hairdresser?'

They walked on, eyes widened and gawking at each other.

'You are a hairdresser,' she repeated tonelessly.

'Hairstylist, actually,' he said. 'I specialize in ladies' hairstyles.'

'And those clients and women you were referring to…?'

'Yeah, they visit me at the salon.'

Oh God.

He unzipped his raincoat, reached into his T-shirt pocket, and passed her a card. 'I've been handing it around to whoever is interested. It's in Juhu, so if you want to book an appointment anytime, just let me know.'

Her head was a swirling mist of daze, guilt and embarrassment. She took his card mechanically.

'You look a little shocked,' remarked Charlie.

'No, no.'

They had walked on a little further, before he turned to her with a curious look on his face.

'Wait, what were *you* thinking?'

'Sorry?'

'You thought I was doing something illegal, right?'

'No.'

'But you just said that.'

'Oh, I say a lot of things, Charlie. Just ignore me.'

She hoped against hope that he would drop the subject. However, they had barely gone past three steps, when Charlie broke into a mischievous grin. 'Ohhh, now I get it! No wonder you were so anxious around me.'

'Charlie, look—'

'One night you see me smoking a joint on the terrace, and you think I'm a drug supplier or something, right?'

She paused, and nodded. 'Yes. Yes, that's me. I just jump to conclusions.'

'Well, don't worry. I am not into any of the hardcore stuff, and even the weed is occasional. Usually, I just chill with a beer.'

'But why on the terrace?'

'Like I said, I don't like closed spaces, especially when I'm drinking. The terrace is the closest thing I've got.'

'How did you open the lock?'

'I broke it,' he replied, and then passed her a smirk. 'Is that illegal too?'

A bus honked behind them. Anupama was surprised to see how much they had drifted to the centre of the road without even realizing it. As they sidled back to the pavement, Anupama cast a look behind. They had left the others quite far behind.

'We should wait for them to catch up,' she said.

'Why? Most of them look like they won't make it anyway.'

'I know, but Mrs Govindikar said—'

Charlie snorted. 'It's not a school trip, Mrs Arora.' He added, 'Unless you want to be with them, in which case I'll move on.'

Anupama glanced back. The Govindikar Walker Association members were all trundling along as a single unit, chattering animatedly to each other. Behind them, some tired residents had begun passing fruit juices and energy drinks amongst themselves in a show of solidarity, even though they were barely five hundred metres away from the starting point. No way was she going back to that sordid troupe.

The notion that others might find her drifting away with some young guy a little inappropriate did cross Anupama's mind, but thanks to the raincoats, it was impossible to figure out who was who from behind. And no one would notice her gone in that crowd anyway. They were used to her absence. She had made sure of that.

'Let's just walk slower, at least,' she suggested.

———

How long had it been since she had had tea in a leaky lean-to chai-stall, perched on a rickety plastic stool, with raindrops pattering all about her? Must have been long enough, for the experience seemed almost exotic to her now. Rajeev was a stickler for hygiene and anything from the sidewalk was frowned upon. After the children had arrived, the regime got even stricter, until the only teas they had outside their home were the synthetic machine-processed ones from overpriced cafeterias. Bland and tasteless no doubt, but at least you didn't risk oral infections from the leftover saliva of previous customers.

That was a long time ago, though. Nowadays, tea was served in little plastic tumblers even in roadside tea stalls, to be discarded after use, along with the saliva. She wouldn't even have known that, had it not been for Charlie's suggestion to grab a cuppa before their return.

The mini-marathon had ended up becoming a micro-marathon as one of the ladies, Mrs Kaushik, began complaining of chest pain as the Olympians drew near the Mith Chowki signal. Panic and hullabaloo ensued as every marathoner jumped to her aid, some offering to take her back in a taxi, others leaping into passing autos so they could get back quickly and arrange for some home remedies, others scurrying into the market nearby to see if they could find a clinic of some sort, and still others making a dash for the Infiniti mall a little distance away, claiming there was a chemist store inside. Within a matter of minutes, three-fourths of the participants had disappeared.

The irony was that, in all the confusion, none of them remembered to take Mrs Kaushik along. The poor lady was left behind in the rain, sullenly rubbing her chest under her raincoat and mulling over what to do next, until Mrs Govindikar took the initiative and declared the marathon a success regardless of its non-completion. They had reached out to the media, which was the important point, and owing to the weather, there were hardly any spectators on the road to illuminate about the cause anyway, so she didn't see the point of tormenting themselves any further. Her proposal was met with murmurs and nods of barely-concealed relief. More autos were hailed, and the few remaining marathoners found themselves packing into groups of twos and threes and hurrying back home.

Anupama and Charlie had, in the meantime, progressed so far ahead that it took them a while to realize that no one was following them anymore. With nothing else to do, she had just suggested turning back when Charlie spotted the tea stall. The euphoria that rose within him at the prospect of sharing a monsoon roadside *chai* was infectious. Besides, Anupama reasoned, it might have looked odd to return with Charlie in full view of all her neighbours. This way, at least they could have some buffer time for everyone to go indoors before they got back.

'This is nice, isn't it?' said Charlie, gazing out at the rains.

'Yes.'

'You should come up to the terrace sometime. It's very pleasant when it's not raining, with the breeze and everything.'

Anupama smiled lightly. 'I am afraid my terrace-crashing days are behind me now, Charlie.'

'Oh, please. You must be, what—'

He hesitated. Anupama turned her eyes on him. 'What?'

'I don't know …' he mumbled nervously, 'early … thirties or something…?'

'Yes. I had my daughter when I was nine.'

Charlie guffawed, spilling a bit of his tea. 'Well, you know what they say. It's not about what's up here,' he said, indicating his head, 'but about what's in here.' He pointed at his chest.

'I'm referring to the heart,' he clarified, a beat later.

'Yes, I got that.'

'And I'm not saying that your head looks old, but that the mental—'

'The explanations are really not necessary.'

Charlie shook his head in dismay while swiping at his wet locks, which had fallen over his forehead again. How did they always maintain their symmetry? 'Sorry, I don't know why I always end up being weird whenever I'm around you.'

For some strange, peculiar reason, Anupama felt her heart skip a beat at that.

'Has it ever happened with you?' he asked, raising his greyish-brownish-hazel-whatever eyes to look at her.

'Hm?'

'This whole messing up when someone's around and you don't even know why. You know what I'm saying?'

All of a sudden, the back of her neck felt like there were ants crawling all over it. She resisted the urge to scratch and casually sipped her tea. 'I don't think so.'

'Yeah, you always seem so calm and collected.'

Anupama looked up to see if he was being sarcastic. The expression on his face seemed genuine enough, though.

'Except for that tiny incident about the cream biscuits,' he tacked on as an afterthought.

'Which we agreed not to talk about.'

'That's true. But while we are on the topic—'

'We are not.'

Charlie fell silent. However, the glazed look in his eyes and the faint smile on his lips left her in no doubt as to what was going on in his head.

'You can't let it go, can you?'

'I'm sorry. It's just stuck in my head.'

'Why?'

'Because of that thing you said: "you don't gift cream biscuits to strangers without knowing their back stories," remember?'

She did. 'No.'

'I'm just curious. What did you mean? Is there really a back story involved?'

'It's personal, Charlie.'

'Okay.'

He started humming a low tune to himself, while Anupama closed her eyes and breathed in the freshness of the clarified rainy air, enjoying the fleeting sense of an unadulterated tranquillity she hadn't felt in so long. When she opened her eyes, Charlie was staring at her.

'What?'

'I just want you to know that the terrace offer was not just a formality. If you ever want to, you know, talk or something, you can come up. I'm there until midnight usually. There's a nice shed area too in case it's raining.'

Great, another wannabe therapist in the making, thought Anupama wryly. It's like she was a magnet for vacant shoulders to cry on. 'Thank you, Charlie, but I'm fine.'

'I'm not saying you're not. I just—'

'I got it.'

They drank the rest of their teas in silence.

———

The moment their auto crossed the HDFC ATM by her apartment block, Anupama kept her eyes sharply focused outwards. She instructed the auto to slow down and stop a few metres past the building gates. Charlie gave her a quizzical look, but didn't comment. As they passed the gates, Anupama caught a glimpse of some ladies seated under the shed of A-Wing. Damn.

Charlie offered to pay, but she was adamant. She paid a few extra bucks in addition to the fare and asked the driver to wait for a few minutes.

'Are you going somewhere else?' asked Charlie.

'No, but I need you to do me a favour.'

'Okay...'

'I will go in now, and I want you to sit here for five minutes or so and then come in.'

'Why?'

'So it doesn't look like we have come back together.'

'But we have come back together.'

'Yes, but it shouldn't look like that.'

'Why not?'

'Because I know people around here, and they might take it the wrong way.'

'But we haven't done anything wrong, so how does it matter?'

'Charlie, it doesn't work that way. You have to be in my position to understand.'

'I *am* in your position. We are both in the exact same position.'

'That's not what I mean. Why can't you just do what I am asking you to do?' she said irritably.

'Mrs Arora?' said a voice behind her.

Anupama's insides turned to ice. Slowly, as if in a nightmare, she turned her gaze around to behold Mrs Mehtani standing beside her auto, peering in. Her right hand was balancing an umbrella, and in her left was a bag of groceries.

It simply wasn't fair.

Of all the people, why did it have to be Mrs Mehtani, the motor-mouth local tabloid of the entire block?

'Are you okay?' asked the wily serpent, barely able to conceal her glee.

'Yes, Mrs Mehtani. I wasn't feeling well so this helpful young man here dropped me back.'

'Oh, but the rest of us returned half an hour ago. Where were you?' she asked in an innocent tone.

'I had to stop for a while. To rest.'

'With him?'

'He happened to be nearby.'

'I am Charlie, by the way,' said Charlie, with a wave of his hand.

Mrs Mehtani passed him a sweet smile. 'Hello Charlie, are you staying here too?'

'Yes, C-704.'

'Oh, same floor as you, then,' she said to Anupama.

'Yes, we are neighbours,' said Anupama, through gritted teeth.

'How nice. But isn't that the one with the leaky pipes?'

'Doesn't make a difference to me, I'm hardly ever at home,' said Charlie.

'And yet, you found the time today to give a neighbour company. Isn't that sweet?'

Anupama clenched her fists so tight she was sure her nails were drawing blood.

'Anyway, chalo, you two carry on. I will catch up with you later.'

With a diplomatic grin and a pronounced twirl of her

umbrella, Mrs Mehtani turned on her heels. Anupama could see the spring in her step as she trotted past the gates. It was like the woman had discovered a new raison d'etre.

She turned and snapped back at Charlie. 'Are you happy now?'

'Huh? What did I do?'

'Leave it, Charlie. Just leave it, okay?' she hissed, clambering out of the auto and flouncing through the gates with furious strides. Behind her, the auto continued to splutter sadly until the sound finally died.

7

'You should have taken separate autos to begin with,' said Neena, over the phone.

Anupama sighed; her mobile balanced between her left ear and shoulder as she sprinkled sabji masala over the sizzling ladyfingers before stirring them in the frying pan. She covered the pan and lowered the heat to allow it to simmer. The chapattis and curd curry were already done. Her eyes drifted up to the clock. Dinner would be ready by 9.15. Thank God, something in her world was still in order.

'My life is over, isn't it?' she asked morosely.

'No, it's not. Gossip comes with its own expiry date. Just make sure you don't get spotted with him again.'

'How can I do that? He lives right next door.' She walked over to her kitchen window and cautiously peeked through the sliver between the newspapers plastered over the pane. Charlie's kitchen was dark. He was probably out somewhere, chilling with friends, having the time of his life, blissfully unaware of the wreckage he had just caused.

'So avoid him then. Sooner or later, he will get the message too.'

'I just feel a little guilty, you know. It wasn't really his fault to begin with…'

'It doesn't matter, Anu. We have to be careful about our image. The problem with these youngsters is that they just don't get it.'

'So, I just cut him off completely then?'

'Absolutely.'

'Won't that seem downright rude?'

'You can't please everyone, Anu.'

'I would rather just avoid Mrs Mehtani, to be honest.'

'That will only make you look guiltier. Trust me on this. Now, what are you making for dinner?'

The bell rang before Anupama could reply. She asked Neena to hold on for a second and hurried to the door. When she opened it, there was an envelope waiting for her outside with her name and address on it. Anupama flipped it over. There were no sender's details. She tore it open to see a single chit with a mobile number and a one-line message: *Call me. Charlie.*

She glanced up in surprise. The corridor was empty. How had he managed to get away so fast? Had he run back to his apartment after ringing her bell? Or was he hiding downstairs? She stared back at the chit.

'He gave me his number,' she murmured into the phone.

'Who?'

'Charlie.'

'What? When?'

'Just now. On a chit. But I can't see him anywhere.'

There was a chilly silence at the other end.

'Hello?' said Anupama.

'You want me to call someone?' said Neena.

'No … it's just his number.'

'Do not call him, Anu. This is not normal behaviour. Inform the watchman, if you have to.'

'About what? That my neighbour asked me to call him? I don't think that even qualifies as harassment.'

'Do you want me to come over? I can bring Deven with me.'

'No, it's fine. Let's not make a big deal out of it.'

'Just don't call him, okay? Under no circumstances should you encourage him any further. Go wash your hands.'

'What?'

'Sorry, Deven just walked into the kitchen. No, beta, let it cool first. Anu, I'll call you later, and be careful. Call me if you need anything.'

Anupama hung up, the note clenched in her left hand, the mobile in her right. She stood like that for a few moments, deliberating. There was no denying the oddness of his actions, but then who was she to comment on odd behaviour? And let's face it: she did owe him an apology. More than one, in fact, if you counted the previous disturbing encounters, to which today's was the crowning glory. Curiosity won over caution, and she dialled his number. What was the worst that could happen? He didn't appear to be the ballistic type anyway.

The phone rang twice, before he picked it up. 'Hello?'

'Hi, Charlie, Mrs Arora here. Why is your voice echoing?'

'I'm in the loo.'

'Oh, should I call later?'

'No, no, it's fine. This will take some time.'

Ugh. She resisted the urge to hang up or do something

drastic yet again. 'Why didn't you just give me your number yourself?'

'I didn't want to risk anyone seeing us together again. This way, things can be completely confidential. Just save my number under a pseudonym and burn up the note once you're done.'

'Look, I know I overreacted, and it wasn't your fault. I just panicked. So—'

'That's okay. I just wanted you to know that the situation is sorted. So, you don't need to panic anymore.'

'You don't know Mrs Mehtani—'

'Actually, I do. Mrs Patil – my client – ranted about her all the time in the salon. She is supposed to be a gossipmonger of some sort, right? Didn't take long to make the connection.'

'Well, anyway, the damage is done so—'

'And it's undone too. Don't worry. She won't be gossiping about us to anyone. I made sure of that.'

She didn't like where this conversation was headed. Neena's warning came back to mind. 'What have you done, Charlie?'

'You're going to love this. I was just coming back from my jog this evening when I saw her buying vegetables from a vendor. So, I stopped by to pick up some too. And then, I made sure to keep pace with her all the way to the building, even though she did her utmost to evade me. And as soon as we entered the premises, I struck up a conversation with her in front of a couple of witnesses as if we had been chatting the whole way.

'The masterstroke was that when we reached her block, I handed her my share of vegetables too, thereby giving all the curious onlookers the impression that I had been carrying them for her. Then I bade her goodbye, said it was a real pleasure and that I hoped we could do it again sometime soon. You should have seen the look on her face!'

Anupama didn't even notice when her jaw had fallen open. All she could do was listen in silence. And awe.

'So, you see?' he cried out happily. 'Now everyone believes that she's the shady one, so even if she does try to slander you, they'll assume it's a defensive strategy or something, 'cause no one else saw us.'

It took her a few seconds to find her voice. 'You … you thought up all of this on your own?'

'No, no. I didn't even care about it. But then I felt bad for you, so I called up my mother. She is a huge fan of these TV soaps and stuff, so I figured she would be a suitable advisor for, you know, the rather dramatic situation we were in. She gave me the idea. Apparently, *Har Ghar Ki Bahu* has a similar track going on right now.'

Anupama couldn't help but smile, which progressed into a chuckle, and the chuckle into a laugh; a laugh which burst out involuntarily from her, as if it was out of her control.

'So, are we cool now?' asked Charlie.

'Yes, we are cool. Thank you, Charlie. That was … quite impressive.'

'I know. I can be pretty awesome that way. Now if you will excuse me, I'm almost done here. Took quite a bit of pressure this time.'

'Charlie, please! We are about to have dinner.'

'I'm fixing my shower head.'

'Oh.'

'Why do you always assume the worst with me, Mrs Arora?'

'Goodnight, Charlie,' she said, with another laugh.

She hung up and turned around, her head and heart feeling much lighter. God bless this boy – at least, for the time being. Her phone rang again.

'Hello?'

'Sorry to disturb you,' said Charlie. 'But I just wanted to inform you that there is a monsoon offer going on at my salon right now. So, if you are in the mood for a makeover—'

'Thanks, Charlie. I'll keep that in mind.'

'There is a free papaya facial too if you get a friend along.'

'All right, bye.'

She hung up and was about to head for the kitchen when her phone buzzed again.

'What?' she asked tersely.

'Whoa, someone's in a foul mood,' said Renu.

'Oh, hi—'

'Neena said you got caught with a hot young item today. Speak.'

'Bye, Renu.'

'What the hell! You can tell her but you can't tell me?'

'I just said it was a mistake. And I never said he was hot.'

'So, he's not?'

'That's not the point.'

'Nice!'

'Could you just turn it off for one second?'

'What's his name?'

Just then, the sound of a door being unlocked reached her ears. Misha walked out of her room, her nose crinkled.

'What's burning?' she asked, sniffing the air.

The bhindi!

She hung up and rushed to the kitchen. With trembling fingers, she lifted the lid to be greeted by the sight of charcoal black bits of bhindi stuck to the iron. Great. She turned on the exhaust fan and poured some water on to the vegetable pyre. Billows of steam rose up in an angry, accusing hiss. It was like someone had cast an evil eye upon her cooking. So preoccupied was she in scraping off the dish that it took her a few seconds to spot Misha still standing in the doorway. They hadn't exchanged a word since their showdown yesterday. She had a thoughtful, uncertain look on her face, and experience had taught her that that was usually never good news.

'Who's he?' she asked.

'What?'

'Who were you talking about? On the phone?'

'It's rude to eavesdrop.'

'So you're not going to tell me. I thought I was at an age where we could both be frank with each other. As friends.'

'It's nothing. Renu was being silly about someone, as usual.'

'She's cool. I like her.'

'I know.'

'And I didn't mean to listen in, by the way. It's just that I heard you laughing back there and was curious. It's been a while. It's great you have someone like her around.'

She was on the verge of clarifying that it wasn't Renu to whom the credit was due when something told her that that was probably not very relevant info for her daughter anyway. Besides, she had a strong feeling Misha was building up to something here.

'And I just wanted to apologize to you. About last night. And this,' she said, pointing to her neck, which was now covered with a scarf.

Relief began to drip over Anupama in tiny, uncertain trickles. So, the ship was returning to the harbour, finally. She wanted to say it was okay, however the thought of someone touching her daughter in that way still gave her the jitters. And God forbid that she give the impression that such an act could ever be repeated again. So, she just nodded quietly and carried the kadai off to the basin, with Misha following her.

'I know this must be tough for you, but you have to accept that I'm an adult now. I can make my own decisions—'

'Like getting that ISI mark of affection on your neck?' She hadn't intended to be snappy, but some things were just too much to take.

'It was a mistake. I thought he was just kissi—'

The kadai slipped from Anupama's hands and clattered heavily into the basin.

'Why are we having this conversation?'

'Because I've realized that keeping things from you isn't fair. So, from now on, I'm going to be totally honest with you about everything. Like I was with Papa.'

The mention of Rajeev alongside the burnt kadai in front of her eyes and the uncomfortable topic being discussed made Anupama feel a rising sense of discomfort. Times like this made her wish she had the liberty to go and lock herself in her room too.

Still, anything was better than being kept in the dark, she presumed.

'So now you know about Mehul,' said Misha.

'I do. And it was a bit of a surprise. I thought you were seeing Tarun.'

'There was a bit of an overlap, but I've broken up with him now.'

'Thank God. I mean, I think you deserve better. Just tell me this new one is unmarried, please.'

'Of course he is,' said Misha. 'Plus, he's smart, mature, sensible—'

'Then how come I haven't heard about him before?'

'He has only just joined the college. It's been about a month.'

'Really? Isn't it a bit late for student transfers?'

Misha let out a tinkling laugh. 'I never said he was a student, Mamma.'

The trickles of relief halted mid-flow to be replaced by a siren of maternal alarm that went off with a wailing cry.

'What is he then?' *Please say librarian, counsellor, caterer, peon – anything, just not—*

'He's our new English lecturer. Came in place of Sapna ma'am. And he's like this super smart, double PhD genius. You should see the way he talks about Chaucer and Tennyson and—'

'You're seeing your teacher,' said Anupama in a choked voice.

'Temp, actually. He is still to be confirmed, which he will be, of course. I mean, the man has taught at Venky and Xavier's and—'

'How old is he?'

'Hm?'

'How old is this man? The one who gave you that thing on your neck?'

Misha waved her hand dismissively. 'Oho, age is just a number, Mamma.'

Anupama could almost feel the neurons ignite inside her skull as her forehead reached boiling point. 'Misha, beta, do you deliberately make such choices to torture me?'

'As in?'

'As in if you want me to die of shock, then just electrocute me in my sleep, na? Why go through so much of a hassle?'

'Here we go with the dramatics. I don't know why I thought we could have a healthy open relationship for once.'

'You want a healthy open relationship with your mother? Stop dating married men and sugar daddy professors!'

'Why do you always have to label *everything*?'

'You are not seeing this man. Period.'

'You can't alter destiny, Mamma.'

'No, but I can call up your principal, so unless you want to see him fired, you'll end it right now. Are we clear or not?'

Misha narrowed her eyes. 'My own mother doesn't get me. What a shame.'

'I am serious, Misha!'

'Fine,' she snapped.

She had just turned to leave when, halfway through, she pivoted around to face her. 'You know, Mamma, one day, when you're able to look beyond the bonds and constraints that this world has put on you, you will realize just what a shell you've been living in. And for your sake, I hope that day comes soon.'

'Amen. Now call your brother. Dinner's almost ready.'

The world felt better after a bath; even if it were only for a short while. Your daughter could have a penchant for attracting the worst possible romantic choices, your son could be hiding every aspect of his post-pubescent life from your eyes, your neighbours could be control freaks and gossipmongers, but in those few lingering minutes of dewy freshness after you stepped out of that shower, nothing seemed to matter. On the days when Anupama missed out on her daily dose of JD's offerings, she would often choose this time to log on and admire the plethora of abs, pecs, and biceps beckoning her, when her children had retired for the night and she was free of all responsibilities for the time being. There was something reassuring about the fact that at the end of the day, no matter how crappy and unstable the world outside may seem, she would still have those glimpses of unchanging beauty waiting to greet her behind closed doors, ready to be summoned at her will. Something so discreetly empowering about that.

Two hundred and fifty-two visits so far.

Had this been a retail outlet, a frustrated store attendant would be trailing her heels by now. *Madam, are you planning to buy something eventually or not?*

She eyed a couple of women-oriented pleasure ads pasted above the home page bar – exotic boudoir scents and lotions, lingerie brands, honeymoon kits and some 'adult wellness' products whose details she had never bothered finding out. What was the point? Firstly, the idea of deriving pleasure from something so – synthetic – turned her off. Secondly, even if anything did catch her eye, she wouldn't be caught dead having it delivered to her place, no matter how 'discreet' they claimed their packaging to be. And what did they imply by 'discreet' anyway?

To,

*Mrs X. Flat no ***.*

Product Description: 'Confidential' (wink, wink)

A particular profile caught her eye. It was of a young man crouched on the ground with his arm wrapped around a Labrador. The face had been cropped out, but she could still see tiny tufts of wavy hair at the base of his neck. He sported a lean physique, cuts and rips in all the right places with barely an ounce of body fat visible in his strong tendon-laden arms. It was a decent enough picture as compared to most of the other profiles, but since he was crouched sideways, Anupama could see the back of his T-shirt had lifted above the jeans, exposing a bit of his lower back and a hint of the CK underwear he was wearing underneath. For some reason, she found herself strangely fixated. There was nothing erotic about it per se, but still some intangible force of familiarity pulled her to it, stirring her desires. And then, without warning, the clouds cleared and a memory popped up in her head, clear as crystal – Charlie, bent over her living room floor, inspecting Misha's foot, his CK underwear greeting her as she entered her home that night. Anupama hastily shut down the profile. The guilt was like a shattering blow to the thin coating of rust that had gathered around her conscience over time. A shudder passed through her. No more JD's.

She logged off and, by way of compensation, decided to visit her Facebook profile to check in on her kids and zone back to the sphere of domesticity and motherly concern. The first thing she did was visit Misha's profile and check all the 'likes' and comments on her previous posts and photos, just to see if that Casanova professor of hers had made any prior contact with her, something her eyes may have missed out on earlier as she hadn't been looking for it. It would be nice to have some evidence too if things heated up to a direct confrontation one day. Thankfully, there was no sign of any Mehul amongst her online admirers. She scanned through her friends' list too, just to be doubly sure. No Mehul, teacher or otherwise. She let out a sigh of relief. At least, they had been wise in this regard. Or maybe the sly old bugger was just too mindful of his tracks. She wished they had PTA meetings in colleges too. That would have given her the ideal opportunity to look the man in the eye and pass him the cold, murderous glance she had perfected over months of escorting her daughter through stations and marketplaces crowded with ogling pervs just waiting to cop a feel.

Her next stop was Nimit's profile, where an unwelcome surprise was waiting for her. He had just accepted a friend request from a 'Daenerys Lover 1992'. The profile picture was Charlie's. And as a mark of mutual amity, Charlie had posted a rather vulgar picture of a tank-top-clad busty blonde promoting the daily consumption of dairy products, with what Anupama hoped was yoghurt splattered across her ample cleavage. What was more, her son had promptly liked and responded to it with an LOL. Her blood boiled. She didn't even know they were friendly with each other. Caution restrained her for a fleeting instant before indignation overcame it, and she commented: 'Do you really think it's appropriate to be posting such images on a minor's Facebook profile?' while tagging Charlie into it. She waited a second or two, and when no response came, she was on the verge of logging out when she found herself tagged on Charlie's reply: 'I don't see anything wrong with passing nutritional advice to a growing boy. Calcium deficiency is a rising epidemic amongst the youth of this country.'

The cheeky bastard. He even got two 'likes' for it on the spot! She typed on:

'So is immoral behaviour thanks to the influence of people like you.'

A second later, she found herself attacked by an array of counter-comments from all directions, including her son, who was apparently still online now: 'Troll spotted', 'Grow a pair, dude', 'Did we, just, like time travel back to the 50's?', 'Go away, Grandma!'

Great. Now she was a pariah in her son's virtual world as well.

Her heart fell. She decided to just let things be and withdraw from the battle before it got any more offensive. Just then, a message popped up on her inbox.

Charlie.

Daenerys Lover 1992: Yo what's ur deal, mate? U sounded pretty upset bk there.

She thought of ignoring it, but the thought of letting him get away with the last word rankled in her, so she decided to take advantage of this more private communication space to have another go.

She wrote: 'Just being a responsible adult. Something you should try too now and then.'

Daenerys Lover 1992: Easy there, buddy. U dnt even know me.

She replied: I just don't happen to have very high opinions of twenty-four-year-olds befriending teens online and treating them as peers, unmindful of the consequences this could have on their psyche.

Daenerys Lover 1992: Seems lk a bit of a double standard. Urs says ur twenty-one urself. N just how do u know Nimit anyway? Wat r u, his guardian angel or smthing? Now *that's* creepy.

She typed: I'm just looking out for him. And I don't have to justify myself to you, Charlie!

There was a moment's pause, before the next message cropped up.

Daenerys Lover 1992: Wait ... how do u know my name?

Anupama froze. In her anger, she had forgotten about his profile ID. Her fingers went numb, hovering above her keyboard, unsure. Another message popped up.

Daenerys Lover 1992: OMG Mrs Arora ... is that you???!!!!!

She panicked, logged off, and slammed shut her laptop. She was engulfed by an overpowering urge to rip the grills off her window and jump out. What had she done? Why? *Why?*

A second later, her mobile beeped with a text message. With trembling fingers, she clicked it open.

Charlie: Dont worry. Ur secret is safe wt me ☺

10

Minutes
Atharva Hari C.H.S Monthly General Meeting

Date: 06 July 2014

Present: Managing Committee headed by Smt. Alka Govindikar, A-Wing residents, B-Wing residents (barring B-203, B-501), C-Wing residents (barring C-704)

Apologies: Mrs Kaushik (B-203)

Absent: Mrs Divya Chatterjee (B-501), Tenant of Mr Gautam Acharya (C-704)

KEY POINTS DISCUSSED	KEY DECISIONS MADE
Mr Desai from A-403 raised complaint of litter being thrown from the balcony of A-503 overhead which gets stuck in his own balcony netting. Mrs Saini from A-503	Board requested members to maintain decorum of meeting by not indulging in personal mud-slinging. Instructed Mrs Saini to be more careful with her litter. Instructed Mr Desai to make sure

refuted allegation, saying that it could be from any of the overhead flats. Mr Desai presented old passport photo of Mr Saini as proof, stating it had dropped with the litter. Mrs Saini claimed subterfuge, said that photo could be from anywhere as Mr Saini had a habit of leaving them lying around all over the place. Mr Desai threatened to make a formal complaint. Mrs Saini claimed mental harassment is wilful revenge for her complaint earlier this year against Mr Desai about his double-parking habits, possibly due to his increased drinking habits, as evidenced by the frequency of beer cans noticed in passing, inside his garbage bags.

the car is parked properly at all times, and to keep in mind his status as a respected family man in the neighbourhood, especially at such a crucial time as when he was seeking a matrimonial alliance for his daughter.

Mr Patil from C-202 raised complaint of strange dragging and creaking noises from flat above between 2.30 and 3.00 a.m. every night. Claimed that it disturbed their sleep and

Board stated that this was an internal matter to be sorted out between the two parties. To comment on anyone's late-night bedroom activities was beyond their jurisdiction. Advised all brought his wife and him much anguish. Mr Sharma from C-302 apologized and claimed sound came because of elderly mother-in-law who needed support to go to the bathroom at night. Mrs Patil refuted that claim by stating that she had visited their flat yesterday and found that the lady sleeps in the next bedroom, thereby rendering their claims invalid. Added that the lady seemed too frail to drag furniture around. Mrs Sharma enquired whether complainant was calling her husband a liar in public. Added that they hadn't complained when the Patils' various havans made the whole building a smoke chamber, and that living in such apartments required a certain degree of compromise.

against any future references to havans or similar religious annotations to maintain secular nature of meetings.

Mrs Tiwari of A-604 raised complaint of young men coming into the premises late at night to visit downstairs

Board instructed Ms Shalini Gupta that any security issues connected to the housing society was the society's business.

tenant, Ms Shalini Gupta, thereby raising security issues. Ms Shalini Gupta stated that who visited her and when was her business. Added that visitors were respectable people and her friends.	Reminded her that majority of crimes against women were committed by people known to them. Added that the single youths residing in the premises had the onus of serving as role models of moral integrity and character for the children around them. Advised Ms Gupta to regulate her visitation hours and have every guest sign in their verified details into the visitors' register.
Mrs Mehtani of C-503 raised issue of the broken lock on her building's terrace door. Said it seemed to be an act of vandalism by one of the residents as terrace contained traces of what appeared to be snacks and cigarette butts. Board asked Mrs Anupama Arora of C-703 if she had any inkling of this since she lived on the top floor. Mrs Arora claimed no knowledge. Mrs Mehtani added that breaking a lock like that would generate an awful amount of	Board made note of this and resolved to enquire further with absent tenant from C-704. Serious action to be taken against the culprit as and when found.

noise and that it was odd
that Mrs Arora didn't hear a
thing. Mrs Arora stated the
probability of her being out
when the incident occurred.

Anupama hadn't felt this petrified since the time she had borne witness to Renu setting off a firecracker in the staff toilet when they were in the seventh grade. She felt like she was thirteen all over again, back in that morning assembly, her arms and legs trembling as the principal made the grim announcement at the podium that the culprits, once caught, would be given an immediate TC, no questions asked. She had been an unwitting accomplice then. She was an unwitting accomplice now.

And the worst part was that she didn't even know why she had done it. The lie had just slipped out of her mouth before she could stop herself, like an impulse. And now it was too late.

She subconsciously felt the collective judgment of all present in the cramped meeting hall boring into her as Mrs Govindikar went on with the rest of the session. A primeval urge rose within her to throttle Mrs Mehtani until that notorious cat-got-the-cream smirk was wiped off her face forever. The bitch. Anupama had a strong inkling that both Mrs Govindikar and Mrs Mehtani knew exactly who was behind the broken lock, but now Mrs Mehtani had some drama to look forward to in her sad, miserable life. She wouldn't be surprised if the viren ended up installing an extra CCTV camera on her floor just for investigative purposes. It was a good thing that she had Charlie's number. She would have to warn him the moment she got out of there.

———

Luck wasn't on her side however, because as soon as the meeting was over, Mrs Mehtani trailed her all the way back to their block, chattering on and on about miscellaneous topics, all the while refusing to take Anupama's lack of attention as a hint. Only when they were inside their block and waiting for the elevator did she drop her voice to a conspiratorial aside.

'By the way, sorry for springing that on you. I hope it didn't inconvenience you or anything?'

'Why would it inconvenience me? I didn't even know about it,' said Anupama, pressing the lift button again in a vain attempt to convince it to descend faster.

'I know, I know. Neither did I until my younger one hit a six that went flying up to the roof. He was the one who told me about the broken lock.'

'Your four-year-old hit the ball eight storeys high?'

'Must be his genes. His father was a district-level cricketer, you know.'

'I know.' She had heard the story seventeen times till date.

'So anyway, I just wanted to warn you. One can never be too careful these days, you know.'

'I appreciate it, Mrs Mehtani. Thank you.'

'Oh please, what are neighbours for?'

Mrs Mehtani hummed a merry tune under her breath as the elevator began its slow descent and the light blinked as it arrived at the third floor. From the way she was rocking on the balls of her feet, Anupama knew there was more coming.

'Speaking of neighbours, what's up with that Mrs Chatterjee anyway? This is the second general meeting she has skipped in a row after her no-show at that marathon. I mean, what's the point of being in a community if you're not interested, no? At first, I thought that was why Mrs Govindikar was looking a bit upset today.'

'Was she?' replied Anupama, with the same non-committal attitude she displayed towards all gossip baits.

Mrs Mehtani nodded, followed by a sympathetic cluck. 'Of course, but then I remembered what the real reason was. Tch. Poor thing.'

The elevator finally arrived. As soon as they were in, Mrs Mehtani started humming again, rocking on her feet. Anupama knew the only way to get the woman off her back was by letting her get it out of her system.

'Why? What happened?' she asked reluctantly.

'Well, you know how she and her husband were planning to visit their son in the US later this month? Turns out, the boy cancelled again. Some sudden commitment or something. So sad, no? They had got their visas and everything.'

Anupama nodded. 'Yes, really sad.'

'And this is the fourth time it has happened in a row since he left. I mean, I don't know anything about the work culture out there, but it does seem like they keep the poor boy a little too busy, right?'

Another click of the tongue.

'It would seem so,' said Anupama.

'Such a brilliant boy, though. I always knew he would go far. How much did Nimit get in his half-yearly?'

'Seventy-something.'

'That's nice. Saahil got ninety-four,' she said matter-of-factly, referring to her elder son who was in Nimit's class.

'That's great.'

'Must be his genes. His father was an ICSE state-level topper, you know.'

It took Anupama a few moments to realize they had passed Mrs Mehtani's floor. 'Are you going up?'

'Oh, yes. I just wish to see if the 704 tenant is in. What was his name again?'

'Charlie. And why?'

'Well, I just had a chat with the board, and they agreed I could handle the inquiry on my own. I have a way with these things, you see.'

Anupama felt her pulse quicken. She had to fight every instinct within her to stop gulping on the spot. Mrs Mehtani had the nose of a bloodhound and the eye of a hawk when it came to spotting the tiniest traces of controversial masala around her. In fact, with her keen espionage skills, the woman displayed all the signs of having been a KGB agent or something just as pernicious in her previous life. Her target area may have changed now, but God had been kind enough to bless her with the same character and qualities that had led to her probable public prosecution and execution the first time around. Add to that the diplomatic immunity she enjoyed thanks to the benevolent shadow of Mrs Govindikar, and you had a formidable foe to reckon with, if you ever made the mistake of getting on her wrong side, as Charlie was about to discover. Anupama prayed for him to be out, and was more than relieved when they stepped out onto her floor to see the lock on his door.

'Well, that's unfortunate,' said Mrs Mehtani. 'Anyway, he will come back sooner or later. Will catch him then.'

'I could inform you when he does.'

'Oh, that's not necessary, dear. I have told the watchman to buzz me on my intercom the moment he sees him walk in.'

'Okay. Great, then.'

'Chalo, you take care. And come over for tea sometime, no?'

'I will. See you.'

The moment she was inside her flat, Anupama dialled Charlie's number, only to discover that it was switched off. Perfect.

She weighed her options, pacing to and fro across the living room as she pondered over what her next step should be. Was she over-reacting? Perhaps it was just a harmless little misdeed, for which he would be fined and let off with a warning. After all, it's not like he had directly harmed anyone. Deep within her heart though, she knew just how vain and ineffectual that hope was. This was the same housing society that had installed grills in every window of every block after Mrs Aggarwal's daughter was caught sneaking out at night. In the case of Charlie, it was going to be even worse, since he didn't even have the backing of being a family man to moderate the magnitude of his transgression. Social arrangements at Atharva Hari were like those deep-sea ecological systems you saw on nature channels. Vividly serene and eye-pleasing from afar, but the closer you got, the murkier the reality turned out to be. In a hostile environment of domestically rooted sharks and killer whales, drifters like Charlie were but mere baby squid, whose only mode of survival was their ability to camouflage and blend into their surroundings. All it took was one error in judgment, and they would get mercilessly devoured and excreted out of the system like they had never existed.

She had to do something. It wasn't just the fear of implication that galvanized her to act now, but a touch of compassion for the poor boy. Anupama felt a bit of relief at the fact that her paranoia now had a philanthropic aspect to it as well.

She thought of waiting for his phone to switch back on, but that was risky and time-consuming. What if he just decided to charge it after getting home? Grim thoughts and morbid speculations raced across her mind as she visualized a tearful Charlie buckling under pressure and confessing, among other things, his rather bemusing encounter with her on the terrace that night.

She desperately dialled his number again, only to have the hated recorded message played out for her again.

Like a familiar ailment, tidal waves of panic began to engulf her. Her pacing picked up in speed as beads of sweat broke out on her forehead. It was a good thing her children were out; otherwise they would have assumed she was having another nervous breakdown. What could she do?

She stopped abruptly. A vague memory of him giving his card to her at the marathon flashed through her mind, followed by a blank when she tried hard to recollect whether she had kept his card or not. Praying for her diligence to have come through for her, Anupama picked up her bag and plunged into it, wading past the layers of cosmetic leftovers, bits of diet chana, ATM receipts, a pamphlet from somewhere, a few coupons from elsewhere and semi-decomposed currency notes, until at the very bottom of the pile – voila! She fished out the rather crumpled card and smoothed it out on the table. The work timings were listed as between 10.00 a.m. to 7.30 p.m., so at least she had enough time to reach him.

Without a second thought, she grabbed her house keys and her purse. Cruel are the tricks fate plays upon us, she mused wryly. Her original intent had been to avoid meeting Charlie for a few days, especially after that Facebook fiasco, but now there was no choice. She didn't want to dramatize things, but if her frenzied chain of thought was anything to go by, the future of two lives was at stake here, and the terrifying part was that everything now depended on the course of action by a guy whose sense of social propriety was just about as high as his tolerance of closed spaces.

11

Up until this moment, Anupama had been under the impression that the general hair colour for any healthy Indian youth below the age of thirty was, well, black. Now, however, as she sat in the waiting room of Charlie's salon amidst a row of young girls with auburn, blonde, brown and mahogany streaks gleaming through their fancy hairdos, she couldn't help but marvel at just how far behind the times she actually was. Even the receptionist sported what appeared to be magenta immigrants warring against the dominant caramel community of her pixie cut. Add to that the piercing on her lower lip and her gothic make-up, and the girl could have served as an ideal ambassador for singles everywhere as per Mrs Govindikar's pictorial encyclopaedia.

Fed up of feeling like a racoon in a muster of peacocks, Anupama picked up one of the magazines from the rack and opened it, only to be greeted by more pictures of ethereal goddesses with gleaming skins and impossible hairstyles. She flipped past them, seeking a worthwhile article to pass the time, and was greeted in the end by a long, thought-provoking piece titled: 'The Urban Woman's Guide to

Surviving Menopause.' In spite of the rather grim reference to her forthcoming physiological phase (as if it were an epidemic contracted from a third-world country), she had to admit she was tempted to go through it for the sake of future reference. However, the moment she spotted the terms 'bleed', 'mucous' and 'dryness', her interest vaporized in a flash, and she plopped the magazine back into the rack. Some things were worth waiting for without spoilers.

'Who was it you wanted to see again?' the receptionist called out to her.

'Charlie.'

'Right. He'll be with you shortly. Is this your first visit?'

'Actually, I am not here for a haircut. I just need to tell him something.'

'We have a monsoon discount going on.'

'Thank you, but I am happy with my hair.'

The receptionist gave her a pitying smile and returned to her work. Anupama surreptitiously and self-consciously checked for any flyaway strands in her hair.

Several minutes passed before Charlie appeared, dressed in a black shirt and jeans with a black apron. He had trimmed his stubble down to a goatee today, revealing the tiny dimple on his left cheek, which seemed to smile along with him as he greeted the waiting customers, who fluttered their lashes at him and beamed delightedly. It was like a light switch had been flipped inside each of their animated faces. Something told her he didn't have to struggle to ensure the loyalty of his customers. The receptionist directed his attention to Anupama, and the moment he spotted her, his jaw dropped.

'Mrs Arora?'

'Hello, Charlie.'

His face tensed. 'What have I done now?'

———

'So, you came all this way just to tell me that?' he asked.

They were seated in the staff changing room. The smell of moisturizers, hair tonics and eleventh-hour deodorants hung heavy in the air, suffocating her slightly, but this was the best private space Charlie could manage at such short notice.

'You don't think it's a matter of worry?'

'It's just a lock. I'll put in a new one if it's that big a deal.'

'It's not about the lock. The society takes these things very seriously. Plus, you're a bachelor.'

'Wait, that's an issue too?'

'That is the main issue.'

'Really? Any other problem areas I should know about? Coloured eyes? Chest hair? Non-veg diet?'

'Charlie—'

'Look, don't get me wrong,' he backtracked. 'I really appreciate your concern and all. It's just … I don't get this whole deal, you know.'

'You don't have to *get* the deal. Just prepare a strong alibi and stick to your story. Don't forget, I am in it with you now.'

Charlie grinned, his dimple appearing again tantalizingly as Anupama struggled not to focus on it. 'Yeah, that was very sweet of you. Thanks.'

'You're welcome. So, you will do something about it?'

'I will do something about it.' He nodded.

She nodded back, and then, to underline the conclusion of their discussion, she gathered her bag.

'Well, I should be leaving then,' she said, rising.

'Seriously?' he asked, surprised.

'Yes. Why?'

'I don't know. At least, let me buy you lunch or something.'

'No, no, that's not necessary—'

'I know it's not, I just want to. I have this one last appointment before my lunch break. Then, we can go out and grab a bite. Or did you have any other plans?'

She had planned to go home, take a shower, down a few shots of cough syrup, check out JD's latest male offerings, and then curl up into a ball on her living room carpet until the kids got home. But then, she could always postpone that to the weekdays. Plus, the thought of sitting in a cramped auto for that whole journey home didn't seem like a very appealing idea to her right now, especially if it was on an empty stomach. Her hesitation was all the encouragement he needed.

He gave a short clap. 'Perfect! It's settled then.'

'You sure it won't be a problem?'

'Please, anything for friends … We *are* friends now, right?'

She shrugged, trying to look nonchalant. *Friends*. Why did the thought seem weird to her?

As they stepped out, Anupama was about to move back into the waiting room when Charlie stopped her.

'Come inside,' he said, pointing at the hairdressing section.

'I don't want a haircut.'

'I know. I just want to show you something.'

Upon entering, Anupama realized the something was rather a someone – namely, the only other absentee from the society meeting today – Mrs Chatterjee. Her hair had little tin foils plastered all over, her eyes glued to the magazine she was reading. Anupama's first instinct was to back away and sneak out, but Charlie held her back.

'Are you mad? No one should see us together!' she hissed.

'Relax. She's not like the others.'

Before Anupama could protest any further, Mrs Chatterjee's eyes fell on her, and she broke into a wide smile. To Anupama's surprise, she didn't seem embarrassed or discomfited in the least.

'Hi, Mrs Arora!'

Reluctantly, Anupama walked over, calculating all the possible ill-consequences of this slip, and cursing Charlie for his idiotic short-sightedness.

'Hello Divya, you didn't come to the general meeting today?'

Mrs Chatterjee rolled her eyes. 'There are better ways to spend a Sunday morning, as you can see.' She flashed her manicured nails. 'Besides, Alka has made her sentiments towards my presence abundantly clear anyway. The last two times that I tried to have a say, I might as well have been a wall. And God forbid any of those other goats should go against madam's boycott of me.'

Anupama realized it was the first time that she had heard anyone call Mrs Govindikar by her first name, and along with it came the dim realization that, technically, she was one of the 'goats' as well.

'Are you here for a haircut too? Make sure you get Charlie. He's a genius!' said Mrs Chatterjee.

'He does seem to be in demand.'

She nodded fervently, her foils bouncing symmetrically along her head. 'Obviously. Haven't you seen Mrs Patil? The woman looks five years younger and four kilos lighter.'

'Really?'

'Well, from the face, at least. I'm told she is even considering participating in Monsoon Goddess this year. Not that she won't have competition.'

She patted her hair and giggled. Anupama smiled warmly, amused yet saddened by the odds of Mrs Patil even making it to the shortlist if a bombshell like Mrs Chatterjee were to participate. The irony of a beauty pageant like the Monsoon Goddess – which was held towards the end of the monsoons every year – was that it was designed to be a friendly local initiative aimed at boosting the morale and self-esteem of all the married ladies in the area by showing them that allure wasn't merely a premarital attribute. Unfortunately, however, it ended up becoming a blood-fest of egos, vanities and insecurities cutting across all ages and income groups. It didn't matter how old or young, or thin or fat, or light-skinned or dark, or rich or poor, or tall or short, you were. The moment you entered the competition, you would inevitably develop the self-confidence of a cauliflower that had been shredded, squeezed and left to rot outside in the sun. The pressure and lure of stepping out of your comfort zone and into the limelight was phenomenal, and the physical and emotional stakes only seemed to get higher each year, with several casualties being reported. Last year, for instance, Mrs Awasthi had almost ended up passing out right in the middle of her talent round performance, the cause later being attributed (in whispers, of course) to the extreme diet regimen she had been following two weeks prior to the competition to lose three inches around her waist (boiled moong dal and lemon water only with half a banana per day).

'Why don't you participate too?' asked Mrs Chatterjee casually.

Anupama laughed, only to realize a moment later that she wasn't joking. 'You can't be serious.'

'What? You've got a nice face, and a figure that would put women half your age to shame. I say go for it!'

'It's for married ladies, Divya.'

'So?'

'So, technically—'

'Oh, come on, Mrs Arora. You really think anyone's going to object on those grounds?'

Anupama stayed mum, uncertain of what to say. Mrs Chatterjee placed her manicured hand on her arm.

'You don't have to be what they think you are,' she said gently. 'At the end of the day, no one really gives a damn. Trust me.'

Anupama glanced up at her, surprised. The look on her face was solemn, knowing. She realized that this was the first time the two of them were actually having a real conversation, having only bumped into each other at society gatherings before, and she wondered why. Had she really allowed herself to get influenced by the same rumour mill she despised? Or had she just been plain afraid? A 'goat', so to speak.

'Ready?'

She turned to see Charlie beaming.

'Ready for what?' she asked.

'You'll see,' he said, barely able to contain his excitement.

———

Five minutes later, Anupama found herself, sipping a watermelon-mint-cooler juice, seated in one of those fancy hi-tech recliners that massaged all the important acupressure points in the body through a series of subtle, rhythmic vibrations. It made the tumbler quiver a bit, but that was a minor inconvenience compared to the state of pure physical bliss she was in right now, especially with those huge stereo headphones playing relaxing tunes which she could select from the playlist displayed on the LCD screen by the armrest. And the best part was that it was all free, as Charlie had managed to negotiate a first-time demo for her with the powers-that-be, using his clout as one of the in-demand, master stylists in the house. It was good to know people in high places.

Anupama opened her eyes. Against the gentle church music flowing in through her headphones, she watched Charlie chatting with Mrs Chatterjee as he shampooed her hair. Her eyes were closed, and she nodded every now and then with a monosyllabic reply, but the expression on her face reflected Anupama's zen state of mind right now – calm, relaxed and wholly at peace. She didn't even feel like she was in a salon anymore. It was more of a spiritual sanctuary, where life had its own pace and all material worries and concerns ceased to have any value.

Floating atop the clouds of this serene buzz, Anupama lazily let her eyes wander around, absorbing the ambience. It was one of those simple yet chic arrangements where everything was done up in white and subtle shades of grey, with sleek overhanging light fixtures and asymmetric mirrors for that added touch of panache. The clouds had broken up briefly outside to release a weak beam of sunshine that filtered into the parlour through the glass walls facing the street, making the white walls gleam even brighter.

Her eyes returned to Charlie. The glaring whiteness surrounding them contrasted starkly with his tanned skin, thick black hair and black uniform, making him look like a dark angel of temptation, smuggled by Lucifer into heaven to lure the weaker souls back into the entrapments of desire and other worldly sins. He seemed eminently suitable for this role, especially with those exotic eyes, that effortlessly charming smile, those sinewy arms of his exposed by the folded-back sleeves – strong, almost brutal – offset only by the delicacy of his long, slender fingers that resembled an artist's, fingers that were now covered with foam and dripping wet as they—

With a jolt, Anupama popped back to her senses, her chain of thought splintering into shrapnel of guilt and disbelief.

Where had that come from? Had they mixed something in her drink?

She hastily changed the music to a less ethereal track and closed her eyes, trying hard not to think of her slip of conscience. There was a limit to getting carried away.

She didn't even notice when she had dozed off, until a slight nudge on her arm made her jerk upright to see Charlie standing in front of her. He gently took the headphones off her and smiled. 'Had a good time?'

'Yes, wow,' she said groggily, struggling to get up. It was like her muscles had turned to jelly.

Charlie helped her up. His palms felt warm and ultra-soft, probably from all those lotions and what-nots that were routinely used on his clientele.

As she got to her feet, her eyes caught a glimpse of Mrs Chatterjee. Her jaw dropped. It was like the woman had been reborn. Her once long and thick mane had been razor-cut into a gorgeous asymmetric bob with ombre highlights, soft medium-length curls cascading down the sides of her heart-shaped face so delicately one would think they were melting off it. Add to that her dusky skin tone and sharp cheekbones, and you had one hell of a head-turner. Mrs Chatterjee's feelings seemed to mirror her own. Her eyes literally *sparkled* as she tilted her face to and fro slowly in front of the mirror, admiring herself from every possible angle. She glanced back at Charlie. She didn't say a word, but the awestruck smile that lit up her features was better than any verbal compliment. Charlie nodded with the satisfied pride of an artist who has just completed his masterpiece, or a surgeon who has just bestowed the gift of life upon his patient. The moment was so intense and personal between them that Anupama felt like she was intruding just by being there.

'Saw that?' asked Charlie, after Mrs Chatterjee left.

Anupama nodded, smiling.

'That's what I do it for.'

———

'...A lot of people think that a hairstylist is just a fancy name for a barber, you know, snip, snip, snip and you're done. But it's not like that. You're not just cutting hair when you're in there. You're creating art. You're changing someone's image, and possibly someone's life. That's a huge responsibility.'

He paused as the waiter placed a bowl of steaming chilli paneer between them. Charlie served her and then himself. Anupama took a bite of the paneer. Too spicy, as was to be expected in a restaurant whose menu covers featured a two-headed, fire-breathing dragon, exclaiming 'Ooo! It's Chilli!' She just hoped they hadn't used any ajinomoto – the sole reason for her avoiding Chinese restaurants – however, Charlie had been profuse in his praise of the place, and she had tagged along without putting up too much of a fight.

'It's like you have to be a painter, a sculptor and a therapist all in one.'

'Therapist?' she asked, taking in a small mouthful of the oily chopsuey.

'Oh, yeah. You won't believe the kind of stuff I get to hear in there. I swear, every session is like a crash course in women's psychology.'

'That must be tough.'

'Well, to be honest, I enjoy it. I tried being a stylist for men too, but it's not the same. You see, most guys already have a preconceived image of what they want to look like, and they don't want any kind of shift from it. But women – they come with their own mysteries. They come to discover, to change, to be surprised. And for that, you first need to break the barriers surrounding them and know them, the real them. That's when you're able to show them the side of themselves that they weren't even aware existed. And boy, do they love it!'

Anupama smiled, rolling her eyes inwardly. Yet another sample of the deluded male perspective that believed that the only way to deal with the female psyche was by either mystifying it to a metaphysical level or dismissing it altogether. Goddess or simpleton – those seemed to be the only two options available most of the time, with women like Anupama opting for the latter, for they found it superlatively better to be underestimated and ignored than to be deconstructed and micro-analysed like some unclassifiable fossil from a forgotten era.

'So how exactly do you break these barriers?' she asked, just to humour him.

Charlie flashed a Mona Lisa smile. 'A magician never reveals his tricks.'

Neither does a fraudster, she thought, glancing out of the large windows. Mercifully, there were no signs of another downpour yet.

'Although, I have to admit,' said Charlie, 'you're turning out to be quite a mystery.'

She looked back at him in surprise.

'Me?'

He nodded. 'Usually, it just takes me one conversation to figure a woman out. Two, at the most, if they are the shy and reserved types. But with you – I don't know – it's like every time I meet you, I see something new, and that's what intrigues me. It's like I can't seem to put my finger on you, you know.'

Anupama tried hard to conceal her amusement. One moment he is describing to her how every woman is a delicious mystery, and the next, he actually begins treating her like one. Subtlety wasn't a strong point with the poor boy. Still, she decided to play along, just for his efforts.

'That's a surprise. I have always considered myself an open book.'

Charlie snorted. 'Oh, trust me, you're not. In fact, if you ask me, you've set the walls around you pretty high.'

'Have I now?' she remarked, feeling peeved at the confidence with which he had announced his psychoanalytical verdict.

'Not that it's your fault,' he clarified. 'It's just that I'm pretty good at reading vibes, and I always get this sense from you that you don't want anyone to get too close. I mean, you're the kind of woman everyone seems to know – because that's what she wants them to believe – but no one really does.'

'So, you're saying I am cold?'

'No, no, I'm not talking about you. I'm talking about your vibes.'

'What does that even mean?' asked Anupama irritably.

Charlie fidgeted in his seat. 'I didn't mean to upset you.'

'I am not upset!'

'You look upset.'

'Are you sure? Or is it just my *vibes*?'

'Maybe we should change the topic. Have you seen *Mary Kom*?'

'No, no, you don't drop a bomb like that and change the topic. What makes you think I am closed up about myself?'

'Well, for starters, it's been about a week since we met, and I don't even know your name.'

It was then that Anupama realized it too. All this while, she had simply been Mrs Arora for him, as the name plate outside her flat suggested … as she had been for so many others before him. How many of them had even bothered to ask her yet? 'Anupama.'

'Anupama Arora. You're Sindhi?'

'No, my husband was.'

'Oh, okay.'

Her eyes scrutinized his face, waiting for a reaction. She didn't know why, but it seemed important. He looked casual enough as he took another bite of his chopsuey. But then his eyes met hers with an enquiring glance, and she guessed what was coming next. The same question she would receive every time she mentioned her husband's name to a new acquaintance. 'If you don't mind—' began Charlie.

'He's no more.'

'—could you pass the soy sauce, please?'

A second of mutual awkwardness passed between them, before she broke her gaze away and handed him the sauce bottle.

'I thought you were—'

'It's okay. So ... happy?' he asked.

'What's that supposed to mean?' she snapped angrily.

One glance at the startled expression on his face though, and she became aware of her faux pas.

'You were talking about the restaurant, weren't you?'

'The food, actually,' he said in a small voice. 'Are you happy with it?'

She nodded and made a show of checking her watch, only to realize she wasn't wearing it. Putting her bare wrist down on the table, she nervously flicked her hair back with her fingers, only to get a strand stuck in her ring, causing her to flinch in pain. All this while, Charlie just watched her quietly with a blank look on his face.

'I think I should leave now,' she said, stopping a man passing by. 'Bill, please.' The man stared back at her.

'He's not the waiter,' said Charlie.

Anupama gave up and held her head in her hands, breathing deeply.

'Are you okay?' he asked.

'No, Charlie, I'm not okay. Every time I meet you, I end up being not okay and I am tired of it.'

'That's okay—'

'No, it's not okay! It's not at all okay!'

'Okay, okay,' said Charlie, raising his hands.

'I am not this person, all right?' she said slowly. 'I am not this neurotic freak and I don't want you to think of me that way.'

'I don't,' insisted Charlie. 'In fact, I love the fact that you're so ... raw.'

'Raw?'

He nodded with a grin. 'The thing is, every day I meet these women who come in hoping for a miracle, to feel different, to look different from what they are, and it just boggles me how desperately they want to change, you know. Not that I've any complaints, I mean my whole business depends on it. And then, there's you – opening the door with that bit of dal on your fingers, getting drunk, screaming on the terrace, stalking on Facebook. It's so ... refreshing! I wasn't lying when I said I had never met anyone like you.'

Anupama scrutinized his face minutely to see if he was mocking her. However, the sincerity she saw in his admiration only served to offend her further. She knew she had been awkward and strange in front of him, but this perceived degree of her lunacy hadn't quite struck her until now. And the fact that he considered it to be such a natural part of her personality merely added insult to injury. Perhaps she should have just thrown him to the dogs and let him fend for himself. She picked up her bag.

'Thank you for the lunch, Charlie,' she said tightly.

'I thought you'd be flattered.'

'Oh, but of course. My neighbour thinks I'm a hormonal hurricane of emotional disorders. What more could I desire?'

'Anupama, you're not listening to me. I like you. I really do.'

She glanced at him in shock. 'Did you just call me Anupama?'

'That is your name, right? Or do you prefer Mrs Arora?'

'No, I mean, isn't that more respectful?'

'You find it disrespectful to be called by your own name?' he asked.

'You know what I'm talking about. I *am* older than you so—'

'So … what, I'm supposed to consider you an auntie now? Please. You're way too happening.'

In spite of her reservations, Anupama felt a tiny flutter of gladness at that, which she did an impressive job of hiding.

'Just don't call me that in front of others.'

'Okay,' he said, checking his watch. 'I should get back to work now. What are you doing at five today?'

'Nothing. Why?'

He smirked mischievously. 'I'll be meeting up with Mrs Mehtani right about then. Do come over. It will be a good show, I promise.'

'Charlie, please don't try anything funny.'

'Anupama, trust me.'

Again, that irritating flutter. What was it about the combination of his voice and her name that made her feel so squeamish? She thanked him for the lunch again, bade him goodbye and rose. As she made her way to the door, she firmly set her eyes ahead, forbidding herself from giving in to her impulse to glance back while her mind wondered whether he was still looking at her. The thought made her incredibly self-conscious. She fervently prayed that she would not stumble and that she could just be a lady for the next twenty metres or so, until she got to the door.

Don't look back, don't look back, don't look back…

Just as she reached the door though, she gave in to her curiosity for a mere fraction of a second – only to regret it immediately, as expected. Charlie was looking right at her, elbows on the table, lips spread in a wide grin, dimple and all. That expression on his face – it was like he was waiting for her to turn. As if he weren't just expecting it, he was certain of it. Was she so predictable?

He waved. She waved back at him with all the grace she could muster and pushed at the door, and then pulled it, and then pushed again, until a hovering waiter came over and helpfully slid it open. This time, she didn't have to turn back to confirm the amused look that must have come over his face. Her cheeks heated up, and she was sure the blush was visible on the back of her neck as well. Small wonder he had never met a woman like her.

———

The minutes ticked by with the weight of a premonition.

It was almost five now. Nimit was in his room, 'studying'. Misha was watching a re-run of one of her US sitcoms on TV. Anupama had given up trying to follow the dialogues a long time ago. Why did these Americans talk so fast? And why was everything about sex in the end? She had thought about objecting at first, but then the memory of Misha watching these same shows with Rajeev occurred to her. They had always had their own thing. And now that he was not in the picture, she felt a responsibility – or rather, a challenge – to fill that gap. Not that she thought it made any difference. She could have been a fly on the wall for all Misha cared. But it felt good to make the effort. And some of the episodes could be quite funny at times. It was just that today her mind was elsewhere.

The clock struck five.

Anupama tried her best to look casual now as the seconds whizzed by. Her legs had started fidgeting. She stopped them. It was absurd for her to feel so wound up. She wasn't directly involved anyway. And Charlie had assured her he would take care of it. Everything was fine. Everything was going to be fine. It was just a minor—

The doorbell rang.

Her heart leapt. She told Misha she would get it and hurried to the door. She peered out through the peephole. Charlie and Mrs Mehtani were outside.

There was no turning back now. She had brought this upon herself. She opened the door.

'Hello, Mrs Arora,' said Charlie brightly. Behind him, Mrs Mehtani had a stiff expression on her face.

'Oh, hello, Charlie. What happened?'

'Not much. We just wanted you to clear some confusion. Have you ever seen me on that terrace or anywhere near it?'

'Huh? No. I said that in the meeting too.'

'Right, because Mrs Mehtani here has a little problem in believing the truth.'

'The truth?'

'He is saying that my Jugnu broke the lock,' cried Mrs Mehtani angrily.

'I'm just pointing out the only possible explanation.'

'He is four years old!'

'And yet, he could hit the ball over seven storeys as per your own statement. So, I'm guessing the kid has some major upper body strength going on for him.'

'That doesn't mean he'll break a lock. He knows it's against society rules. No one can open the door to the terrace.'

'So why did he even bother coming all the way up? Didn't he know there would be a lock on the door?'

Mrs Mehtani opened her mouth to retort, only to think better of it and pursed her lips. All this while, Anupama was just following their arguments with the avid interest of a bystander in a heated legal battle.

'He—he is just a kid—'

'Exactly. And you know how kids can be. But you know what? It's okay, Mrs Mehtani. I'll take care of it. I'll even get a new lock for the door and no one has to know. What do you say, Mrs Arora?'

It took Anupama a second to find her voice.

'I think that's a good solution, yes.'

'N—no,' mumbled Mrs Mehtani. 'No, that's not right.'

'I know it's not, but four is too young an age to get implicated and tried for such an offence. Imagine what Mrs Govindikar will say. I'm just considering your and Jugnu's best interests,' said Charlie with a straight face.

Mrs Mehtani turned her hapless gaze to Anupama, who merely shrugged.

'Fine,' she huffed. 'Fine, we'll get a new lock.'

Her cheeks had puffed up and reddened with the effort of restraining herself from bursting out. Without any further ado, she turned on her heel and marched down the stairs, not even waiting for the elevator in her fury. Charlie discreetly turned and left for his flat too, but not before passing her a triumphant wink and smile. Anupama felt her spirits rise. Relief flooded through her senses. She closed the door and turned back to see Misha staring at her from the couch.

'Was that Charlie?'

'Yes, and Mrs Mehtani.'

'Something wrong?'

'Not anymore.'

'Why are you smiling?'

'Just like that.'

She strolled over to the kitchen and for the first time since he had moved in, she opened the windows wide, letting in the dewy fresh air. Opening the faucet, she washed some curry leaves and set them aside to dry. She was in the mood for some hot, steaming upma now. With adrak chai. And some fried, salted green chillies. Ah, bliss!

After a moment's thought, she took out her mobile and fished out Charlie's number, texting him:

Anupama: D'you like upma?

A second later, she received a reply.

Charlie: U kiddin'? I was almost in a relationship wt it once.

Anupama: Come over then. I'm making it.

Charlie: Super!!! But wat abt ur bestie Mrs Mehtani?

Anupama: I dnt think she wl b coming up anytime soon thanks to u. Besides, I can always say u came to visit Nimit.

Charlie: Now, aren't u an evil genius? :D M impressed, Anupama.

Anupama: ☺ Cm in 20 mins. The weather's too nice to be alone.

Charlie: Ha ha , if I didn't knw u better, dat wud hv almost sounded romantic :D :D

Charlie: Anupama?

Charlie: Arey, that was a joke! I swear! Didn't u c the smileys??

Charlie: Anupama? U there? Hello?

Charlie: ???

Charlie: So … upma/ no upma?

Anupama: I will pack urs separately. Come in 20 mins to collect it.

Charlie: Ok

13

The downpour a few days later transcended everyone's expectations. The Central Line from Kurla to Bhayander was suspended. Traffic ground to a standstill in most of the suburbs, with the previously waterlogged streets now turning into a diverse patchwork of flowing streams and stagnant ponds. The Arabian Sea flowed with wild abandon over and beyond the Marine Drive boundary walls in vindictive waves, splattering over-enthusiastic selfie-clickers and their ill-fated phones. Five people were reported injured across the city. Cars submerged into flooded ditches, bicycles rode on bicyclists rather than the other way around, mewling kittens were rescued in vegetable baskets. And Anupama found herself stuck at home with her kids, wondering why her ceiling was dripping from some of the unlikeliest of corners.

Her meeting with Renu had been cancelled owing to the impossibility of travel in this weather, and the southeast corner of her living room, which seemed to have taken these tidings badly, was weeping profusely in zigzag patterns of moist misery.

'Why don't we just call someone?' asked Nimit.

'I've already called someone. No one's coming in this weather.'

'Perhaps we could call Charlie.'

'Why? Is he a mason?'

'He fixed my ankle,' suggested Misha.

'Your ankle wasn't leaking.'

Deep in her heart, she cursed Facebook for strengthening the bond between Charlie and her kids in a way that was so effortless that it made her wonder if they weren't all kindred spirits with links from a previous birth. The number of 'likes', smileys, thumbs-ups and LOLs that they shared between each other on a daily basis (thanks to Charlie's lethal combo of humorous double-entendre status updates, impeccable photography and selfie-taking skills, and GoT – Game of Thrones – mania) seemed more than the sum total of real-life smiles she had received from both of them post-puberty. What further complicated the scenario was that she couldn't even actively discourage her kids, as that would mean blowing her online cover. Charlie had kept his word to keep her secret. And, in any case, to the best of her knowledge, her kids barely interacted with him in real life.

Anupama nudged the small mopping bucket aside, replaced it with a deep-bottomed saucepan, and moved the bucket below the new third leak, which had erupted in the five minutes they had spent staring at the ceiling. This had never happened before. She had spent fourteen years in this apartment, and not once did the climatic vagaries adversely affect any part of her home.

'This is so depressing,' said Misha. 'I'm going to my room.'

'Yes, because going to your room solves everything.'

'What do you expect me to do then?'

'Suggest a solution.'

'Call Charlie.'

'What is your obsession with Charlie?' Anupama cried out at her children. 'Weren't our lives going on just fine before him? Why don't you just ask him to adopt both of you until the monsoons get over?'

Midway through her rant, she realized she was overreacting, but by then the momentum had built up and she couldn't help but finish her tirade. Her children, as expected, gaped uncomprehendingly; the silence in the room interrupted only by the sad drip-drip of the leaking ceiling. Anupama steadied her breathing.

'It's just a question of one or two days,' she said. 'We can manage.'

A loud bang made them all jump. She looked up to see the whirling ceiling fan emitting sparks in sporadic bursts of light and energy. The putrid smell of burnt plastic pervaded the air.

'We are all going to die in this house,' moaned Nimit.

'Just turn off the fan.'

He didn't need to because, barely a second later, the fuse blew, plunging the three Aroras into a static semi-darkness. Plop-drip-plop went the drops, long-sufferingly in the background.

'Now what?' asked Nimit.

'It's just a question of one or two days,' said Misha tonelessly. 'We can manage.'

Anupama parted the curtains, although it didn't make very

much of a difference thanks to the gloaming of the overcast weather outside. Behind her, the chorus of mutters and moans reached a new crescendo.

'Are we seriously expected to live here without electricity?'

'How will I charge my mobile and laptop?'

'You know how humid it will get by afternoon?'

'And there will be no WiFi!'

'If you two just keep quiet for one second, I might be able to think of something,' snapped Anupama.

Three firm knocks resonated across the room at that moment, making them all glance at the door. Nimit ran over and opened it to reveal Charlie standing outside. Nimit leapt into his arms, enfolding him in a tight embrace.

'Duuude!'

'Heyy,' said Charlie. 'Sorry, I was just passing by when I heard a bang. I tried ringing your doorbell, but I don't think it's working.'

'The electricity's gone. And our roof's leaking,' said Misha.

'It's okay. We can manage,' said Anupama.

'I could have a quick look at your switchboard, if you like,' offered Charlie. 'I've fixed quite a few electrical snarls in my day.'

'That's really not necessary—'

'Yes, it is. We don't even know where the switchboard is,' cried Nimit.

Anupama pursed her lips and folded her arms. She locked eyes with Charlie and gave the tiniest of nods. Charlie turned on the flashlight on his mobile, located the switchboard cabinet on the wall behind the entrance door and opened its shutter. He started flipping through some of the switches.

'Hmm ... seems fine ... nope, definitely not an overload...'

'Be careful,' said Misha.

He rose on tiptoe to peer closely at the tangle of wiring within and that was when Anupama noticed that he was barefooted, having left his shoes at the door.

'Shouldn't you be—' she began, only to be interrupted by the clatter of his phone dropping to the floor. She waited for him to pick it up, but he didn't. He just stayed there with his hand in the switchboard. It took her a moment to recognize the tremors passing through his frozen body.

'Omigod, he's being electrocuted!' screamed Misha.

Nimit let out a high-pitched howl, and leapt to his feet. He lunged at Charlie instinctively, but Anupama yanked him back and shoved him to safety. She hoisted the spindly-legged wooden side-table that stood by the door with the presence of mind provided by the surge of panic-triggered adrenaline. She swung it forward and struck Charlie hard in the abdomen, detaching him from the wall. He collapsed on to the floor and lay there unmoving, his eyes closed. Anupama, Misha and Nimit hovered anxiously over him.

'Is ... is he dead?' asked Nimit in a quivering voice.

Anupama checked his pulse. 'Call doctor uncle from downstairs.'

———

His vital signs were stable, thank goodness, and there seemed to be no damage to his body other than the bruise where she had struck him. Nevertheless, it would be advisable to have a thorough check-up done as soon as he regained consciousness, recommended Dr Patkar. The switchboard had been boarded up with rubber-gloved hands and black tape, to be examined only by a certified professional with life insurance. The kids had been packed off to a friend's place for gadget-charging and other recreational activities with the guarantee that she would call them the moment he awoke. And now, with candles flickering about them in the semi-darkened room, Anupama sat beside Charlie, staring at his calm face as he dozed on Nimit's bed.

Now that his eyes were closed, she noticed that he had significantly long lashes for a man. What was it her mother had told her about men with long eyelashes? Oh yes, don't trust them. Mole by the upper lip? Don't trust them. Wide-toothed smile? Don't trust them. Coloured eyes? Don't trust them. Prominent Adam's apple? Don't trust them. Bell-bottomed pants? Don't trust them. Heavily bearded? Don't trust them. Clean-shaven? Don't trust them. Gelled/oiled hair? Don't trust them. The closer she approached puberty, the longer the list of untrustworthy characteristics became until she reckoned that, at this rate, the only people she could trust would be, well, women. And that was when her mother's masterplan came to light. Thank God for Renu during her growing up years; otherwise, the closest she would have got to sex education was a clandestine viewing of *Ram Teri Ganga Maili* with her giggling cousins.

Charlie stirred. Tiny beads of sweat were forming on his forehead and neck. She fervently hoped he wasn't running a temperature. After a moment's hesitation, she put her hand on his moist forehead. Somewhere in a dim corner of her mind, she registered the thought that this was the first proper physical contact between them, barring that one time he had saved her from tripping during the marathon. His temperature seemed fine. She felt his cheeks and neck too, just to double check, and then she felt his forehead again. His skin was surprisingly soft, like a child's. Perhaps he was uncomfortably hot and therefore sweating. She considered removing the sheet that covered him; but that would leave him quite exposed. In their clumsy, desperate struggle to carry him to the bed, most of the buttons on Charlie's shirt had been ripped off, and the couple that remained had been undone by Dr Patkar in order to examine him. He lay there now with his shirt open, a crepe bandage wound around his midriff where the bruising had turned faintly purple.

Charlie groaned softly. He did seem to be in discomfort. Perhaps she should remove the sheet. What difference would it make? They were both adults, and anyway, she was more like a ... like a friend to him, wasn't she? And it *was* getting dreadfully humid indoors. She would replace it when the kids returned, or when he woke up, whichever happened first. Taking a deep breath, she rose to her feet and gently lifted the sheet by the edge before sweeping it off in one swift move. Charlie stayed inert, much to her relief.

There, that wasn't so bad.

She picked up a magazine and began fanning herself with it. Then, she widened the arc of her fanning to include Charlie. A thin whistling sound came out of his nose as he exhaled. She giggled. How surreal was this situation? She could just about picture the expression on Mrs Govindikar's face if she were to see her now, seated at the bedside of her comatose, shirtless neighbour.

A mosquito hovered above his forehead and she shooed it away with the magazine. However, when the pesky insect persisted in buzzing over Charlie, with a swift swipe she grabbed it in mid-flight above his nose and squeezed it in her fist, all accomplished soundlessly. A moment later, she felt Charlie's warm breath strike the underside of her wrist. An overwhelming ticklish sensation swept through her, followed by gooseflesh breaking out all over her body. She withdrew quickly and settled back in her seat. The humidity inside the room seemed to have suddenly risen because she was sweating now. She tried reading the magazine with which she was fanning herself, only to find her eyes straying from the page and onto the specimen now lying with his face turned towards her. There was a greyish hint of stubble on his cheeks and his hair was all sticky and mussed up. Even so, the whole tableau reminded her of those sensuous posters of men's colognes, the kinds which were deemed too expensive to buy for one's husband unless it was a silver jubilee anniversary or something of that magnitude. What had she got for Rajeev on their twenty-fifth anniversary? Was it a tie? It was a tie, wasn't it?

She sat up straight as Charlie turned towards her in his sleep. Her eyes involuntarily slid towards his waist where his jeans had receded slightly. That was when she noticed two tiny curved black lines above his left pelvic bone, disappearing into his underwear lapel. She looked at his face to ensure that he was still unconscious before moving closer to peer at the marks. What was it? A mole? Or a tattoo? From here, it resembled the antennae of some bug, or perhaps the antlers of an animal. Her face was only a couple of inches away from his—

'What are you doing?'

Her head snapped back so hard that her neck cricked. The pain, of course, was nothing compared to the excruciating embarrassment of seeing Charlie staring at her with a mixture of surprise and uncertainty.

'You scared me!' she cried.

'*I* scared you?'

He tugged up his jeans self-consciously.

'I was just – checking something.'

'Yes, I could see that.'

'Charlie, please.'

He glanced down at his bare torso. 'What happened to my shirt?'

'The buttons were ripped out.'

He cast her another suspicious look.

'Oh, for God's sake, I saved your life,' snapped Anupama.

'What?'

'Don't you remember? You were being electrocuted.'

Slowly, realization dawned on his face, followed by a sheepish grin. 'Oh…'

'What?' asked Anupama.

'I wasn't really … I thought you knew – I was just kidding.'

Anupama stared at him, astounded. '*What*?'

'How could I get electrocuted? There is no electricity in your house, remember?'

'But you blacked out!'

'Because you knocked me out!'

Anupama shook her head in disbelief and anger. She had half a mind to knock him out again.

Charlie tried to rise and winced with pain. 'Could you help me up, please?'

Anupama cradled his back as he levered himself upright. His pecs came to life, swelling up his chest and defining their contours clearly. Without even realizing it, her eyes remained fixated on this phenomenon until—

'Seriously?' cried Charlie.

A cold trickle of sweat ran down her back.

'My eyes are up here, Anupama.'

'I—'

'I'm just saying, you know, I'm not a piece of meat.'

'I wasn't—it's not—'

What happened next happened so fast that she wasn't even sure it had happened – Charlie rose swiftly from the bed, his lips touched her lips for one lingering, surreal instant, before he slowly subsided back into the bed, his eyes riveted on hers. It took Anupama a couple of moments to realize she wasn't breathing. She inhaled, exhaled, and then stared blindly at him. There was a twinge in the back of her head, but the rest of her body had gone numb. It was the closest she had come to an out-of-body experience.

They both stayed like that, unmoving. A hint of a smile appeared briefly on Charlie's lips, before fading away when it met with no response.

'You okay?' he asked, finally.

Anupama didn't reply. The expectant expression on Charlie's face rapidly withered to an apprehensive one. 'I … It just felt right, you know…'

'You kissed me.'

'More of a peck, actually.'

'You kissed me.'

'It—it could be a friendly kiss if you want. I mean—'

'You *kissed* me.'

'I'm sorry, I don't know what—'

His words were abruptly cut off by a stinging slap. Perhaps it was the perspiration on his cheeks or something, but the sound seemed to reverberate like thunder in the muggy stillness of the room, seeming much louder than the impact. Again, both of them froze. Anupama didn't even know why she had reacted like that. She was feeling more shocked than outraged, and it just felt like the right thing to do – instinctively speaking. But now that she had done it, she couldn't help but feel a rising sense of trepidation deep inside. Charlie was staring at her, his hand on his cheek.

'I'm sorry,' he murmured.

'You should be.'

And then, she kissed him.

Or rather, lunged at him, devouring his lips in one go. She could feel him stiffen at first, too stunned to respond. Then, slowly, his lips parted and he wrapped his arms around her waist, drawing her close. She kissed him with a hunger she hadn't even known existed within her. The stubble over his upper lip was pricking her a bit, adding to her ecstasy, for it was a sensation quite alien to her. Rajeev had always been clean-shaven, his cheeks and jaws as smooth as a baby's. Why the hell was she thinking about Rajeev now?

She pulled away, breathless.

'What are we doing?' she panted, her mind a complete blank and her heart a raging beast. 'What are we doing?'

'I … I don't know—'

And then, she pounced at him again.

They were barely a few seconds into the kiss when three hard raps jarred the silence. Someone was at the front door.

'Wait here,' she gasped.

'S—Sure,' he panted back.

Like a sleepwalker, Anupama detached herself from a stupefied Charlie and drifted to the door and opened it to see … Mrs Govindikar standing outside.

The sight of her matronly figure, rigid and tight-lipped, was enough to punch her hormones back into harsh reality.

'Good afternoon, Anupama.'

'H-Hello, Mrs Govindikar.'

'I heard about the power outage at your place. Do you need any help?'

'No, no—'

'Why are you sweating so much?'

Before she could reply, Mrs Govindikar touched the side of her neck with a plump finger. 'Your temperature's high too. Do you have a fever?'

Anupama shook her head, her pulse rate rising by the second. 'No, it's just really hot in here, you know.' She fanned herself with her hand to justify her statement. Her other hand remained on the door knob, ready to slam it shut at the first opportunity, but Mrs Govindikar stayed firmly put. Her eyes probed inward.

'Where is he?'

Anupama's throat went dry. 'Who?'

'Charlie. I heard he was accidentally electrocuted.'

'He's fine now. He's resting.'

'Where?'

'Inside.'

'In your bedroom?' A hint of censure in her tone.

'No, Nimit's.'

Mrs Govindikar's gaze stayed locked on hers. Anupama felt like a novice drug dealer facing the head of the Narcotics Control Bureau. A fresh trail of sweat tracked down the side of her forehead. The seconds ticked by heavily, until finally, Mrs Govindikar blinked.

'I'll send my electrician over, just in case,' she said in a leaden voice. 'In the meantime, you can wait at my house. He'll call you when he wakes up.'

'Sure, I'll be there in five minutes.'

Mrs Govindikar turned on her heel, the nightmare on the verge of ending, when a crooning, folksy voice filled the air.

O re khevaiya … paar laga more saiyaan ko…

Charlie's mobile.

Anupama's heart stopped, as did Mrs Govindikar's feet. They both did an about-turn in time to catch sight of a sweaty, bare-chested Charlie rushing into the living room, his unbuttoned shirt flapping behind him.

'I'll take it, I'll take it,' he said, grabbing his cell phone and saying 'hello' as he casually returned to the bedroom. He shut the door behind him.

The emotional rollercoaster of the past few minutes fused together to take its toll on Anupama. A nervous giggle escaped her lips, then another, and then another. She was far from amused, let alone happy. She was aware on some level that her social reputation, as she knew it, was history. Yet the inane chortling wouldn't stop. It's like someone was tickling her from

the inside. What was this – some sort of defence mechanism?
A glance at Mrs Govindikar's outraged face and she burst into
another gale of laughter.

'I don't see the humour in this situation,' snapped Mrs
Govindikar, and that triggered another paroxysm of mirth.

Charlie stepped out of the bedroom, phone glued to his
ear, staring at them. 'What's going on?'

'Anu, control yourself. What kind of behaviour is this?'

'Why is she laughing?'

'Anu! Are you listening to me?'

Anupama nodded, her eyes swimming with tears now, but
for the life of her, she couldn't stop laughing.

'Call the doctor,' Mrs Govindikar ordered Charlie.

He dithered in the doorway, uncertain.

'What?'

'Who's the doctor?' he asked.

Anupama collapsed into the sofa and doubled up, barely
able to breathe, wiping her eyes, still chuckling in merriment.
She was convinced she was going to die. Oh well, at least, it
was a jolly way to go.

14

She didn't die.

However, she did manage to introduce a funereal darkness to the surroundings within a matter of minutes, with neighbours thronging in droves to witness the debacle of the first ever nervous breakdown within their settlement. Word of death and illness spread like greased lightning in this neighbourhood, its pace being determined by the peculiarity of the causes and symptoms and/or the source of the news, and Anupama had scored highly on both counts, the second time since Rajeev's stroke. Mrs Govindikar had been beside her the whole time, energetically massaging the invalid's hand as the residential doctor performed a preliminary check-up on her and prescribed further tests to rule out a stroke or Alzheimer's or worse. Thankfully, her merriment had been summarily routed by Charlie's abrupt exit (Mrs Govindikar had practically shooed him out of the apartment before anyone else arrived), only to be replaced by an all-pervading mortification. At the same time, she felt a hint of relief too – at the fact that her hysterical outbreak had overshadowed the rather grim circumstances in which she was discovered by

Mrs Govindikar. She didn't know for how long the diversion would last, but was grateful for it all the same.

The electricity was back on. Her children, after confirming that there was nothing fatally wrong with their mother, had retired to their respective rooms, affording her some privacy. Dr Gupta had concluded that while all her vital signs were fine, her heart rate was still quite high. Questions were posed to her regarding any possible triggers and recent causes of stress or excitement. If only they knew. Her breath caught in her throat yet again as she recalled the incident with Charlie. The mere recollection of that memory was enough to send the blood pounding to her temples. Try as she may, she still had trouble believing it had actually occurred. It seemed like a distant dream, a dream within a dream. A truth so surreal that one is certain that it would never really sink in.

A barrage of frantic queries kept popping up in her mind with increasing frequency: Why? How? And most importantly – what now?

She had crossed the point of no return, hadn't she? No matter what she did, she couldn't undo what had passed. And … should she? Why should she? It had been a matter of mutual consent, hadn't it?

Consent. He had *wanted* to kiss her. Charlie. Charlie had kissed her. Charlie wanted her.

Her. Her and Charlie.

Charlie.

Charlie with those abs and those dimples and those eyes. *That* Charlie wanted her. She felt like her stomach was on zero gravity. Of all the people in all the world – Charlie…

Funny, handsome, unpredictable, young Charlie. Young.

Young.

Young.

The word stuck in her head, swirling and bouncing off the corners of her mind until it took on a grim implication that she hadn't considered before. The fog lifted off her consciousness, and her nerves began to act up in a jangled fusion of dread and panic.

What had she done? Oh God, what had she done? What the hell was she thinking? The poor boy.

No, wait, what poor boy? He had started it. In fact, he should count his stars lucky she hadn't thrown him out of her home. He had practically molested her, if one were to look at it that way. But then, what had she done? Molested him back?

So sticky and ugly the word sounded … mo-lest-ed … mo-lest-ed.

Mrs Govindikar entered, bearing a cup of tea and all of Anupama's prior misgivings. She had forgotten that the woman was still here.

'How are you feeling now?' she asked, handing her the cup.

'Much better, thank you,' said Anupama. She took a sip. It was stronger than she would have liked.

Mrs Govindikar sat by her side. 'That was quite a scare you gave us, my dear.'

'Yes, sorry. I don't know what happened.'

Mrs Govindikar nodded thoughtfully, her tiny fingers smoothing out the edges of the bedcover. 'Good thing I was here, right? Otherwise who knows what could have happened?'

Anupama gingerly raised her eyes to look at her placid, unaffected face – or was it? She had never been good at telling the difference between coldness and blankness. She took

another sip of the scalding tea and set the cup aside, wondering
how best to ask to be left alone now without committing yet
another social solecism. Before she could think of a suitable
method to evict the woman, Mrs Govindikar placed her hand
over hers. Her eyes, which had now taken on a sagacious
look, levelled themselves at Anupama's, holding her in their
penetrating glare.

'Remember who you are, Anu,' she said. 'Remember what
you have.'

Anupama nodded silently.

'We are all prone to make errors from time to time. That's
what makes us human. But that is exactly why it is imperative
to keep things in perspective. Before things get out of hand
and it's too late.'

'I agree,' replied Anupama, with another nod. Her heart was
like a piston gone out of control, but this was the worst time
to show any signs of weakness. Damn the clammy forehead.

Mrs Govindikar's gaze never faltered, her pitch-black irises
burrowing into Anupama's very soul. 'So, I trust this will never
happen again then?'

'What will?' asked Anupama, her voice a bare croak.

'You make a rather terrible liar. The least you could have
done was to wipe your lip gloss off his mouth.'

Icy fingers crept up from her toes to her scalp. Perhaps it
would have been merciful providence to have died right there
on the spot. She wanted to say something, but her voice had
deserted her.

'You really thought I had no idea?' asked Mrs Govindikar
coldly. 'By now, you ought to know that nothing escapes my
eyes, dear. I've had my sights on you two for a long time

now, right from the moment when you first sat on his bike. I knew it was Charlie who had broken the terrace lock, but I didn't pursue it because I knew that you were there as well that night.'

How could she? What was she, a ghost? Or were there hidden CCTV cameras in the building she didn't know about? Either way, did it really matter anymore? Anupama found herself pinching her arm discreetly in the dim hope that she would wake up, for the moment had all the makings of a classic nightmare where one's worst fears manifest without warning. However, there was no reprieve to be had. This situation was the worst nightmare of all – it was real.

'Won't you say anything?' asked Mrs Govindikar relentlessly.

Anupama lowered her eyes, her temperature rising again, along with her blood pressure. Her nerves felt like they were on fire. What could she say? She waited or rather hoped, in vain, for another bout of hysteria to come to her rescue. She stayed frozen. Mrs Govindikar patted her hand gently.

'I know it's been tough, my dear. But you need to understand, you're not just a woman. You have a family, a reputation, responsibilities. Do you really think it's worth throwing all that away on … on an *urge*? How long do you think these things can stay hidden? No matter how emancipated we consider ourselves, you know the kind of society we live in. Have you even considered the repercussions of your actions on you? Your family?'

And just like that, the few, tiny residual sparks of desire that still flickered inside were extinguished into nothingness. The shame in her heart was not the shame of discovery anymore, but rather the shame of guilt. Dimly, she wondered if she would ever be able to look Mrs Govindikar in the eye again.

'Please don't tell anyone,' she murmured weakly.

'Of course, I won't, Anu. I care for you, which is why I have been silent so far. But this needs to stop. You understand that, right?'

Anupama nodded, feeling the last few trickles of sweat making their way down the back of her itchy neck.

Several minutes after Mrs Govindikar had left, Anupama sat paralysed not daring to move. She reached for her mobile. Six missed calls from Charlie. She took a deep breath, straightened her shoulders, steeled her resolve, and pressed the dial button. He picked it up before the first ring was over.

'Hello?'

'Hi, Charlie.'

'Are you all right?'

'Yes.'

'Thank God. What happened to you back there?'

'It doesn't matter. Listen, Charlie, what happened between us—'

'Was amazing! I mean, I can't even tell you, Anu, how much—'

'Charlie,' she said, a little more firmly, 'what happened between us, I trust you will keep it to yourself?'

'Sure, of course … if you want me to.'

'I do. And just to make things clear, it will never happen again.'

There was a short pause. 'O-kay, bu—'

'I wish it hadn't happened, but now that it has, there is nothing I can do about it.'

'You make it sound like a mistake.'

'It was.'

Another short pause. 'Oh, okay.'

'Let's just forget it ever happened, all right?'

She could hear him breathing at the other end, as she waited for a response.

'If that's what you want,' he said, finally.

'It is. And, Charlie?'

'Yes?'

'Maybe it's better if we keep our distance from now on. It's just getting too complicated, if you know what I mean.'

'Did Mrs Govindikar say something to you?'

'It's not about her. It's about me.'

'So … this is what you want? You're a hundred per cent sure?'

'Yes.'

'Fine, then. It was nice knowing you, Mrs Arora.' His voice was even, measured.

'You too, Charlie. Take care.'

She hung up, and it was only then that she dared to acknowledge the tightening in her chest – like a coil being wound up way beyond its capacity, threatening to rip apart any second. She told herself that it was only her guilt at unintentionally hurting the poor boy. She told herself that this was ultimately for the best, the only thing that she could do, and this feeling of her head and her heart being at odds would eventually subside. After all, this conflict wasn't supposed to exist within her in the first place, was it? For she wasn't merely a woman anymore, was she? She was so much more…

It was only when Misha knocked on her door that she realized just how long she had been sitting still on the bed like that. Almost two hours. How the time had flown by.

'Mamma, you okay?' she asked, from outside.

'Yes.'

'It's five forty.'

'So?'

'So … I don't know, don't you usually have chai at five thirty?'

She wasn't aware that her daughter had noticed her routine enough to know this. 'Yes, I'll be right out.'

'I could make it if you're feeling tired or something.'

'No, it's fine. Thank you, beta.'

She took a deep breath, forced her limbs to mobilize, and then carried herself into the bathroom. Once inside, she wondered why she had entered the bathroom in the first place. She didn't need to pee, being dehydrated significantly over the past few hours. It was a glass of water she needed actually, more than anything. She caught sight of her haggard face in the mirror and realized she couldn't step out of her room looking like that. She splashed her face with water from the faucet in the washbasin. She repeated the procedure several times over, but it felt like it wasn't enough. Something was missing. Something essential.

She opened her eyes and noticed that the large, floral-patterned, plastic bucket by the shower was filled to the brim. Yes, of course. She knelt by it, shut her eyes, and slowly immersed her face in the water until it clogged up her ears. In the dead silence that followed, she imagined herself sinking deep into the heart of the ocean, her body weightless like a feather, her limbs askew, hair adrift, her blank, wide-eyed gaze staring at nothing as the blackness surrounded her. The thought brought with it an unexpected sense of peace and calm, and after what seemed like an eternity, she felt truly relaxed. So relaxed, in fact, that she didn't notice that she was still immersed until the water entered her nostrils. Sputtering and coughing, she emerged from the bucket, gasping for air and feeling embarrassed at what was probably one of the stupidest near-death experiences ever.

She felt mortified. Imagine what the neighbours would have said if they had found her body like this. Slapping herself back to her senses, Anupama got to her feet, ignoring the protests of her knees and the rest of her numbed, tired body.

———

She decided to go with cinnamon instead of ginger this time. Its bittersweet aroma rose in fumes as Anupama added the powdered spice to the bubbling tea and waited, head bowed low in thought, leaning against the cold kitchen platform.

In the five minutes that it took for the tea to brew, she had made a couple of firm resolutions to herself, because the moment seemed ripe to make a crucial life change. She resolved to live a life of dignity henceforth. She would be the woman her mother wanted her to be. She would be the lady Mrs Govindikar expected her to be. She would be a pattern-card of what she ought to be. She would never indulge in any childish nonsense ever again, no JD's, no inebriated encounters, no … anything. The only thing that would matter would be her responsibilities, the tasks at hand. She wouldn't think about the past or the future; she would stay focussed on the present. And as of now, her only present was the pot of tea, after which she would soak the rice and dal for dinner and shred the cabbage. Just like in the good old days, when life was simpler.

A faint rustle reached her ears. The papers she had plastered across her kitchen window had come loose from their moorings; the frayed edges hanging off the pane. With a speck of trepidation in her heart, she decided to fix them, promising herself that she would not sneak a peek outside. And miserably failed the moment she reached there. She moved in behind the cover of the paper and glanced out through the opening.

She paused.

For the first time since he had moved in, Charlie's kitchen windows were covered – plastered all over with newspaper, just like hers were.

15

By the time she finished getting ready, she had forgotten what she was supposed to go downstairs for. The initial idea had been to hop down to the departmental store and be back in two minutes flat (rather than calling them and waiting for ten to fifteen minutes for their delivery boy); but then she remembered she hadn't applied any lip balm. It was almost six in the evening. Mrs Govindikar and her troupe would be returning from their evening walk. There was no point in looking like a hobo if she happened across them. No sooner had she moisturized her lips than she became aware of the state her hair was in. After much deliberation, she decided to pin it up in a chignon. But now that her hair was up, her eyes were clearly visible and the dark circles and puffiness beneath were all too apparent – an issue she rectified with the judicious use of a concealer and an eyeliner. The problem now was that she was too made up for her casual top and leggings, therefore off they came and she changed into more appropriate attire. She was just about to leave when her eyes caught sight of a stubborn crease in the lower left corner of her kurta, which obviously had to be ironed out. The ironing done and all colour-coordination completed, she checked the clock. 6.20 pm. Where had the time gone?

In her haste, she forgot to follow her customary practice of ensuring that the coast was clear through the peephole before stepping out into the corridor – an oversight she regretted immediately. For standing in front of the elevator was Charlie with a tall, skinny female in five-inch stilettos, who resembled an aggressive giraffe, and chattered away in an excited, high-pitched voice (an unfortunate characteristic of most girls in her age group these days). So engrossed was she in her narration that she barely registered Anupama's entry as she walked up and stood beside them. Charlie gave her a polite nod. She nodded back. As they waited, the young lady yakked on.

'And then I was like, whatever yaar, if you can't handle your shit then like, don't pass your shit to me. Seriously…'

The elevator arrived. Charlie slid the doors open. Anupama entered, followed by, like, her and Charlie.

'…and then she was like, why are you being such a bitch, and I was like, excuse me? You can't talk to me like that…'

Anupama silently calculated the speed at which the elevator would crash down if the metal cables holding it were to snap at that very instant. It didn't help that ever since their split a week ago, she had been keeping a frosty distance from Charlie. He had tried calling and texting her a couple of times, but she had been steadfastly unresponsive. Neena was right. It was better to establish and maintain firm boundaries from the very outset. They continued to courteously exchange formal pleasantries whenever they bumped into each other, but that was about it.

'This is Madhu, by the way,' said Charlie to her. 'Madhu, Mrs Arora.'

'Oh, I'm so sorry,' squeaked Madhu. 'Hello, aunty.'

'Hello.'

'That's such a cute top. My mother has one just like it.'

'Thank you.'

'So where was I?' she said, turning back to Charlie. 'Yeah, so she just went like, totally crazy, and I was like, what's up with you, you know…'

Charlie started humming. Anupama knew the tune. It was the song he had hummed during their first shared elevator ride. Something about a *khevaiya*, if she could recall correctly.

'Why are you singing?' asked Madhu.

'I just like this song.'

'You're such a weirdo. Seriously, aunty, how do you live next to this guy?'

Anupama smiled tightly. 'God alone knows.'

The elevator reached the ground floor. Madhu turned to Charlie with a pouty look.

'Babe, could you open the door please?' she whined. 'I just had my nails done.'

And that was all the cuteness that Anupama could handle. She grabbed the steel handle, and wrenched the gates open with a force that shook the whole elevator.

'Thank you, aunty!' the creature cooed and teetered out on her stilts. Anupama held the door open for Charlie.

'You first,' he said.

'That's okay. You go.'

'No, no, it's fine.'

'Charlie, *go*.'

And so he went. Unfortunately, he had parked his bike outside, so she was doomed to share the walk up to the gates with the duo. However, she was saved the effort of having to make inane small talk with her new acquaintance because, as they stepped into the driveway, Madhu's phone rang, and she plunged into an animated conversation with the caller in a tone that lay somewhere between horror and ecstasy, and interjected with a lot of 'likes'.

'Heard Nimit's birthday is coming up,' he said.

'Yes.'

'He called me.'

'Okay.'

'I'm thinking of coming over if it's okay with you.'

'Fine.'

'You're sure it's not an issue, right?' he asked pointedly.

She shrugged. 'All of his friends are coming. If you want to come, come.'

His brows rose a bit at that. He actually looked hurt. For a moment, Anupama faltered in her resolve, feeling a twinge of guilt, when a high-pitched wail interrupted them.

'Baaabe, which one's your bike?'

'It's the Fazer!' he called out.

'The what?'

'Never mind, I'm coming! I'll see you then,' he said to her, before hurrying over to the bikes parked in a row.

'Bye, bye,' said Anupama, but he was already out of earshot.

A peculiar feeling came over her as she saw him trot over to Madhu and guide her towards his motorbike. She couldn't quite place her finger on the emotion, mostly because she couldn't – or rather, didn't want to – but it seemed halfway between disappointment and annoyance. He would probably lend her the same floral raincoat that he had given her that fateful day, she thought. She noticed the old watchman staring at her from his cabin, his eyes enlarged and gawking behind his thick glasses. His gaze irritated her – blank yet assessing. She scowled at him and he hastily turned back to his intercom phone. Unfurling her umbrella, Anupama walked on, only to realize that she had forgotten what she had come down for. Not wanting to dither in front of the watchman who kept throwing suspicious glances her way, she resolutely made her way past the gates. By the time she stepped out onto the street, Charlie and his friend were gone.

'Toilet paper,' she muttered to herself, finally recollecting her errand.

16

The next morning, Anupama woke up to a raging fever and felt immensely grateful for it as it afforded her the best excuse to go incommunicado without raising too many questions from friends and family.

For the next three days, she kept herself shut inside her bedroom, except when she had to step out for her meals with Misha and Nimit; the food supply mostly taken care of by an intricate neighbourhood delivery network overseen by Mrs Govindikar and her troupe of concerned homemakers, who took turns sending out Tupperware boxes full of whatever high-protein, low-carb delicacy they had prepared for the day (thanks to the shadow of the Monsoon Goddess pageant looming over most of them), which was followed by a return visit from their kids or domestic help to reclaim the cleaned containers. On two occasions, there were 'Get Well Soon' cards along with the deliveries, hand-drawn by one of the art 'prodigies' in the benefactor's household. Both times, it had shown her depicted as a round-headed, smiling pencil-stick figure of a woman wearing a salwar kameez with her two smiling pencil-stick children figures playfully prancing beside her in a garden full of butterflies and daisies, while the smiling sun shone over them all. She wondered whether the format of the cards had also been predetermined by Mrs Govindikar.

Her children, although visibly curious over her state, kept their queries to themselves. Misha, in particular, looked quite intrigued, and Anupama often caught her staring at her when she thought she wasn't looking. Once or twice, she caught herself wondering whether Charlie knew about her indisposition, only to shake the thought away. It didn't matter, she told herself.

On the morning of the fourth day, the fever subsided completely, leaving her miserably refreshed and cured. She would have gladly faked illness for a few days more, had Renu and Neena not paid her an unexpected visit to fathom the reason for her failure to respond to their calls and messages. After a cursory check-up to confirm that everything was fine, they whisked her out for a surprise, ignoring her feeble protests.

The rain was falling hard and erratically when they stepped out, their huge round umbrellas dangling above their heads as they made their way towards the gate. Halfway through, Anupama caught sight of the old society watchman staring at them from his cabin – or more specifically, at her. He had a peculiar look in his eyes, somewhere between fear and uncertainty. She didn't have much time to think about it though, as Renu hustled her into her car and drove off with the sleekness of a secret service agent transporting a defector across the border.

She didn't even bother to ask her about their destination, for she knew that when Renu resolved to keep something secret, nothing and no one could pry it out of her. It was for this reason that Neena still laboured under an illusion of Rajeev as a good family man, and for that Anupama was thankful. Not that it had been easy to get Renu to swear to keep her mouth shut.

The ride was as terrible as she had expected it to be and more. At every turn and intersection, they found long traffic jams, people who were drenched and too tired to honk, yet too annoyed to not do so occasionally. All along the way, Neena hummed cheerful tunes and did her utmost to make small talk with a barely-interested Anupama, while Renu cursed and ranted at every obstacle they met. It really was a horrible day to travel, especially if the aim was stress relief. The more graphic Renu's profanity grew, the merrier Neena's tunes became, in an attempt to counterbalance the mood of the outing. Not that it made a speck of a difference to Anupama, who gazed out of the window in stony silence. To be honest, she couldn't quite understand why they were both so hell-bent on cheering her up in this drastic fashion. She had had down days before, and it had usually been confined to a pep-up phone talk or an impromptu tea visit, at the most. They knew she liked to have her space. In fact, if they really knew her, they would have taken the kids out instead and given her the privacy to curl up on the floor and stare at the underside of her sofa until her mind blanked out. And this time, there would have been no unexpected new neighbours to disturb her either. No one would have bothered her. No one.

A few hours and a couple of random stops later, Anupama began to get a sneaking suspicion of the master plan. Renu was taking them to all their old haunts as collegians; the idea obviously being to relive their carefree days and rekindle the joy of youth within their souls. It was another matter that every spot they visited – from Abu Mastana's kulfi stall to the local theatre to the chai tapri near Pedder road – had either shut down, collapsed or gotten demolished and renovated into a residential complex. The final result was that rather than feeling young again, they got to realize just how much time had slipped by, and how ancient and outdated they had become – a thought that ended up depressing the other two as well, while Anupama tried to remember just how much cough syrup was left in her medicine bottle back home. Would she need to buy a refill on the way?

It was a sombre group that made its way back to her building at around ten in the night. Anupama thanked them both for the lovely day and courteously invited them upstairs for tea just as a formality, and was relieved when they refused.

She entered her home to find another surprise waiting for her. Misha had made dinner. Maggie noodles with boiled veggies and scrambled eggs. The eggs were cold and the veggies slightly undercooked, but Anupama was grateful all the same. The kids seemed to be rather attentive and pampering towards her too, which made her even gladder. So glad was she, in fact, that it almost made her suspicious. She had fallen sick a couple of times before – much sicker than she had been over the past few days – and yet never had the pleasure of witnessing such unexpected feats of kindness. And what with the sudden nostalgia tour organized by her friends, the timing just seemed too serendipitous to be a coincidence. Still, as long as things remained idyllic, who was she to complain? The answer, if any, would come to her sooner or later anyway, so she might as well just enjoy the moment while it lasted.

Later, out of habit, she logged on to her Facebook account before going to bed. And that was when the reason for all the tender, loving care became as clear as day. Her euphoria drained away in an instant.

Her page was alive with two status updates from her kids, each wishing their late father a very happy birthday, and hoping that his soul was resting in peace.

It was Rajeev's birthday today.

Her children had assumed that she was depressed because she missed having him around on this, his special day. That it had made her feel so low that she fell ill. And so did her friends.

Poor old Anu. Pining for her lost soulmate. Longing for their times together. Pining for him. Loving him. And wasting away.

And somewhere, in that fifth dimension, she probably was lamenting her loss. Maybe in that parallel universe she hadn't made out with the young man next door on an impulse and gotten ill obsessing over it, oblivious to everything else, including her late husband's birthday. Conceivably in that world, at this very moment, both her perceived and actual realities were in perfect alignment, and things were actually making sense.

Anupama longed for that world. She would have given anything to be there. But she wasn't. She was here. Alone. *Lost*.

Suddenly, the world around her, everything she knew, seemed so alien and incoherent. Her heart lurched with a fear she couldn't quite place. She had felt lonely before, but she had never felt this … disoriented. It was like she had just woken up to discover that her entire life had been someone else's dream. That she herself had been a figment of her imagination, seeking the truth within a reality that never existed. Why was everything so wrong? Why didn't anyone know her? Or was it the other way around? Were they the ones who were right, and she, the one who needed to get a grip? Was their perspective of Anupama the true version of her? Then why didn't it feel right at all? Why couldn't she persuade herself to be who everyone thought she was? Wouldn't that be simpler? Wouldn't that be *right*?

She could feel the unmistakeable onset of a panic attack, and that scared her even more. She felt choked, suffocated. The walls seemed to be closing in on her. She had to get out right now. She had to talk to someone, anyone. Someone who would listen, just listen, and not judge her. Someone who didn't, or at least thought he didn't know the real her. A stranger, perhaps. A stranger she could trust, if ever there was such an oxymoron. Her mind frantically grappled with these turbulent thoughts, even though a part of her had already arrived at the answer she sought, like a long-forgotten instinct. Her head refused to accept it of course, but it was there.

She had promised herself she wouldn't go to him. She *couldn't* go to him, not after all that had transpired. Besides, wasn't he the reason for all this chaos in the first place? Damn him. No. Anyone but him.

———

Five minutes later, she found herself walking up the stairs to the terrace in her nightgown, half-dazed, half-intrigued, still wondering whether this was real. Even if it wasn't, she was curious to see where it would all lead to. Her heart beat wild against her ribs, in sync with the aggressive hammering of the rain outside. She wondered whether he would actually be up there in this weather. The terrace door was wide open; the topmost steps gleamed wetly with the rainwater. She took a deep breath and resolutely walked up.

Charlie was perched on the ledge with his back to her, holding a huge umbrella above him. Tiny tendrils of smoke from his joint emerged from the cover of his umbrella and dissipated into the rain.

She stood rooted to the spot in the doorway, as she tried to evaluate the consequences of the next few steps. She could turn back at this moment and he would never know. No one would. Her routine would return to normal, as would her stability. Life would go back to being the same that it had been all these years. With Rajeev. Without Rajeev.

The same. The exact fucking same.

She took a step forward, then another, feeling the cold rain wash over her with torrential force. For the first time, she wasn't afraid of getting wet. The feeling comforted her rather.

It took Charlie a few moments to notice her standing behind him, soaked to the skin.

'Mrs Arora?' he exclaimed.

'Anupama,' she corrected softly.

He quickly tilted his umbrella to shield her, but she moved it away. He asked her if she was okay, and she shook her head.

'You may fall ill again,' said Charlie, the worry deepening on his face.

So, although he knew she had been unwell, he hadn't

bothered to contact her; but wasn't that exactly what she had asked of him? She had lost him for good. Just like she had wanted. Her strength left her, as did her restraint. The rain camouflaged her tears, but not the trembling of her lips or the sadness in her face.

'Hey, hey,' said Charlie, getting up and embracing her. She pressed herself against the warmth of his body. She knew she was making his T-shirt wet, but he didn't seem to mind. He was about a foot taller than her. His skin on the side of his neck on her forehead was as soft as she remembered it, slightly bristly at the point where his stubble ended. Slowly, she raised herself on tiptoe, her eyes shut, gently running the tip of her nose against his cheek, until they were both at eye level. She opened her eyes. Charlie was staring at her with an expression that mirrored her own feelings. The umbrella was no longer in his hand and now he was just as wet as she was. Neither of them cared.

The moment hung between them for one delicious instant; the tension between them an almost tangible entity now, breathing, waiting, coaxing them on.

And then their lips touched. A shudder passed through Anupama as she submitted herself completely to the overpowering onslaught of her senses – the sensation of Charlie's warm breath upon hers, the feel of his lips, the taste of his mouth mingled with the raindrops trickling in between them. The world had not existed before this, and if it had, it had been a poor parody. A travesty. An illusion. Suddenly, everything was real. *She* was real. That was what it was. She had been alive for a long time now, but for the first time in her life, she felt *real*.

She didn't know how many seconds or minutes the kiss lasted, but when they drew apart, she knew one thing for sure. Something had changed inside her forever. Her tears continued to flow, but their essence had changed. There was no more misery left inside her, just the soothing hollowness of relief.

Her fingers still clasped behind his neck, Anupama gazed up at Charlie, at the loving tenderness in his beautiful grey-green-hazel eyes that percolated into the depths of her soul. Mrs Govindikar was right. She wasn't just a woman anymore. She was a human, a soul, a wanderer, a lover.

She loved this man. She wanted him like she had never wanted anything in her life. It didn't make sense, and it didn't have to, for that was a truth that would never change whether she accepted it or not.

'I think I'm in love with you,' said Charlie.

And Anupama just smiled.

Gradually, like the fragmented remnants of a fading dream, the surroundings began to impress themselves upon her. The rain had slowed down to a drizzle. She became aware of her wet nightclothes clinging to her skin, the chill in the air, Charlie's umbrella lying forgotten by the terrace wall … and beyond the terrace wall, down below, the old watchman peering up at them from his cabin by the entrance gates, his glasses unmistakably trained up towards them.

Anupama froze, more out of surprise than fear. In a flash, she understood the secret behind Mrs Govindikar's omniscience. Her spy at the gates. No wonder he wasn't able to look her in the eye this morning. She waited for the old man to avert his eyes sheepishly, but he didn't. He seemed to be looking right at her, at them. Charlie followed her gaze and immediately saw the old man. 'Oh crap!' He glanced back at her anxiously. 'Should we—'

'Kill him?' asked Anupama, half-jokingly.

'I'm sorry.'

'For what?'

'I ... don't know.'

Anupama turned back to see that the watchman continued to stare at them insolently. Fine, two could play at that game. The zone she was in right now permitted no panic or concern. She felt indestructible. Besides, the damage, if any, was done already, might as well reap its benefits. Charlie's eyes widened as she drew him closer.

'You know what they say,' she said. 'Whether you commit one murder or two...'

———

Twenty minutes later, she was lying on Charlie's futon, spent and exhausted.

Their lovemaking had been frantic, clumsy, erratic and pleasurable in a way that made her toes curl. She could still feel the trail his lips had followed across her entire body, the firmness of his fingers as he held her close to his body, the hard yet yielding fluidity of his muscles – his limbs, his chest – the pace and frenzy of his movements that almost seemed feral ... For the first time in her life, she had had two orgasms in a row – a fictional fantasy that she thought was limited to the adult entertainment industry. She had sighed, she had moaned, she had even screamed at one point, clutching him for dear life, and through it all Charlie had been with her, one with her, carrying her along on a dizzying trip of newer and newer heights of ecstasy from which she never wanted to return.

Anupama let out a deep sigh. She had draped a sheet over her naked body, even though he had assured her that it wasn't necessary, the room was semi-dark anyway. Anupama had forbidden him from turning on the lights, and they had only had the light filtering through from the street lamps. But now that the high was gone, she could feel the familiar twinges of self-consciousness returning. It didn't help that the man lying next to her was a prototype of a male anatomy lecture. She didn't want him to regret anything. The moment was so perfect, so blissful … and that was how she wanted him to remember it. She wished he would say something, but his eyes looked upward at the ceiling, arms folded behind his head, face serene as his chest moved up and down rhythmically.

'Say something,' she said, finally.

'Like what?'

'Anything … how are you feeling?'

'Good.'

'Good?'

'Yeah, like, really, really good. Awesome, actually.'

'Okay …' she said, trying to hide her disappointment.

'What about you?'

'I'm good too.'

'Great.'

With that, the conversation concluded. Was it mandatory for men to lose their passion and depth along with their sperm? Not that she had had experience enough to make a comparison, but she did have high hopes of him. Was it wrong to expect the ones who made you feel special, to be special in their own way? Perhaps, it was. Perhaps, this was just the way things were.

'Should I turn on the lights?' asked Charlie.

'Wait.'

As she felt around blindly for her nightgown in the darkness, she bumped into some of the packing boxes lying on the floor and wondered why he hadn't bothered to unpack them yet. Finally, she found her wet garment and slipped it on, just as the lights came on. She was adjusting the straps over her shoulders, when two strong arms gripped her tightly in an embrace from behind. A second later, she felt Charlie's nose and stubble rub against the back of her neck, raising gooseflesh all over her body.

'I was right,' he whispered in her ear. 'You *are* different.'

And that was all, all that she needed. Brimming with relief and joy, Anupama turned around and kissed him deeply. 'So are you.'

17

It is darkest before dawn. And vice versa. Although the latter is a truth that not many care to acknowledge.

Having basked in the life-giving rays of dawn, it was now time to face the darkness of an enduring dusk.

Although she had no regrets about last night, for that was a threshold she had crossed permanently, neither was she under the delusion that her actions would have no consequences, especially now that there was a prime witness to her fall from grace. She half expected a crowd of accusatory spectators to be gathered outside her window right now, pointing and whispering. Judging. Witnessing. Chronicling.

In a few hours from now, she would be infamous.

She had thought about having a talk with her children about it in the morning; but then decided against it because they were getting ready to go to school and college. There was no need to send them off with such a heavy burden on their minds. They would get to know about it by lunch time anyway, if Mrs Mehtani had anything to say about it.

So, all she could do now was wait for the guillotine to fall with her hands folded on her lap and a dignified smile on her face. If she had to go, she would go with her head held high and the blissful memory of a double orgasm with a Greek god who loved her, which wasn't such a bad way to go anyway. She only hoped that the slut-shaming rituals would end by 3.00 p.m., because she and Renu had a client meeting scheduled for the evening.

The problem was that while her mind was fearlessly rational about the whole situation, her heart was a whole other story. The roles had reversed. Earlier, it was her heart that was egging her on and her mind, holding her back. But now that the point of no return had been breached, her head was now in a rather progressive and liberal mood (possibly as a damage-control measure), while her heart was incessantly pumping adrenalin into her system, gearing her up for a battle of a magnitude she was yet to estimate.

The doorbell rang.

Anupama braced herself, trying hard to ignore the chill in her veins. The moment of reckoning. The hour of judgment. Time to face the music.

She smoothened out her kurta, straightened her shoulders and walked to the door; her subconscious already dealing with the inquisition in the offing.

Yes, it's true … Yes, it's him … How? The way any two consenting adults do it … Don't worry about my kids. I can take care of them myself … Why him? Why not … I don't think that's any of your business, to be honest with you … No, I will not move out. I am not a criminal … Yes, of course it was consensual … What does Rajeev have to do with this…

She unlatched the bolt, twisted the knob, and swung open the door to see – Gopal, the building superintendent, standing

172   Debashish Irengbam

outside with a sombre look on his face. He appeared to be alone and unarmed, so she opened the door wider.

'Yes?'

Gopal wordlessly handed her a folder containing a single document. Anupama glanced down curiously.

ATHARVA HARI C.H.S MANAGING COMMITTEE

This is to report the sad and tragic loss of our loyal and dedicated society watchman, Mr Banwari Lal, who passed away last night in his security cabin after more than fifteen years of service. According to the coroner, the death was painless and due to natural causes attributed to old age. Since Mr Lal has no kith or kin to speak of, the society has decided to organize a collection drive for his funeral and last rites. You are requested to donate as much as you wish towards these expenses. The shortfall will be extracted from the society's corpus fund.

Thank you for your cooperation.
Mrs Alka Govindikar
Chairperson

Anupama stood frozen, the paper clutched in her hands, reading and re-reading the circular, until she realized that Gopal was patiently standing by for her response. She asked him to wait and went back in. In place of the reservoir of retorts and replies that had been occupying her mind just a few seconds ago, now only questions remained. She wondered what time he had died last night. Was he even alive when she saw him? Had her boldest act of defiance been witnessed by a corpse? Was that the reason for his motionless gaze, his lifeless eyes watching their rebellious passion? Or had her sexuality been too much for his frail shell to handle? She felt her stomach contract at the thought of her sensuous rendezvous being the last sight the poor man beheld before shuffling off his mortal coil.

A shudder passed through her as she retrieved a five-hundred-rupee note from her purse and gave it to Gopal. He informed her that the funeral would be held at 5.00 p.m. at the local crematorium, in case she wanted to attend. Anupama thanked him and locked the door.

It took a while for the apprehension and nausea that had been bottled up since morning to subside. When they did, the vacuum in her mind made her feel giddy. It dawned on her that, despite the rather morbid and tragic nature of this unexpected development, the bottom line was, her secret was still intact. As far as the world was concerned, she was still the same. Nothing had changed. A load lifted off her chest, and for the first time that day, she breathed freely. Was this a sign? A second chance, so to speak?

Now that matters didn't seem quite so direly irrevocable, she wondered whether she had been foolhardy last night. It wasn't wrong, of course, but was it wise? Eventually she would have to tell her friends and family no doubt, but why do it in a way befitting of an erotica thriller, especially when she, as a person, was anything but erotic or thrilling? Charlie and she would have to take it slow now, she decided, slow and discreet. And for that, there needed to be rules. Lots of rules.

That night, Charlie hopped up on the terrace to find a long list of procedural rules and regulations waiting for him.

'So … three seconds is the maximum amount of time I can make eye contact with you?' he asked, going through the list.

'In public, yes,' said Anupama.

'Why three seconds specifically?'

'Because two would seem too fidgety and four would be too attentive.'

'Is it okay if I use a stopwatch for the purpose?'

'Charlie.'

'I'm just saying … d'you really think people have nothing better to do but keep us under micro-surveillance?'

'I've spent the better half of my life here. You have spent one-and-a-half months, in which you have managed to almost get kicked out twice.'

'Touché.'

He returned to the list, studying each point very carefully. Try as she might, Anupama couldn't help but feel distracted by the sight of his lips moving as he quietly mumbled the words under his breath. For someone who smoked so frequently, he had a nice, well-shaped pair of—

'So, every time we go out, I have to pick you up from Mith Chowki?' he asked, interrupting her reverie, his beautiful eyes flashing up at her.

'Yes.'

'Isn't that a bit far? I mean, you will literally be spending forty-fifty bucks for an unnecessary auto ride when I could just pick you up from the first intersection outside.'

'Charlie, I'm not taking any chances.'

'And what if we are going the other side towards Mira Road?'

'We will not go towards Mira Road.'

'Why not?'

'Because Rajeev's parents and relatives stay in Bhayandar.'

'That's almost twenty kilometres away.'

'Charlie, I'm not taking any chances.'

'Wouldn't it just be easier if you wore a burqa and I wore a mask just like any other normal couple?'

'I'm glad you're finding this amusing.'

'It's just that … after last night, I thought things would be different.'

'Things *are* different. I have accepted us. I just need some time to make others accept it too.'

'And how will that happen unless we tell them?'

'That's what I need time for. To figure it out.'

Charlie shook his head in dismay. 'I just don't get what the big deal is. It's not like we are doing anything illegal. This is the twenty-first century, you know. You *can* have a younger partner without getting stoned to death for it. In fact, I don't think anyone even gives a shit anymore.'

'How many couples do you personally know like us?'

Charlie opened his mouth to reply, before pausing to think. The seconds ticked by.

'Exactly,' said Anupama. 'So please spare me the liberal speech and just focus on the plan of action, which I have carefully thought through. Trust me, this is the right way.'

'Fine,' he said, folding up the list and putting it in his pocket. 'So what is the timeline we are looking at?'

'I'm thinking let's wait until the Monsoon Goddess pageant gets over, at least. The worst thing to do would be to test those ladies' open-mindedness while they are suffering the pangs of hunger and carb-withdrawal.'

'So, another month of secrecy, then. I could do that. What about your family?'

'What about them?'

'Do we tell them along with the neighbours or before? If we do it now, I could even start coming over to your place and—'

'Are you mad?'

'What? It's bound to happen sooner or later, right? In fact, the sooner it happens, the more time they will get to absorb the fact that I'm … you know … sort of … their future…'

DON'T, Anupama wanted to scream, but it was too late.

'…daddy.'

Her insides lurched horribly at the word. The thought of Charlie being Misha's – she couldn't even say the word – made her feel queasy and nauseous. How come she hadn't considered this obvious scenario before?

'You okay? Your face has gone pale,' remarked Charlie, looking at her with concern.

She took a deep breath, trying to steady her nerves. 'I think we're going too fast.'

'I'm not saying it has to happen tomorrow. But eventually—'

'Stop. Just stop.'

Charlie stopped. His face darkened. 'I'm sorry. I just assumed – you do love me, right?'

Anupama nodded silently.

'Then – this is a serious thing, right? Like, with a future and all? I mean, I just want to be clear,' he said tentatively.

'I love you,' said Anupama, more to herself than him. 'I do. I know I do.'

'Great,' said Charlie, his face beaming again. 'So we will cross that bridge when we get to it. Okay?'

She nodded quietly again. He smiled warmly and wrapped her in an embrace, her ear and cheeks pressed against his chest, listening to the sound of his even heartbeat.

'Don't worry. It's going to be okay,' he murmured.

And Anupama nodded quietly, yet again.

18

'There's something different about you,' said Renu, squinting at her from across the coffee table. They had just concluded a successful meeting with yet another socialite from the posh 'Townie' community who wanted to convert her Bohemian chic penthouse into a rather sombre minimalist design as a tribute to the late Chico, her favourite Persian cat, recently deceased. Anupama remembered reading a piece about the feline's extravagant wake in the *City Highlights* two days ago, attended by all the Who's Who of Page 3 in the city. The most expensive funeral parlour in the city had been booked for an entire day; a projector screen had played slideshow images of the cat's happiest moments, with Mozart's '*Requiem*' playing in the background, while mourners (read: fellow socialites and employees) paid their respects to the deceased as it lay peacefully in its teakwood-walnut casket, complete with satin inner padding and intricate brass-work lining running all along its polished edges. At the other end of the spectrum was the paltry 3,475-rupee community-sponsored ceremony awarded to her society watchman after his fifteen years of dedicated service, and Anupama found herself teetering on the brink of despairing for humanity's humaneness.

Not that she or Renu objected to the exorbitant paycheque. In fact, considering that the said millionaire had three more elderly cats (read: future interior renovations) queueing up at the pearly gates, Renu could finally plan out the further extension of her office in Oshiwara and corporealize her castle in the air. The final clincher had been Anupama's masterstroke suggestion of having a monochrome painting of Bastet (the Egyptian cat goddess) in the living room. It had nothing to do with vaastu, but the bereaved millionairess had been delighted. Her only condition was that Chico's face be superimposed on top of the goddess's body, which Renu had no problem with.

So here they were, celebrating their victory in a café with whopping mugs of cold coffee, comprised of slim milk, decaf coffee, artificial sweeteners, and low-fat ice cream (practically zero calories according to Renu). They had asked Neena to join them as well, who was on her way. Sipping her coffee, Anupama was wondering when and how to break the news to her friends about her secret romance, when Renu broke in on her thoughts with her observation.

'What do you mean?' asked Anupama.

'I don't know, but something has changed. I can feel it.'

'Really? So, you're an aura expert now? Maybe we should add that to our list of services'. Anupama laughed.

'Whoa.'

'What?'

'You just cracked a PJ and followed it up with a fake laugh.

I haven't seen you do that in a while. You're feeling guilty about something.'

'Please. Why don't you just join the CBI or something,' said Anupama, with a light laugh and a nervous flick of her hair.

'You did it again! What is it?'

'Nothing.'

Renu's eyes popped out, her lips parting in a wide grin. '*Oh ... my ... God!*'

'What?'

'Who is he?'

'Who?' asked Anupama, turning to look behind her.

'The one you banged. You slept with someone!'

'What?!'

'Anupama Arora, don't bullshit me. I know that look like I know the back of my hand. Spill the beans before Neena gets here, or you will have to go through a group confession.'

'There's nothing to tell!'

'Fucking hell, you're blushing! It's someone we know. Someone controversial.'

'Are you mad?'

'Is it one of JD's studs?'

'No!'

'One of our clients? No, they were all married, and I know you well enough to know that ...' She paused midway, a look of realization crossing her face. Anupama desperately tried to focus on her coffee as Renu brought her face inch by inch towards her, her mouth a perfectly symmetrical 'O'.

'Oh, bloody fuckin' ... *Charlie*?!'

'Shhh,' hissed Anupama, more out of instinct than necessity, since there was no one around who she knew anyway.

In a dramatic gesture, Renu cupped her mouth with both hands, her eyes wide as saucers. Anupama tried to repudiate her allegation, but her jaws were glued shut, her whole face a burning furnace. They both sat like that for a few quiet seconds, each numbed by their own overpowering emotions, while the low-fat ice cream in their coffee dissolved sadly into low-fat goo.

'You sly little minx,' said Renu finally. 'No wonder you didn't need JD's services!'

'It's not like that,' snapped Anupama. 'It's a rather … recent development. And it's not even about the sex—'

'Yeah, right,' she said, rolling her eyes.

'Fine, the sex is great, but the thing is, it's not just about that. He's a great guy—'

'Uh-huh.'

'And we have this really incredible connection—'

'I'll bet.'

'Keep that up and you won't hear another word from me.'

'I just don't get why you have to justify it. He's hot, right?'

'Yes, but—'

'But what? It's okay to have a sex drive, darling. And I'm really really happy for you. Proud, in fact. Way to go!'

She gleefully passed her a double thumbs-up from across the table. Anupama gave up on any further explanations, as she knew it would be a futile exercise while she was in this kamikaze mode. She would have to wait for her batteries to die down a bit before resuming the topic again. In the meantime—

'You can't tell Neena about this,' said Anupama. 'I love her, but you know how she can be.'

'Obviously. The last thing you need is a moral lecture right now. Besides, we can't expect everyone to share our levels of maturity, right? So how big is he?'

'How big is who?' asked a voice from behind.

They both swivelled to see Neena. An awkward pause followed in which three sets of blank smiles were exchanged amongst the trio.

'Heyy, nice kurta,' gushed Renu.

'Yeahh, what is it? Fabindia?' gushed Anupama.

'Cottonworld. How big is who? And why are you changing the topic?'

Renu glanced surreptitiously at Anupama. Ad libitum was not her forte.

'Someone,' said Anupama, realizing that ad libitum wasn't exactly a character strength of hers either.

'You two are hiding something from me,' said Neena accusatorily, seating herself without taking her narrowed eyes off them.

Renu scoffed derisively and turned her attention to the menu, while Anupama laughed lightly and nervously flicked her hair. Neena's jaw dropped open.

'Wait a second. You're feeling guilty,' she observed. 'And Renu's obviously hiding something.'

Great, déjà vu, thought Anupama with foreboding.

'Either Anu's found someone, or—'

'I'm pregnant,' cut in Renu.

This time, Anupama's jaw dropped open too, as Renu struggled to keep a straight face. Impromptu was *really* not her strong suit.

'You're joking, right?' cried Neena.

'Nope. It's true,' she said, passing Anupama a double wink with her left eye.

Anupama looked at Neena and nodded with pursed lips.

'But how?' exclaimed Neena, stupefied.

'What do you mean how?'

'I mean wha—who's the father?'

'Oh, you don't know him,' said Renu nonchalantly.

Neena passed Anupama a horrified glance. Anupama shrugged, doing her utmost to look sympathetic.

'And that's all? That's all you have to say about this?'

'Well, what can one do? Shit happens. You guys want to try the chocolate mousse?'

'Renu, this is huge! You – have – a – baby – in – your – womb! This is an actual human life we are dealing with.'

'And I think it's craving chocolate. So, you want to share or not?'

Neena shook her head in disbelief, eyes bulging, mouth opening and closing like a halibut in the throes of death. Finally, she turned to Anupama. 'Aren't you going to say something?'

'I can share the mousse,' said Anupama.

'To hell with the mousse!' yelled Neena. 'Renu, this is a huge commitment. Your life is going to change. And what about the father? You're not … I mean, you're not planning to raise it on your own, are you?'

'And what if I am?' shot back Renu. 'Is that such a bad thing?'

Anupama felt a bit taken aback by the annoyance on Renu's face, while Neena sighed gustily.

'D'you remember that money plant we gifted to you?' asked Neena darkly.

'Oh, for God's sake—'

'All you had to do was water it twice a week and you couldn't even do that! How will you take care of a child?'

'Because the child won't get hidden behind my curtains. Besides, you did it. How hard could it be?'

Neena's eyes narrowed even farther. 'What's that supposed to mean?'

'Why don't we try the brownie sizzler this time?' Anupama butted in hurriedly.

'I'm just saying, you know, try stepping off your pedestal every now and then. Just because you were happy settling down as the Sati Savitri of the household doesn't mean that you get to judge us every time we fail to adhere to your established norms of feminine morality.'

'Excuse me,' snarled Neena. 'Just because I don't offer my body to every—'

'Oh, enough with this bullshit, I'm seeing Charlie!' snapped Anupama.

A deathly silence fell across the table. Anupama felt the pendulum of attention swing its way back towards her like a wrecking ball.

'What?!' exclaimed Neena, looking horrified for what seemed like the zillionth time in five minutes.

'My neighbour, Charlie … the one I told you about. I'm seeing him. We are dating, actually. Not publicly, but in a way. Technically.'

'What?'

How much clearer could she have been? With a stoic face,

Anupama waited as the gravity of her confession sank into her latest confidante.

'But he's what, twenty-one?'

'Twenty-four,' said Anupama defensively. 'And he will be twenty-five this September, so…'

Slowly, Neena leaned back in her chair. She leaned forward, picked up her glass of water, took a sip and put it down carefully before leaning back again. All this while, her eyes restlessly darted around, taking in every inch of the café, other than the spot where they were seated.

Nature abhors a vacuum, as Aristotle rightly said. The void that was created in Neena's mental stress furnace by the relief of Renu's pregnancy dismissal was now rapidly replaced by the astonishment of this new – and even more scandalous – revelation.

'And … how long has this been going on?' asked Neena in a measured tone, drawing arabesques on the glass table top with her index finger.

'A while. I mean, it just became official recently but, you know, it's complicated.'

'I see, I see. And … have you … you know?'

'Done *it*?' interjected Renu helpfully.

'Not that it's any of my business, but—'

'Yes,' replied Anupama.

Neena took another, longer sip of water, her eyes riveted on the fascinating table top. 'Is he serious about this?'

'Yes.'

'And you?'

'Of course.'

A deep, ponderous exhale followed, before Neena finally raised her eyes to look at Anupama. 'Fine, then. I'm happy for you.'

Anupama's eyebrows flew up the same distance that Renu's jaw dropped down. 'Seriously?'

'Of course. I mean, obviously, it's not the most … expected … of situations, but as long as you are both adults and happy and fulfilled, who am I to object?'

'So, I get the cosmic shit-storm and she gets a supportive shrug?' cried Renu.

'She is in love. You're an unwed mother-to-be.'

'And you are a pompous ass.'

'What are you getting so worked up about? You're not even pregnant.'

'It – doesn't – matter!' shrieked Renu.

It was then that Anupama realized that for the first time in years, Renu had suggested celebrating at a coffee shop instead of a pub. Now that the thought was in her head, she couldn't help but notice how flushed Renu looked, and as it turned out, it probably wasn't just out of stress.

'Renu, you're not really … ?' asked Anupama, as Neena's eyes widened.

'What! Mad or what? Why don't you two just open up a pregnancy guessing centre or something?' said Renu, with a tinkling chortle.

Anupama and Neena exchanged a meaningful look. A PJ followed by a fake laugh. They glanced at Renu to see that she was no longer smiling. An uncomfortable silence followed.

'I'm fucked, right?'

'No, no, you're not. We're here for you,' said Anupama,

grasping her hand supportively. They both turned to Neena, whose face was expressionless. A moment or so passed before her features relaxed, and she nodded with a sigh.

'Just tell us what we can do.'

'Well, for starters, you could order me a *fucking chocolate mousse!*'

———

Twenty minutes later, Anupama found herself seated in Renu's car, both of them gorging on their second helpings of chocolate mousse that they had picked up for the road. They could see Neena through the glass doors of the chemist shop outside, where she was selecting pre-natal vitamins and other medication over the counter while engaged in an animated discussion with the chemist. The rain had turned into a slow, steady drizzle of vapour-like drops.

'She's a good friend,' sighed Renu. 'A bit of a prude, sometimes. But we need someone like her.'

'I know.'

Renu twisted around to face Anu. 'By the way, you didn't have to lie to her, you know.'

'About what?'

'You know, the whole "being serious about Charlie" thing. What you're doing isn't wrong, and eventually she will have to accept that too.'

'But I am serious about him.'

Renu chuckled. 'Anu, please. You can't be *that* naïve.'

'What's that supposed to mean?'

'Look, no offence, you *are* a catch. But guys like Charlie –

they aren't really options for settling down. At least not at this age. You know that, right?'

'You haven't even met him,' said Anupama tersely.

'Anu, he's twenty-four. That's all I need to know. You know how guys were when we were twenty-four. And that was one generation ago. Can you imagine how they would be now?'

'But he's not—'

'Like the others? That's what they all say, honey.'

Anupama bit her lip, resisting the urge to snap at her, attributing Renu's acerbity on prenatal hormonal fluctuations.

'I'm just saying – have fun, enjoy it, see how it goes,' Renu went on. 'Just take it slow. You don't want to repeat the same mistake, do you?'

Anupama glowered at Renu. She had touched a nerve, the one nerve that was off-limits to her – to anyone, for that matter. She could already see the remorse on Renu's face, but it was too late. The pure, unbridled rage, which she hadn't felt in quite some time, flooded back into her system with a vengeance. She crumpled her mousse and flung it out the window.

'Anu—'

Swinging her door open, she stepped out of the car and marched away, conscious only of the blood thundering in her ears. She could faintly hear Renu and Neena's voices calling her back. But she had to get away from them. She had to go.

19

Sometimes, it's in the most crowded of places that we find the solitude we need.

She had tried most places – parks, beaches, spas, saunas, yoga houses and even the occasional ashram or two. Nothing worked; mainly because it wasn't the silence she was seeking. She already had more than enough of that in her life and felt haunted by it. No, it was the noise and the hustle and bustle that she craved. An anonymity in the chaos, urgency and energy of a crowd.

Who would have known that sitting on a bench in a packed inter-state platform in the CST railway station during rush hour, would give her the fleeting sense of peace for which she so desperately yearned?

Every time she felt like she was going to crumble and fall apart, Anupama would retire to this secret sanctuary, watch the trains come and go, while folks scrambled to get on and off them. She would observe lost, nervous, hopeful, blank, or worried expressions on people's faces, the frantic pace, the sweat on their brows, the neatly folded handkerchiefs, the worn-out footwear. Each had their own stories, their own worries and their very own routines. Nobody gave her a second glance. She was just another nobody to them. She could die right now, and no one would even notice it for a while. The thought comforted her. Being anonymous was a privilege that she had never enjoyed.

For a couple of years now, she had been wondering what it would be like to live life as a perpetual stranger. Being a wanderer, never getting attached to anything or anyone, never letting anyone know who you were. As she watched those dusty, faded crimson trains entering and exiting the platform with mechanical regularity, she ruminated about how easy it would be to leave it all behind. Right then, she could choose to just cut and run and never come back. She wondered where she would go and whether it even mattered.

How easy it was, she reckoned, and yet how difficult. Impossible, even. It was a futile thought. She was too far gone now. There were people depending upon her. Relationships, responsibilities, reputations.

She knew it could never happen, but she liked to fantasize about it anyway. Forty-two years of her life had flown by and she had never travelled on her own. Not even once. She wondered why.

The last time she had asked her mother for permission to go on a college trip with her classmates, her life had changed drastically in a way she could never have foreseen. Her mother had extracted all the details about the male-to-female ratio (both students and teachers) amongst the group and contacted most of them personally to confirm their identities. She even obtained the landline number of the lodge where they would be putting up, the bus service they were to use, the contact numbers of the nearest police station in the area. At the end of the whole exercise, Anupama wondered what all that fuss was about because her mother refused to grant her permission to join the expedition anyway – something about it being 'improper' for her to travel in the company of men; and so far away from home; and at her age. When the issue of propriety threatened to turn into a heated debate, her mother had stonewalled with 'it wasn't safe', and having convinced her husband of her fears, that was that and the matter was laid to rest.

By then, Anupama's mother's sleuthing skills had become the talk of her college, and for the next few months, Anupama found herself the butt of jokes. It was the early nineties back then, after all. *Jawani Zindabad* and *Baaghi: A Rebel for Love* had been released. Nirvana and Rage Against the Machine were ruling the charts. Rebellion against authority was as much in vogue as fringe cuts and high-waisted denims.

This humiliation and the subsequent squabbles that followed at home, made up the final straw for Anupama, who had always held her mother's iron hand with a rising contempt and bitterness. She decided to rebel, and in the worst way that her mother could have imagined. She got herself a boyfriend. And not just the exchanging-notes-in-class sort, the full-on going-out-in-public kind.

Within a fortnight, she revolutionized her image from that of a timid mommy's girl to a bold free spirit, much like her forward friend, Renu, who had changed two boyfriends in her first year in college. She was officially a 'girlfriend' now, and she loved the attention and awe it garnered around her social circles.

His name was Rajeev Arora. He was a third-year student, just like her, but from the Commerce wing. He was stable, self-assured and smelled nice. And for a girl who had never known the joys of being committed to someone, he was an invaluable ticket to a new world. Not that he was even remotely like the romantic heroes she saw in movies, but that was okay. Her mother had assured her long ago that that sort of stuff existed only in fiction. In real life, practicality was what mattered. And practical he was, no doubt about it. He knew exactly what he wanted his life to be and had assured her that there would be a space in it for her as well.

Her mother had had a hissy fit, as was expected. However, the more she raged, the braver Anupama had become. The harder she tried to convince her that it was a mistake, the more hellbent Anupama became to make it work. She actually began to take pride in her nonchalance towards her mother's indignation. She wasn't a timorous little girl anymore, was she? She was going to do what she wanted to do. And what she wanted to do was to prove her mother wrong, more than anything else.

The problem arose when her friends began to give her mixed signals. While Neena wholeheartedly supported her choice, Renu didn't quite hide the fact that she believed Anu could do much better. There was nothing wrong with him per se, she explained, but that was exactly what was wrong with him. He was too … right. Like the antiseptic and sterile food that was served in hospitals. Nutritious, of course, and good for you, but not something you want to stick to for the rest of your life.

Fine, then, Anupama had decided, she would rebel against

her friends too, if that's what it took. She liked hospital food, and their opinion didn't matter. Rajeev treated her well, said he loved her, and more importantly, he wanted to be with her. Forever. After a lifetime of feeling inadequate, here was a person who not only accepted her the way she was, but even claimed to like her for it. If that didn't make him a catch, she didn't know what would.

Shortly after Neena's wedding, Rajeev had popped the question. He had got a high-paying placement in a good financial firm, and under some particular government scheme, he could even buy an apartment of their own if they got married before the end of the year. A person whom Rajeev knew had assured him that he could make the necessary arrangements to get this flat, provided Anupama's father agreed to cover the shortfall in Rajeev's resources to finance this investment. That had been his proposal. It wasn't exactly moonlight-and-roses, but they were on a strict timeline here, so she said yes. After all, they had known each other for almost two years now, and so far she had had no issues.

In the weeks to follow, the atmosphere at home had been cold, to say the least. Her mother stopped talking to her altogether; her father became the only source of communication between the two ladies in the household – a role that he swiftly came to resent. Not that Anupama minded the estrangement. In fact, she revelled in it. She felt bold, strong, liberated. She felt vindicated for all those times when her mother had forbidden her from enjoying the simple pleasures of life, when every advice had been a command and every rule, unquestionable. And here she was now, silenced finally.

It was only on her wedding day, right before she was to leave for the pandal, that her mother deigned to break her silence, only to reiterate her warning.

'You have no idea what you have done to yourself,' she said with an air of finality, before planting a chilly kiss on her forehead and leading her out of the room.

She still had the wedding photo framed on her bedside table. She and Rajeev sitting next to each other on their 'thrones', with Rajeev's parents on the right, and hers on the left. The only one smiling in the picture was her mother.

Her phone buzzed yet again. Assuming it to be Renu or Neena and planning to cut the call, she fished her mobile out of her bag, when her eyes fell on the ID. Charlie.

'Hello?'

'Hey, 'sup? Just wanted to know if we have any plans for tonight,' said Charlie. 'Coz it's Shivani's birthday today, and she's giving us a treat at this joint nearby which has a two plus one on drinks going on. *And* it's karaoke night.'

'It's okay. Go ahead.'

'You sure?'

'Yes, of course. We can meet up later.'

'Thanks a lot! Love you!'

'Love you too.'

She hung up to see nine missed calls from Renu and Neena. She would have to call them tonight and apologize, yet again. They would be livid for a while, but then eventually forgive her, and life would go back to normal. Well, as normal as it could be. For a moment, she felt tempted to go home and take a swig out of her cough syrup bottle. But then she chastised herself for the thought. That phase of her life was over. She had someone now. She wasn't lonely anymore. Was she? She wasn't, she decided. She wasn't. She couldn't be. Not after all that had happened.

With a sigh, Anupama rose from the bench and joined the travellers swarming towards the exit. Time to return to the daily grind, she mused.

20

The new society watchman was a lot younger than the previous guy, in his twenties, with an avid interest in the translated works of Kafka and Dostoevsky, and a rather disinterested view of the world around. He wouldn't smile or chat and seemed to completely ignore the comings and goings of the residents in the building. In other words, he was a godsend for the discreet romance blossoming between the occupants of C-703 and C-704.

Anupama knew that his insouciance wouldn't last long, not if Mrs Govindikar had her way, which she inevitably would; so it was vital to make the most of this break she had been granted for the time being. After receiving the endorsement from her friends (Renu was still a bit sceptical), her relationship with Charlie had reached a new level of legitimacy – a fact that both elated and terrified her.

They were 'officially going out' now, to use her kids' terminology. Their first bona fide date had been at a quaint little bakery situated deep within one of the cramped, graffiti-decorated alleyways of Chapel Road in Bandra West – a place suggested by Charlie and validated by Anupama as 'safe' for their rendezvous. She wasn't proud of it, but she had nearly gone round the bend preparing for this evening. She had read up on the latest news reports and film reviews, researched on dating tips and articles pertaining to usual guys' interests and had even looked at the odd sports article or two, which was tough, because she had no idea whether he was into cricket or football or racing. In spite of having met him several times now, the thought of being with him in a predetermined romantic context for a specified period of time scared her witless, and she was determined not to appear dull or uninteresting for even a minute, no matter what it took.

Head filled to the brim with stats, figures, headlines, punch lines, popular discussion topics and a general checklist of men's issues, Anupama had reached the venue on the dot, only to sit waiting for twenty minutes before Charlie showed up, sweaty and irritated, having been held up in the rush-hour. They ended up spending the evening discussing the morbid traffic situation in the city and cursing its congestion, pollution, heat, civic infrastructure, public common sense, hygiene. At one point, they had even debated over the merits of paper bags versus plastic for some reason. And surprisingly, it had been ... fun. In fact, Anupama couldn't remember the last time she had been so enthralled by a conversation with someone over something as impersonal as sanitation and commuting. It was only when Charlie dropped her at the junction of S V Road and Linking Road that she realized they hadn't even touched on the burning topics of the day that she had so painstakingly rehearsed. It simply hadn't mattered.

Their next few meetings were of a similar random and unpredictable nature, with the topics of conversation and debate ranging from the mundane to the bizarre – why were some of the African tribes so tall, where did they get their height from? What was the difference between a Marathi upma and a south Indian upma? Why was the concept of pickles so different in India and the US? Why was kissing termed 'making out' when most of the time it happened indoors around here? Why did people find sunsets romantic and sunrises philosophical? Did a caterpillar know from its hatching that it was going to become a butterfly? Did it look forward to the metamorphosis or dread it? Why did the idea of travelling to an unknown place scare some and invigorate others? Why did people live a life that didn't make them happy?

They never discussed Syria, or the US presidential elections, or the Indo–Pak tensions, or any other trending topic of the week. They had their own little circle of interest and discussion, where no research was required to sound interesting, and no thought was required to begin a discussion. There was no script to be followed, no wit to be displayed. The things they talked about, the way their queries and responses flowed into each other, the simple joys and complex emotions that stirred up in both of them, the little mischievous hints, the annoyed pauses, the meaningful glances and smiles – everything was so natural, so effortless, that it seemed like child's play in its simplicity. This was the way it was always meant to be, wasn't it? Where had this openness and honesty been all her life? When had the awkwardness and the formalities seeped in? Why couldn't it be like this all the time, at least with the people she cared for?

Of course, she was also aware that her meetings with Charlie had a beauty and joy that was exclusively theirs and theirs alone. No one else could have understood its meaning or value. To an objective bystander, their chemistry may have appeared weird or un-relatable. However, it was this very unconventionality that made her feel all the more special for being with him, for having him in her life, and for – what was the word she was looking for – *fitting*, yes, fitting with him in a way that she herself could not have foreseen until very recently. The phase of her physical infatuation with him had evolved into something more essential and deeper. She still beheld his beauty with a familiar sense of awe, like an artist anonymously observing his own masterpiece amidst a crowd in the gallery, but now, it was these meetings that she eagerly anticipated. In her heart, they were a resounding success, and that delighted her beyond anything.

Using the exit-meeting-return procedures that she had formulated, they could even afford to go to safe zones like the North-West corner of Juhu beach, or the rear of the food court in Infiniti, or even certain restaurants, provided they weren't anywhere near Charlie's salon, because his workplace had turned into a hotspot for most of the ladies in the block now.

After the success and envy of Mrs Patil and Mrs Chatterjee's makeovers, Charlie had become something of a secretly revered maestro in the neighbourhood. Word of mouth spread fast, especially if the medium of communication was hushed whispers. Within a matter of days, Charlie found his appointment book brimming over with ladies from the A, B and C blocks of Atharva Hari, along with a few others from the neighbouring housing societies. Even his longstanding clients found it difficult to squeeze themselves into his schedule, especially if it happened to be during the office and school hours of the Atharva Hari husbands and children.

With an inkling of Mrs Govindikar's and Mrs Mehtani's antipathy towards the rather good-looking bloke with the 'nice eyes' and the 'magic hands' in C-704, the ladies had been cautious in approaching him. However, it was a given that the secret wouldn't remain under wraps for long, especially when the elaborate bangs and curly tresses began making their appearance across the parks and the streets and the elevators.

Unsuspecting husbands would return from work to behold their wives nonchalantly sporting brilliant beige and feisty crimson highlights, elaborate chignons, spiral waves, textured locks, tousled ringlets, victory curls and hairstyles with names that sounded like exotic ice-cream flavours. Upon enquiry, all they would get in response was an enigmatic smile that would have put Mona Lisa in the shade. Blow dryers, paddle brushes, hairsprays, pomades and curling irons began to make an aggressive appearance across dressing tables. Teenage daughters began to consult their mothers about the latest hairstyle trends. The departmental store owner downstairs began to get orders for mousses and serums with French and German names that he couldn't even pronounce. And overall, domestic household budgets rose by an average of fifteen to twenty per cent with certain 'miscellaneous' additional charges that would have to be borne at least until the Monsoon Goddess pageant got over.

None of it escaped Mrs Govindikar's beady eyes of course, especially when all the members of her walkers' group, with the exception of herself and Mrs Mehtani, began to sport hairdos they wouldn't have dreamed of attempting even in their heydays. The most remarkable aspect of this makeover was the change in their personalities as well. Some of them even seemed to have become taller overnight, if that was possible. Their shoulders were straighter, their gait bolder, heads held higher with a subtle sense of pride. Ladies who could barely look people in the eye before were now confidently strutting about, flicking side-swept bangs off their forehead and acknowledging the flattering attention they received as their due. Mrs Govindikar didn't want to sully her image by seeming too curious, so she got Mrs Mehtani to do her dirty work and make the inquiries. The reply was the same every single time. A 'visiting' stylist who was no longer in town.

The intricate home-cooked food delivery network operating within the housing society also became secretive towards Mrs Govindikar; every now and then, Charlie would find a new Gujarati, Marathi, or Sindhi delicacy waiting outside his door as an anonymous thank-you gesture.

Anupama found her hands full as well, what with Nimit's birthday on the horizon, and volunteering to help out in the upcoming Monsoon Goddess pageant. It wasn't so much volunteering as being railroaded by Mrs Govindikar into providing her services, because the matriarch believed that it was crucial for Anu to participate in the socio-cultural life of the block. She would have politely refused as she was wont to do every year, except this time Mrs Govindikar had some additional artillery in her depot, and Anupama didn't want to push the envelope too far. The more involved she seemed in these mundane affairs, she reckoned, the less the attention and suspicion she would attract. Mrs Chatterjee, Charlie and some of the single tenants in the Atharva Hari Cooperative Housing

Society had offered to lend a hand as well, only to fall on deaf ears. Anupama suspected that if Mrs Govindikar could have had her way, Mrs Chatterjee would have been blackballed from the competition this time; but then that would have belied the democratic principles that she set great store by. Nevertheless, Mrs Govindikar spearheaded the jury panel, which greatly diminished Mrs Chatterjee's chances of defending her crown this year, despite being one of the strongest contenders in terms of beauty, confidence and personality.

'I don't see your name on this,' Mrs Chatterjee had remarked as she signed up on the application form.

'I'm not participating, Divya.'

Mrs Chatterjee shrugged. 'Would have been nice to see some new faces for a change.'

Anupama had hoped that the issue had been laid to rest, but little did she know of the degree of Mrs Chatterjee's tenacity, for at the next general meeting, Divya raised the topic of how more ladies should be encouraged to participate to uphold the spirit of the competition, and of course, increase the chances of their housing society winning the crown again. This recommendation would have been promptly trashed had she not singled out Anupama as a classic example of hidden potential. The moment the spotlight turned its baleful eye on Anupama, things changed. It was unanimously agreed that the poor widow leading a secluded life with the problematic daughter and the academically average son was the perfect poster-girl for their event. Although no one had a clue what this 'hidden potential' was, since when did humanitarianism need a clear motive? Noting the general mood of the masses, Mrs Govindikar took a call immediately and urged Anupama, who at that moment wanted nothing more than to nuke the entire gathering, with a special explosive reserved for Mrs Chatterjee's big mouth, masked the desire for murder and mayhem within her soul with a hesitant smile, which was received with a thunderous applause.

———

'I think it's awesome. Congrats,' said Charlie, as they both shared a bhutta between them, the distant Worli sea link bridge looming over the misty Arabian sea behind them.

They were perched on a stony perimeter wall at Bandra fort, yet another certified safe spot considering that the only folks to be seen here were young couples looking for a cosy archaeological niche to make out. Not that they had any such intentions, considering Anupama's aversion to any display of affection in public. The clouds had cleared up a bit for the afternoon, letting in a trickle of watery sunshine.

'It's not awesome,' argued Anupama. 'It's charity. I'm going to be the bloody ambassador of public compassion out there. "Oh, look at me. Sad, old widow trying to fit in. Please love me, accept me." Might as well wear the obligated white sari too.'

The smile faded off Charlie's face. 'Don't talk like that.'

'What do you mean?'

'I don't like it when you talk about yourself like that,' he said sullenly.

'Like what? I'm just stating the facts here.'

'Really? So, is that what you are? A sad, old widow in a white sari? How many times have you worn a white sari? How many times have you even worn white, for that matter?'

'It's not about the sari, Charlie.'

'No, it's about you wanting to be something you are not.'

'Are you drunk or something? Do you think I *want* to be a widow?' snapped Anupama, her volume rising with her temper.

'No, I think you want to be what you think everyone wants you to be, and that's what's stopping you from being what you actually want to be.'

'What?'

Charlie took a deep breath. 'Look, I know you're probably going to hate me for this, but the fact is that no matter how much you want to believe it, you are not the stereotypical mourning widow you think you are. And that's fine. In fact, there's nothing fine or not fine about it. That's just the way it is. So why pretend?'

And there it was. The all-too-familiar nervous-breakdown rage that threatened to make her a psychotic murderess every time. All it took was the one trigger. *Pretend.* He thought that she was pretending? Her grief, her struggles, her misery, all that shit she had been through – it was all a mere pretence for him? He was her last ray of hope; someone who accepted her the way she was, without judging her. And here he was, on a whole other tangent.

'So you think I'm a fraud.'

'No, I think you're different. And that's great. So why try to change it?'

'Different as in – I don't have feelings, at least not for my dead husband. Is that right?'

'Anu, you're twisting my words.'

Anupama picked up her purse and slung it over her shoulder wordlessly, her lips pursed tightly.

'Where are you going?' asked Charlie.

Without a word, she stepped off the wall to walk off, when he grabbed the strap of her purse. 'Anu, wait—'

'Let go, Charlie.'

'Why are you walking away?'

'Don't make a scene—'

'Arey, but—'

'Mamma?'

Anupama froze, her insides congealing into brittle crystal. She didn't have to glance at the horrified expression on Charlie's face to guess who it was. Slowly, inch by inch, she turned around to see her daughter, Misha, staring at her. She wasn't alone. A rather distinguished-looking gentleman in his fifties was standing beside her, wearing a leather satchel on his shoulder, reflecting her look of horror on his face. Anupama didn't have to guess who he was either. Of all the ways and all the places where she could have met her daughter's beloved Mehul sir, it had to be this one.

'What … are you doing *here*?' asked Misha.

'I—' said Anupama, glancing at Charlie for support, and receiving only a blank stare in return. He had frozen into immobility, his hand still clutching the strap of her bag. She needed words, wit, conviction, time, anything, yet all that came out her mouth was another, 'I—'

'Oh – my – God,' breathed Misha, her eyes oscillating manically between Anupama and Charlie. 'Oh, my *God*.'

'Beta, listen—'

'*Oh, my God*!'

'It's not what you think it is…'

'Then what *is* it?'

'Her friend is pregnant,' blurted out Charlie.

'So?'

Charlie drew a blank again.

'It's mine,' he said, desperately.

'Oh, shut up, Charlie!' cried Anupama.

She turned to face her gawping daughter head-on. Firmness was the need of the moment. She couldn't be weak. She couldn't be ashamed. She had practised for this scenario a dozen times in her head. She could do this. 'Well, so now you know. And before—'

'You are such a hypocrite!' shrieked Misha.

'Excuse me?'

'So, you can get a boy toy for yourself, but I can't even date an older man without raising your BP?'

'Okay, first of all, he is not a boy toy. We are in a relationship.'

'Since when? He came, like, yesterday.'

'It's been two months, actually,' said Charlie, from somewhere in the background.

'The point is – I am a grown woman. I know what I want. I know what I am doing,' said Anupama, spouting her well-rehearsed lines.

'Well, ditto!'

'No, not ditto. You, young lady, were in an affair with a married man!'

'MAMMA!'

'If I may,' Mehul cut in politely, 'I think it would be better if we took this conversation elsewhere.'

It was then that Anupama and Misha became aware of the pin-drop silence around them; all the canoodling couples in the vicinity had paused in their foreplay to watch the rather intriguing family drama unfolding before their eyes.

'There is a rather nice coffee shop nearby. Perhaps, we could all sit down and have a calm discussion about this,' he suggested in a voice that was placid, yet firm.

Feeling like a toddler facing her school principal, Anupama just nodded, resentful at the ironic shift of authority. She glanced at Charlie, who had developed a sudden interest in the pebbles by his feet, his ears an interesting shade of crimson. A kitten marooned on a floundering raft couldn't have looked more vulnerable.

———

Moments after they stepped into the café, it began to rain, hard.

The barrage of drops gave the sea a rippling appearance of unrest on the surface, underlining the calmness of the currents beneath. A diametrically opposite scenario pervaded the table of customers watching the silvery waves through the glass walls of the café, where the calm silence of the four occupants seated around the gate-legged table concealed the blizzard beneath the surface. Even in the tension and anger of the moment, Anupama found herself pinching herself in the arm for the fourth time, just to make sure she wasn't dreaming. The surrealism of her situation hadn't escaped her. She had pictured this moment of revelation to her children along more sensitive and tender lines. And yet, the fates had seated her facing her daughter and her elderly partner across a coffee table, with her own dirty little secret seated beside her, fidgeting with his napkin. It was just too absurd, too chaotic. In fact, it seemed that ever since she had met Charlie, her life had been pure chaos, a series of uncontrolled events that she could not have imagined even in her worst nightmares.

'It's so nice to finally meet you, Mrs Arora. Misha has said so many nice things about you,' said Mehul, in a cautious attempt to break the ice. Neither of the ladies responded, their eyes fixed on the sea.

'So, what do you do … sir?' asked Charlie tentatively.

'Please, call me Mehul. I am a professor of English literature at Misha's college. That's where we met.' He smiled warmly at Misha and moved his hand towards her, when a stern sideways glance from Anupama made him rethink his move. Misha noticed this, and firmly reached for his hand, her eyes daring her mother to challenge her.

'Cool,' said Charlie.

'And how did you two meet, if you don't mind my asking?'

'On the terrace,' said Charlie with a grin. 'It's quite a funny story—' Anupama shot him a vitriolic glare. 'Which I will narrate some other time.'

'You know why this is happening, right?' said Misha, smiling coldly at Anupama. 'It's karma.'

'What?'

'All your life, you fenced us in with all your rules and regulations, ensuring that we always, always, toed the line. Well, where are your precious rules now?'

'For your information, those were not my rules, they were your father's. And the only reason I made you follow them was to keep the peace in the house.'

'Please. Don't even try to put this on Papa. He was totally chilled out.'

'Because he had someone else doing the dirty work for him!'

Misha scoffed, turning to Mehul. 'This is so like her. She always has an excuse for everything.'

'Hey, you talk to me directly.'

'Madam, cappuccino?' asked the waiter, arriving with their orders.

'Here,' said Misha.

'Two café lattes. Regular.'

Anupama and Mehul nodded. The waiter placed their cups in front of them and turned to Charlie. 'Have you decided what you want, sir?'

'Er, not yet,' said Charlie, glancing at the menu.

'Just take a cold coffee,' said Anupama.

'Yeah, Charlie, you had *better* take a cold coffee,' sneered Misha.

'Misha—'

'I'll take a cold coffee,' Charlie said hurriedly to the waiter.

'Mocha, caramel, vanilla?'

'Er—'

'Just get a plain cold coffee,' said Anupama irritably.

'With ice, without ice?'

'Doesn't matter.'

'Ice-cream, non-ice cream?'

'*Leave*,' said Anupama in a tone so frosty that the waiter strategically retreated without another word.

'And this is on a good day,' Misha stage-whispered to Charlie.

'Talk to me directly, or don't talk at all.'

'Sorry, but there's one thing I don't get,' said Charlie. 'If the rules were set by your husband, then why do you still need to follow them? I mean, why does it even matter anymore what the rules are?'

And just like that, the spotlight was back on Anupama.

'Because I have a responsibility.'

'What responsibility?' asked Misha.

'You won't understand.'

'That's convenient.'

'I don't have to justify myself to you, Misha.'

'Fine, then. What are we even sitting here for?'

Grabbing her bag, Misha rose from the table, followed by Mehul. They had only gone a few steps, when Misha paused and turned on her heel to face her mother.

'Oh, just so you know, I'm bringing Mehul to Nimit's birthday party. You might be comfortable keeping your double-life a secret from the world, but I am not.'

And with that, she marched off, leaving behind a stunned silence. The thought struck her that this was the first time that her daughter had rebelled against her so brazenly. Up until now, their squabbles – no matter how bitter – had been confined to within the walls of their home. Come to think of it, that was a rule too, wasn't it? A rule she had set to maintain their decorum in society, as far as she and her family were concerned. Not that she was in a position to dictate the terms of social propriety anymore.

A tumult of contradictory impulses rose within her, as she saw her daughter walking off hand in hand with that man. She wanted to run after them and call out to her daughter, while at the same time she wanted to run away and hide, to cry in solitude. On the one hand, she wanted to chastise Misha, while on the other, she wanted to understand the young girl's turmoil. She wanted her daughter to uphold her mother's rules, while she herself wanted to be accepted for defying them. She wished someone could just point her in the right direction, for neither her mind nor her body were in gear and she felt like she was coasting at breakneck speed. Would it be total anarchy at home now? Would mother and daughter ever be able to look at each other in the same way again?

The waiter arrived with Charlie's cold coffee, and she realized he had been sitting quietly next to her all this while, looking as uncertain as she felt.

'Are you okay?' he asked.

She shook her head, closed her eyes, and took a few deep breaths.

'Do you have it?' she asked quietly.

'What?'

'That … that thing you smoke. What do you call it?'

Charlie's eyes widened for a fraction of a second. 'Ganja?'

'Yes.'

'You want to smoke weed?'

'Do you have it or not?'

'No, but I know a place where we can get it. And I think I have some paper strips in my bag to roll up. But … are you sure?'

'Let's go.'

21

'Why are you with me at all? I mean, seriously, why?'

'That's the twenty-seventh time you have asked me that question.'

'You're counting?'

'It was an approximate figure.'

'It didn't sound approximate.'

'Yes, I'm counting. Sorry.'

'Why?'

'I guess I just like to count.'

'No, I mean why are you sorry? Why are you apologizing to me all the time?'

Charlie opened his mouth to say something, then stopped. Anupama smiled. 'You were going to say sorry again, weren't you?'

He smiled sheepishly.

'I'm not a ticking time bomb, Charlie. You don't have to defuse me all the time.'

'I know. Sorry.'

Anupama giggled. Charlie chuckled.

Giggle, she thought to herself, taking another deep drag of the joint Charlie had expertly rolled. What a girly word. Giggle. Girls giggled. Men chuckled. But she wasn't a girl, though, was she? She was a woman. And yet, she giggled. Fuck this world of giggles and chuckles. She would do as she pleased. If she wanted to chuckle, she would, and if she wanted to giggle, she would. *Giggle*.

She took a deep, deep breath. Her head and body felt so much lighter. Gently, she ran her fingers through Charlie's hair. He was lying beside her on the rough gravelly terrace, the intermittent moonlight breaking through the clouds and lighting his features with a soft, silvery glow. She loved the feel of his hair in her fingers. She loved the liberty of touching him wherever she wanted, whenever she wanted – the sheer power of it. She loved the clean, sweet breeze flowing over their bodies. And more than anything, she loved the idea of the two of them here. *Here*, of all places. It had been a risk, but boy, had it been worth it.

For the terrace upon which they lay was not in their building – although that had been Charlie's initial plan. It was her college.

The place that had changed her life forever without intending to. The place where it had all started – her new life, story and identity. It was a place that had intimidated her as a youth, with its stern lecturers, strict dress rules, grim stone walls encompassing the entire perimeter and a library that was quieter than a cemetery at all times. The years may have faded its academic relevance and standing, turning it into one of those quaint little heritage institutes surviving on government subsidies that no one really cared for anymore, but there was still an ominous austerity about it that you could sense even from outside its now rusty, wrought-iron gates. In a lot of ways, to her the college represented socially what her mother stood for domestically – an inexorable authority. Omnipresent, omniscient and omnipotent. It was for this very reason that Anupama had chosen this location for her first tryst with marijuana. It just seemed befitting on so many levels.

Anupama was well familiar with the one chink in this fortress, thanks to Renu – the lower left corner in the southwest segment of the boundary wall had collapsed a long time ago, leaving a gap just big enough for a person to crawl through. Although this had been haphazardly filled with loose bricks and stones, all it took was a slight shove and you were in. If one quietly replaced this makeshift repair after exiting, no one would even notice the transgression. She marvelled that this flaw in the superstructure of this magnificent edifice had survived all these years and wondered how many generations of students had taken advantage of it. As for getting to the terrace was concerned, the archaic security systems were no match for Charlie's lock-breaking skills.

So here she was, on this moonlit, monsoon night, with a boy, lying on her college terrace, doing something in her forties that she wouldn't have dreamt of doing in her twenties. And people said miracles were pure fiction.

'So, what happens now?' asked Charlie, staring up at the sky.

'I don't know. And I honestly don't care. At least, not right now. After all that's happened today … after all the years spent worrying, fretting and caring ... for these few moments, I just want to be me.'

Charlie tilted her face towards his, his eyes trapping her attention.

'I wish you could be you forever,' he said softly. ''Coz when you are you, there's no one like you.'

Anupama smiled and traced his eyebrow with her forefinger, feeling the velvety softness. She didn't know if it was the weed, but for some reason, he looked singularly beautiful tonight. She was afraid to pinch herself again. If this was a dream, she would rather stay asleep for a little longer. 'Why are you with me?' she asked in wonderment.

'Twenty-eight,' said Charlie, with an amused grin. 'I could ask you the same question, you know.'

'I think the answer would be a little too obvious.'

'So, it's all about the looks, is it?'

'No, of course not. I mean, you are beautiful, it's true ... and I'd be lying if I said it didn't matter ... but, how do I put it, there is this thing about you ... I feel I can trust you, or rather, that I can connect with you. And more than that, I feel like I know you. I mean, it's absurd, of course. I don't even know your full name yet or where you come from, but from what I have seen of you, it's just ... you and me – it just seems to fit, you know. Am I making any sense?'

Charlie smiled, nodding. 'More than you know.'

'There is another slightly more selfish reason.'

'What?'

'When I am with you, I remember what it was like – back in the days when I would dream and fantasize about what it would be like to fall in love, to be in love. It's like I'm living all those fantasies now. Flights of fancy that I had summarily dismissed and forgotten. That's the thing about you, Charlie. You remind me of a forgotten me.'

She took another drag and gazed up at the heavens, which seemed extraordinarily spectacular to her eyes that night. A distant star twinkled feebly every now and then from between the scudding clouds, to wink at them, like a mischievous little celestial spy. A sniffle reached her ears. She turned sideways to see Charlie hurriedly wiping his eyes.

'Are you crying?'

'What? No, of course not!' he protested, rubbing his nose tightly. 'Must be a cold or something.'

Amused, Anupama passed him the joint and watched him take a long drag.

'Chandrashekhar Dhillon,' he said, releasing a grey cloud of smoke.

'What?'

'My real name. It's Chandrashekhar Dhillon.'

Anupama stared at him. 'Chandrashekhar?'

Charlie nodded. 'Dhillon.'

'How did that become Charlie?'

'My mom wanted to name me Charlie, my father wanted Chandrashekhar, and I was too young at the time to voice my opinion, so.'

Anupama observed him closely. 'You don't look like a Chandrashekhar.'

'I don't feel like a Chandrashekhar, either. But you know how fathers can be, right? It was either his way or the highway. So, when I turned seventeen, I just said fuck it, I will be what I want to be.'

'And so you became a hair stylist.'

'No, I became a singer.'

Anupama's eyes shot wide open. 'What?'

He grinned. 'I forget how little you know about me. I tried my hand at singing when I passed out of school, you know. Went into formal training and everything. I was pretty good too. At one point, I was even performing at local competitions and weddings and stuff.'

'Wow.'

'Nothing really wow about that. The place where I come from, they aren't very many options. But yeah, it felt nice to be appreciated.'

'So why did you quit?'

'I don't know. I guess I just got bored. After a point, everything just became too repetitive. Everyone wanted to listen to the same songs, the same melodies. My heart wasn't in it anymore.'

'Sing something for me.'

He burst into a throaty chuckle. 'Oh, come on.'

'What? I want to hear you. Please.'

His eyes turned to her eager face, before looking heavenward in exasperation. 'Fine. I might be a bit rusty though. It's been a while. What do you want me to sing?'

'Whatever you like.'

A thoughtful look crossed Charlie's face. After a few seconds, he sat up cross-legged, his back straight, while Anupama propped herself up on her elbow, facing him. He closed his eyes, cleared his throat, and took a deep breath. What emanated from his mouth next was a slow, rather soulful-sounding Punjabi song. She didn't understand some of the lyrics, but from the rather quivering tenor of its melody and the few words she could discern in between, it seemed to be a song of separation between two lovers and the angst that followed. Charlie's brows were furrowed, his head swaying in sync with the scale of the tune. Anupama watched in silent awe, at the intense concentration reflected on his face and the power in his voice. It wasn't just a song she was listening to, it was a story. This wasn't mere talent, she realized, it was an art, and even in those few lines that he had sung, she could make out the passion he felt for it. This was a facet to him that she couldn't even have guessed at before, and she wondered just how many more secrets lay beneath that seemingly uncomplicated front, waiting to be discovered.

Anupama closed her eyes, absorbing the mood and the moment, letting his soothing voice take over her senses. She had never been much of a musical person and had a very poor memory of tunes and lyrics. But deep in her heart, she knew that she would remember this melody forever. This melody and this moment, when the man she loved sang for her.

Charlie ended the song on a crescendo, his voice reaching a high pitch before fading into quietness. He opened his eyes and looked at her, the serenity on his face replaced by the impish grin she had come to recognize so well.

'That was beautiful.'

'Thanks, although I missed a few notes here and there—'

Anupama kissed him, swiftly silencing all his doubts and self-criticism. When they parted, she had a look of amusement on her face.

'What?' asked Charlie.

'I just realized – I am kissing a boy in my college.'

'*And* smoking up. You're one hell of a badass, Mrs Arora.'

'And you're one hell of a bad influence, Charlie,' she said softly, reaching for the top buttons of his shirt.

22

By the time she returned home, it was almost half past eleven at night, a record of sorts because she couldn't remember the last time she had been out after ten. Charlie was to arrive forty-five minutes later as per their arrangement. She felt deeply sorry for him because he had to wake up early for work tomorrow; but hey, you win some you lose some. And considering the 'gains' they had both enjoyed tonight, he was in no position to complain. It had taken quite some time and effort to get the gravel out of their hair.

Very quietly, she inserted the key into her door and opened it. To her enormous surprise, the living room lights were on, and to her even greater consternation, Misha was seated on the couch, stiff and stony-faced.

'Why are you still up?'

'I was waiting for you.'

'Do you know what time it is?'

'I could ask you the same question.'

'Misha, it's late, and you have to go to college tomorrow.'

'Seriously? After all that's happened, *that's* your main concern?'

And with that, the bubble of bliss popped, and she found herself facing the cold reality, where explanations were due and conflicts unresolved. With a heavy heart, she plopped her bag on the table. 'Let's go to my room.'

Without a word, Misha marched out, leaving Anupama behind to turn off the lights and follow her.

She entered her room to find her daughter sitting on the bed, clutching a pillow, lost in thought. The expression on her face – more perturbed than angry – made her look young and vulnerable. Anupama had a brief flashback of all the times she had seen that very same look on her daughter's face, and each time it had involved a confession or some other private conversation of an equally disturbing nature. She walked in and sat in front of Misha, facing her. Misha's eyes stayed downcast. For a few moments, neither of them talked, breathing in the silence that surrounded them. Misha turned to look at the framed, wedding photo on Anupama's bedside table.

'That's the only photo of Dad you have in your room,' she remarked.

Anupama stayed quiet, watching her daughter as she turned back to her.

'You did love him, didn't you?'

'Yes,' replied Anupama without hesitation.

'Till the end?'

'Misha, what I have with Charlie has got nothing to do with your father.'

'I wasn't talking about that.'

'Then why are you asking such questions?'

Misha shook her head slowly, the pillow still clutched

tightly to her chest. 'I know you think I've been oblivious, but I've not. I knew there was something wrong, even though you both tried your best to hide it from us.'

'Misha—'

'I'm not a child anymore, Mamma. I know things. You never talk about Dad, and the few times that I – or for that matter, anyone does – you get disturbed. I had come to regard this distance as a normal part of our relationship, but it doesn't work anymore. Enough with all the secrecy, Mamma. Just tell me the truth. For once, let us be open and honest with each other.'

Anupama gritted her teeth, trying hard to control her emotions. She could feel the onset of another passionate onslaught, but it wasn't rage this time. It took her a moment to steady her breathing and calm herself enough to talk.

'Beta ... I love you, and I've always wanted the best for you and Nimit ... so trust me when I say that whatever I have done or not done, there has always been a reason for it ...' She looked her daughter in the eye. 'Trust me. The truth doesn't always make things better.'

'You're talking about the affair, aren't you?'

A chill coursed through Anupama as she stared at her daughter's expressionless face. She must have misheard. There was no way she could have known about that. She had done her utmost to make sure no one knew, least of all her children.

'Don't worry. It's just me. Nimit has no idea,' said Misha.

'H—How...?'

'I told you. I know things. In fact, I had known it for quite some time, perhaps even before you did.'

Was this entity really her daughter? All Anupama could

do was gawp helplessly, for as it turned out, her whole life so far had been one long, farcical illusion of being in control.

'When did you get to know?'

Misha pursed her lips, her fingers digging deep into the soft pillow. 'A…a year before he … passed away.'

A year? Anupama had found out just a *day* before Rajeev's demise.

'Then why didn't you say anything? Why didn't you tell me?' she cried.

'Because I'm a bitch, okay?'

'Misha—'

'He swore me to secrecy. And I could see that he was happy after so long, and that was all that mattered to me … at the time. Trust me, it hasn't been easy for me at all, because I realized what a horrible thing had been done to you and still having to face you every day … but that's the way it is. I just … I just wanted him to be happy. Okay? So now you can scream and hate me all you want and … and…'

Her words and anger tapered off as her emotions choked her. Anupama wrapped her arms around her. She could feel Misha stiffening in her embrace, but she held on to her daughter, feeling her shuddering. Slowly she melted in her mother's arms. Mighty sobs wracked her slim frame. It took a while for the overwhelming guilt to be dispelled and to calm down.

Suddenly, it all made sense. Misha's unexpected coldness and hostility towards her ever since Rajeev departed, the increasing distance between them and the resentment simmering just beneath the surface … Anupama gently rocked her to and fro as she had when Misha was a young child.

'I'm sorry,' she whispered.

'It's okay,' said Anupama, caressing her hair. 'It's okay.'

Misha straightened up, wiping her eyes. 'It's not. You didn't deserve that. He shouldn't have—'

'It doesn't matter anymore.'

'I don't know why I still love him and miss him.'

'Because he was a good father to you and Nimit. And he loved you too.'

A slow smile spread across her teary face. 'I love you too, Mamma. I know I don't show it, but … I do.'

'I know, beta. I love you too.'

'And I just want you to know that – you have my support, a hundred per cent. I can understand why you didn't want to let us know about you and Charlie, but trust me, it's okay. Really, I'm happy for you.'

'Thank you.'

'Did you like Mehul?' she asked shyly.

'He seemed very mature – no pun intended,' said Anupama, making Misha chuckle. 'And I have to admit he handled the situation very well.'

'That's just the way he is. Once you get to know him, you will see how special he is, in his own way.'

'Does he make you happy?'

'Yes.'

'Then that's all I need to know.'

Misha smiled widely, her eyes welling up again as she leaned forward to hug Anupama.

'I'm so happy,' she sighed. 'I can't believe this is happening.'

Neither could Anupama. They had bonded more in the past five minutes than they had in the past couple of years.

Somehow, somewhere deep inside, she had always known a time would come when her children would become her friends. She had never reached that point with her mother, but for some inexplicable reason, she could see it happening in her own family. She hadn't known how or when it would happen though, and had someone warned her that it would be in this fashion, she would have probably hopped on that train at CST station for real and disappeared ages ago. However, now that it had, nothing seemed more natural than to be sitting here, wrapped in her daughter's arms – just two women battling their demons the best they could.

She had her own demons as well, although that was a story which her daughter didn't need to know, no matter how honest and open she wanted to be.

Later that night, as Misha slept peacefully beside her on her bed, Anupama lay wide awake. The day which she had been trying to forget for so long, had finally come alive and how. There is something rather unfair about memories, she reckoned. The good ones formed and faded easily, while the bad ones were seared into the subconscious forever – every tiny, painful detail painstakingly preserved.

As far as Misha was concerned, her father's illicit relationship had been an error of judgment, a wrongdoing committed in passion and a moment of weakness. A mistake, to be forgiven and forgotten.

But Anupama knew that Rajeev's affair was merely a symptom of a much larger problem lurking beneath the surface of their lives – a disorder they were both fairly familiar with. For 'stability' is a double-edged sword: on the one hand, it immunizes one against the bumps and blows of an unpredictable future; on the other, it diminishes the pleasure of looking forward to the newness of each day, for you know exactly how it is going to be. That was what was essentially wrong with their marriage. It wasn't lack of love. It was an over-abundance of stability.

She had dealt with it by resigning herself and making the best of what she had. He had dealt with it by finding adventure elsewhere.

She wished she were angrier, or miserable, or heartbroken, but as Charlie had said, she couldn't pretend to be something she was not. She did feel resentful, although it wasn't directed towards her husband. Rather, it was her mother, may her soul rest in peace. She was aware of how ridiculous it sounded. It was her own fault and her own decision. She had not been bulldozed into it. In fact, her mother had opposed the union from the outset. And how right she had been in her forecast! And it was for that very reason that Anupama hated her. Half her lifetime thrown away in trying to prove a point to her mother, only to realize how futile the whole exercise had been, and in the end the only loser in this deal was herself.

The dark truth (the one that had taken eons for her to accept) was that the day she had found out about the affair, she had been relieved, more than anything. It had been right after they had had their usual evening tea and cream biscuits at five thirty. And to give the devil his due, Rajeev had confessed to her himself, as he couldn't live with the burden of keeping such a huge secret from her anymore. Her first reaction had been shock. Her second had been relief. After such a long time, she had finally found a legitimate and blameless way out of a life that she hadn't chosen. Outwardly of course, she appeared devastated (perhaps at some level, she actually was), shunning his tears, apologies and explanations, and declaring that they would have to separate because she couldn't go on with this farcical marriage.

Yet that night, as she lay in bed with her husband, both facing away from each other, the thought struck her that for the first time in years, she had a chance to be something other than what she was. She tried to quell the joyous anticipation bubbling within her, and to convince herself that she ought to be outraged (which to an extent, she was). She thought of her kids and felt extremely sorry for them, for they didn't deserve any of this misery. Yet, beneath it all, the thought of a new beginning was too overwhelming to ignore. She wouldn't need to be Mrs Arora anymore. She would be Anupama. She would be free, unfettered by any baggage. It wouldn't be easy. There would be a lot of pain along the way. But it would be worth it. Filled with these euphoric thoughts, Anupama had shut her eyes, thinking about how the next time she opened them, her life would change irrevocably.

And it did; only not in the way she had imagined.

She had woken up to find Rajeev lying still in bed, his limbs twisted awkwardly, eyes half-open and unblinking.

It had been a massive cardiac arrest, the doctor had declared later. While he was still asleep. There was nothing anyone could do. It was no one's fault.

And that was true, medically speaking. Medical science only looked at the arterial plaque build-up and cholesterol levels. It didn't care about the hurtful news one had broken to the deceased right before his death. Hippocrates didn't concern himself with one's resentment towards the deceased moments before his unfortunate demise. Medicine and insurance policies could only go so far, couldn't they? The underlying causes of the cardiac arrest lay in what couldn't be put down on paper and that was a burden exclusively reserved for her. She had never known who the other woman was and she didn't care.

On that unforgettable morning, her fate had been sealed. She was going to be Mrs Arora forever. The gods couldn't have thought of a more fitting punishment.

And then, out of the blue, Charlie happened.

Was there any point to planning one's life at all?

She glanced at her daughter's face. She had always been a restless sleeper even as a child – arms and legs twitching, eyelids fluttering, strange little moans, giggles and groans escaping her lips as she dozed fitfully. Sometimes, when her murmurs got too loud, Anupama would walk into her room and cradle her in her arms, rocking her until the turbulence had passed. Rajeev had told her that there was no need. They were only dreams, and the more she fussed over her, the longer it would take her to grow out of it. But she couldn't resist. Misha wouldn't remember any of it in the morning of course, when she would cheerfully wish them both good morning and exchange a friendly hi-five with her father.

Tonight, she seemed at peace. A million questions sped through Anupama's mind, mostly related to how their lives would change now, with all these new developments. However, the only effect all that pondering and contemplation had was to give her the initial threatening throbs of a migraine. Besides, hadn't she just decided that there was no point in planning anything anymore? There was only one thing left to do, the *only* thing she could do.

Go with the flow, she chanted to herself, turning off the bedside lamp as she settled in for the night. *Just go with the flow*.

23

The morning routines done, Anupama began to make a mental checklist of all the people who knew about her and Charlie. She wasn't sure what she intended to do with it, but it would help to have some clarity, at least.

Her daughter knew.

Her best friends knew.

The dead ex-watchman of her building knew.

And if all that stuff about our loved ones in heaven were true, then so did her ex-husband, her mother, and the rest of her extended family – the thought of which gave her a rather wry, sadistic pleasure. She considered changing Rajeev's framed picture in the dining room to a more cheerful one. His eyes looked too piercing in this.

And of course, there was Mrs Govindikar. Now, *there* was a complicated situation. Technically, she knew, but then Anupama had also assured her that she wouldn't continue with the relationship any longer, a misconception she was probably still labouring under unless she had other spies of whom Anupama was unaware. At some point, she would have to tell her the truth as well. She could plan ahead for it, but then again, what was the point? It wasn't like she had had to tell any of the others who knew so far. They had all got to know in their own mysterious ways as ordained by destiny. So why not include Mrs Govindikar in that divine scheme of things as well? The universe would inform her, probably at the most inconvenient time possible, going by the current trend.

Her phone buzzed with a message.

Kay: Heyyy just heard. Checked him out too. Ga-yorr-gee-yussss! You, sweetheart, are my new hero!!

Anupama sighed in exasperation. So now Kay knew too. *Thanks, Renu.*

Given the speed at which Charlie was being accepted within her inner circle, she might as well make him a nominee in her will and insurance policy in the near future.

Breathing deeply, she massaged the tight knots in her neck. She could convince her mind that she wasn't stressed, but her body was a whole other matter. Just as she was contemplating going in for one of those Swedish massages at the local spa, her phone beeped again. With rising dread, Anupama opened the message.

Charlie: Heyy, got an off today. My place in half an hour? I got upma ☺

Anupama smiled, her spirits lifting instantly with relief and anticipation. It being a weekend, her children were still asleep, and if her past experience was anything to go by, they wouldn't wake up for another hour, at least. She could always tell them she had gone for a walk, if either of them even bothered to ask.

Screw the massage. This was what she needed.

———

'God, this is nice upma,' sighed Anupama.

She was on Charlie's futon, her legs stretched across his as they both gorged on the free samples from the new south Indian restaurant that had opened two blocks away. As always, he was in his boxers and she, in his oversized T-shirt. She liked the feel of it on her skin after sex and the fact that it smelled faintly of him was an added bonus. Besides, it had seemed like too much effort to look for her clothes in that pile of T-shirts, toiletry, comics, magazines, stationery items and other guy stuff that Charlie had lying around. The rest of his bedroom floor space was occupied by the sealed packing boxes. In his living room, the bean bag, coffee table and couch were the only items that had been extracted from their crates, and they were surrounded by several sealed packing boxes as well.

'You really need to tidy up your place,' she remarked. 'And why haven't you unpacked as yet?'

'I have. I just took out all the stuff I need right now.'

'What's in those boxes?'

'Stuff I don't need right now.'

'Will you need them later?'

'I don't know.'

'Then why don't you just throw them away?'

'Just because I don't need them now doesn't mean I won't need them later.'

'Actually, that's exactly what it means. Unless you prefer to live in clutter.'

'It's not clutter.'

'Then what is it?'

'It's stuff. Why can't stuff just be stuff?'

'Why are you getting irritated?'

'Because you're not letting it go.'

'How can I? You've been here for more than two months now, and every time I come here, I have to look at all this mess.'

'Oh, so now it's an issue.'

'I'm just trying to help, Charlie.'

'No, you're trying to be my mothe—'

He stopped himself quickly, but it was too late. Anupama froze. 'What did you say?'

'Nothing.'

'Did you just call me your…?'

'No! No, of course not.'

Slowly, Anupama put her plate down. Swinging her legs off the edge of the futon, she stood up, trying hard to absorb what had just happened. Behind her, Charlie stayed still – petrified.

'I didn't mean it,' he said. 'It was just a generally offensive statement. Like, you know, I am such a dick, or she's such a witch. Nothing literal about it.'

Her head was spinning. A sudden bout of weakness came over her, as if her blood sugar had dropped. The rational part of her mind tried to meekly suggest that perhaps she was overreacting, only to duck for cover as her emotions hurled their full fury at it. She sat back down on the bed, pressing her temples. Charlie crept up behind her and tried to hold her, but she pulled away.

'I'm sorry,' he said.

'No, don't be. You're right. You're absolutely right.'

'No, I'm not. I'm idiotically wrong.'

'It's okay, Charlie. I agree. I was trying to be your mother. And why shouldn't I be? Right? I mean, how old is she?'

'Huh?'

'Your mother. How old is she?'

'Er, I'm not sure.'

'How old was she when you were born?'

Charlie stared at her uncertainly.

'Answer me.'

'I don't know …' he said. 'Twenties, I think.'

'Oh God.'

She rose from the bed, clutching her head. 'Oh God … oh God.'

'What's happening?' asked Charlie.

She glanced back at his befuddled face – his young, boyish face, gorgeous even in its puzzlement. 'What are we doing, Charlie? Mrs Govindikar was right. What are we doing? What am I doing?'

'Okay, you need to relax.'

'No, I have relaxed for too long. That's the problem. I have let a lot of things slide. But we need to think, Charlie. We need to think where this is going.'

'I thought we were taking it slow.'

'Well, we can't slow down time, can we? I mean, what happens twenty years later, when I'm sixty and you're – what – forty?'

'Forty-four.'

'I don't care about your single digits!' shrieked Anupama.

Her kurta was lying on the floor. She picked it up in a huff, followed by the rest of her clothing.

'What are you doing?'

'Where's my bra?'

'Over there, by the coffee mug.'

Rolling her eyes, Anupama hobbled over to it. She had

just removed the tee and strapped it on, when her eyes fell on Charlie – and the rather prominent tent in his boxers.

'Seriously? Now?' she snapped.

'Well, I'm sorry but this isn't in my jurisdiction! And if this is happening in spite of all your disturbing Freudian motherly talk, then just imagine how much I must be attracted to you!'

She paused. It took all her willpower not to laugh at that, yet an involuntary, transient trickle of a smile did appear on her lips, and that was all the encouragement Charlie needed.

'Just … sit down for a minute,' he said. 'I'll make some coffee. We'll talk. That's all I ask.'

'I don't want coffee.'

'Fine, then, just sit down for a minute. 'Coz if you step out in this mood and someone sees you, I'll probably get booked for assault or something.'

She had to admit he had a point. Huffily, she sat down, expecting Charlie to cajole and reassure her. Instead, he got up from the bed and headed towards his packing boxes.

'What are you doing?' asked Anupama, as he ripped open the taping on one of the boxes.

'I just want to show you some of the stuff I keep.'

'That's not necessary.'

Charlie ignored her and continued undoing the tape. Finally, when the box was open, he rummaged through some of the items and finally came up with what appeared to be a photo frame. He came back, sat down beside her and placed it in her hand. To Anupama's surprise, it was a picture of Charlie taken from a while ago. He was on stage, but he wasn't singing. Clad in a white Bengali-style dhoti and kurta, he seemed to be in a rather dramatic pose, his hands flung up at the sky, his face darkened with bitterness and despair.

'This was me as Devdas when I was part of a travelling theatre group in Kolkata,' said Charlie. 'Probably one of the most memorable experiences of my life.'

'You were an actor too?' asked Anupama, amazed.

Charlie nodded, gazing reminiscently at the picture. 'I dabbled in theatre for a while. This was my first lead role.'

'How old *are* you, really?'

Charlie laughed. 'This was two years ago, before I came to Mumbai.'

'And the singing?'

'Right after school.'

'Anything else I should know about?'

Charlie fetched out a green cloth strip. 'My green belt from my karate days in Delhi, when I wanted to be a professional martial artist.'

Anupama held it in her hands, fingering the fabric. How did a guy go from all this to styling ladies' hair in a salon? How many cities and professions had he changed in the past few years? And how could one change one's ambition so swiftly?

'Were you good at it?' she asked, handing him back the belt.

'Well, I don't like to brag, but by the end of my second year in training, I was one of the top two in my class. My sensei even thought I had the capability to compete in international competitions if I kept at it.'

'So, why did you quit? I mean, if you were so good at all of these things, why would you leave?'

A ponderous look came over his face as he replaced the belt in the box and shut it. 'Remember that thing I told you about how I hate closed spaces? I guess the same funda applies to my life as well. What's the point of having a passion if you don't feel passionate about it anymore, right? If there's one thing I can't stand, Anu, it's the feeling of being trapped.'

'But maybe if you had just stuck with it—'

'But why? We are all here for a short while. Why waste time over things that don't interest us anymore? My biggest fear is regretting in the end that I didn't live the life I wanted. I know this is all in the past and I'll never go back to it, but I just like to keep this stuff around for the sake of nostalgia. That's it.'

'I see,' said Anupama grimly. 'So tomorrow, if you start feeling trapped here—'

'I won't. Because I'm happy.'

'For now, you mean.'

He sighed. 'What do you want me to do? Give you a written guarantee?' Charlie cupped her face in his hands, locking eyes with her. 'You're not a talent or an experience I'm trying out, Anupama. What we have is unique, it's real. What we have can't be put in a box and sealed away.'

She wanted to believe him. She really did. But somewhere, deep within, the germ of a fear had sprouted. And try as she might, she found it difficult to eradicate it.

'You do like being a hairstylist, don't you?' she asked.

Charlie smiled. 'I love it. From the bottom of my heart, I do.'

'And you're so good at it,' added Anupama. 'It's such a nice field too. Everyone loves you.'

'Anu, I'm not running away.'

He held out his arms, and she sank into them, burying her face in his chest.

'It's just … this whole week has been so heavy,' she

murmured. 'It's just … too much information, too many changes. I feel like everything's getting out of hand. Things are moving too fast and I can't control them.'

'Then don't,' said Charlie softly. 'Just try going with the flow for a change.'

Anupama scoffed. 'Trust me, I am trying. But it's hard when you don't know which way the flow is headed.'

'That's … kind of the idea, you know.'

She hugged him tighter. 'I'm just scared. I know it sounds bizarre after all of the neurosis I just displayed, but the truth is I don't want to lose you.'

'And you won't. Trust me, I am as serious about this as you are. In fact—' He paused abruptly.

'What?' asked Anupama.

'Never mind. We'll talk later.'

Something about that sounded rather ominous. Slowly, Anupama stood looking at him anxiously. The wary expression on his face confirmed her suspicions. 'Tell me, Charlie.'

'Seriously, we don't have to talk about it right now.'

'What have you done?'

'Nothing. I just wanted to suggest something, but it's okay.'

He tried to pull her in again, but she stiffened. The suspense was killing her. 'Charlie.'

Closing his eyes, he let out a resigned sigh. 'I was just wondering if you'd like to meet my mother.'

'Say what?'

'She's coming here in a few days to visit me, so I thought—'

'You thought why not introduce her to your forty-two-year-old girlfriend within two months of your relationship?'

'She has met all my girlfriends so far.'

'And how many girlfriends have you had?'

'Can we please stick to the topic?'

'Charlie, it's too soon. I mean, I'd love to meet her obviously, but there is a place and time for everything. Besides, it might take her some time to get used to the bizarre idea of you being with someone like me. So, let's just take it a bit slow, okay.'

'Hm.'

'What?'

'Nothing.'

Again, that abashed look came over his face that suggested something dreadful had happened. And the only dreadful thing she could think of at this point was, 'You have already told her, haven't you?'

Charlie nodded sheepishly. 'But if it helps, I didn't mention the age thing at all.'

'Oh, brilliant.' Anupama groaned. As the horrors of this new and unwelcome surprise gradually dawned on her, she added another unexpected name to the mental checklist she had prepared only this morning – Charlie's mother.

Someone above was really having a laugh.

Just then, the doorbell rang. Both of them froze, staring at each other.

'Were you expecting someone?' asked Anupama.

Charlie shook his head.

'Go, see who it is,' she whispered, nudging him, just as the bell rang again.

She watched him cautiously approach his main door and peer through the peephole. A second later, he turned back to her with alarm writ large on his face.

'It's Mrs Mehtani!'

'What?'

'I don't know what she's doing here. There's a man with her too.'

Terror flooded through her veins in a freezing tide. She was trapped! The bell rang again, impatiently.

'Just stay there. I'll make sure they don't come in,' whispered Charlie.

Anupama nodded and slammed the door shut just as Charlie opened his main door to behold Mrs Mehtani and a grumpy-looking man in a khaki uniform, with what appeared to be a cylinder with a sprinkler strapped to his back.

'Yes?'

'Hello, dear,' chirruped Mrs Mehtani, 'mandatory pest control inspection. May we come in?'

'Actually, this isn't a good time.'

'Ah, unfortunately, this is the only time Shambhu can manage. And we have strict orders to make sure that none of the flats are left uninspected. I'm just trailing along to make sure he does his job right. Doing my bit for the society, you know.'

'So why don't you come back in five minutes?'

'Because we have other things to do as well, dear. Yours is the only flat left. Why? Is something wrong?'

'No—'

'Perfect! This will only take two minutes,' she said, nudging the door open gently yet firmly as Charlie struggled to protest. 'Come, come, bhaiya.'

Inside the bedroom, Anupama's heart stopped as she heard their voices down the hallway. They were in! She could hear Mrs Mehtani guiding the pest control guy.

'You can leave out my bedroom,' said Charlie. 'It's completely pest-free, I assure you.'

'Nonsense, dear. You can never be too sure. Bhaiya, just check those corners and then we can go directly to the bedroom.'

'Really, Mrs Mehtani, don't you think this is an invasion of my privacy?' he said tersely.

Mrs Mehtani paused, the smile on her lips turning frigid by degrees. 'Excuse me?'

'I'm just saying, you know, this is my personal space. And I do believe you are intruding.'

'Oh, is that so?' she said sweetly, approaching him until they were standing nose to nose. 'So of all the tenants and residents in this housing society, you think you're the only one who needs to guard his privacy? Because no one else had an issue? What does that really imply, I wonder.' Her eyes drifted to the closed bedroom door.

'I just—'

'And if that's too much of a hassle for you, then I could call Mrs Govindikar here right now to resolve the matter.'

That silenced Charlie. Helplessly, he watched the smirk deepen on Mrs Mehtani's face as Shambhu announced he was done with the kitchen and living room.

'Great. Follow me,' she said in a sing-song voice as they both headed for the bedroom.

Time had never moved more slowly for Charlie. With rising dread, he stared at them, drawing step by step closer to the inevitable discovery that would—

Mrs Mehtani swung the door open and stepped into

the bedroom, swiftly scanning her surroundings. Messy as before, and empty. Charlie swiftly followed on her heels and peeked in, feeling momentarily relieved. However, the en suite bathroom door was shut and he knew it was only a matter of moments before the fox noticed it. Just as he feared, Mrs Mehtani immediately trotted up to it and turned the knob, only to realize that it was locked from the inside.

'Huh, that's interesting,' she remarked, turning to Charlie. 'You didn't tell me you had a guest.'

Before he could reply, she turned back to the door and knocked on it. 'Hellooo? Who's there?'

In the bathroom, Anupama was on the verge of hyperventilation. Why, oh why, hadn't she just crawled out of the bedroom window instead? It would have been a risk to her life, but at least, she wouldn't have been cornered like this. What was she to do now? She knew for a fact that Mrs Mehtani wouldn't leave until she had exposed her completely. There was nowhere to run, nowhere to hide. Was this the way things were really going to end after all those precautions? Outside, the knocks continued.

'Hello? Are you all right? Can you hear me?' called Mrs Mehtani, tapping on the wood.

She turned back to face the men. 'Who's inside, Charlie?'

Charlie gaped at her mutely, eyes unblinking, jaws clammed shut.

'Okay, I'm getting worried now. Shambhu, d'you think you could break down this door? Or else I could call—'

'Wait!' cried Anupama, from inside.

Mrs Mehtani's eyebrows rose in a mixture of astonishment

and barely concealed delight. She swivelled on her heel just in time to see the door opening and Anupama stepping out, harried and defeated.

'My, my,' drawled Mrs Mehtani. 'What's this?'

'Look, Mrs Mehta—'

'Finally, you're out!' came Misha's voice from behind them. Everyone whipped around to see Misha standing in the bedroom doorway in her nightdress, toilet kit and towel in hand. 'I've been waiting forever.'

'What's going on?' asked Mrs Mehtani, confused.

'Our bathroom is messed up. Something to do with the piping. Charlie kindly offered to let us use his until the repairs are done. Mamma said she wanted to go first,' said Misha.

The spotlight was back on Anupama, who nodded weakly. 'Yes, that's right. Thank you, Charlie.'

'Oh—please—what are neighbours for?' said Charlie, smiling nervously.

'Then why didn't you answer when I was calling out?' demanded Mrs Mehtani.

'Because I was embarrassed. Can you imagine what this situation would look like to a cheap, narrow-minded, soulless gossipmonger with nothing better to do? Not everyone is as mature as you, Mrs Mehtani.'

Mrs Mehtani's eyes narrowed. 'You don't have any toiletries, though.'

'I just came to use the washroom.'

'If you like, you could inspect their loo too, perhaps with a plumber in tow,' suggested Charlie innocently.

With her tightly-pursed lips and clenched teeth, Mrs Mehtani managed the best twisted smile she could.

'Maybe next time,' she declared coldly, storming out of the recently disinfected premises with Shambhu trailing behind her.

As soon as they were out of earshot, Misha turned to acknowledge the grateful smiles. 'Next time, give me a heads up. It will make life so much easier.'

24

'Smile wider, ladies … that's it … let the joy reach up to your eyes … your Inner Woman needs to know that you love and embrace her…'

The instructor's soothing voice reverberated mystically in the acoustics of the large, mosaic-tiled auditorium in which Anupama, Renu and Neena were sitting cross-legged on the floor with a dozen other ladies in more or less (mostly less) the same age range.

After zumba, ballet classes and power yoga, the latest fad to hit the upmarket segment of women's fitness in the city was this Inner Woman routine – the aim being to unleash one's feminine potential and embrace the woman residing within using a combination of workouts, dances and meditation techniques. Neena had had her eyes set on the program the moment she spotted it in the 'Upcoming Events' section of her paper, and more so when she discovered its benefits for pregnant women. She wasted no time in contacting Renu and Anupama and suggesting that they make this a group activity, for Renu's sake. The registration fees had already been paid by her, and all they needed to do was show up. Renu, in turn, wasted no time in replying that her ear fluids had gone out of balance so she couldn't come, while Anupama claimed her head was hurting. The next day, Renu claimed she had suffered a massive stitch in her lower left diaphragm and was bedridden, while Anupama claimed her ankles were hurting. The day after that, Renu was struck by a mysterious case of vitamin B-12 deficiency, while Anupama claimed her back was hurting. The day following that, Neena showed up at both their places with bottles of multivitamin pills and pain relief sprays and bundled them into a waiting cab, before they had a chance to muster up their individual maladies of the day.

So here they were now, breathing deeply, suffering equally and trying hard to hold on to their weeping Inner Women in the burning hell of achy joints, cramped muscles and bladders that were crying out for relief.

'Breathe in deeply, ladies,' said the instructor. 'Experience the beautiful enigma that is your body.'

'Mine's a bloody slaughterhouse right now,' rasped Anupama. 'Why did we have to do this in the middle of my period?'

'Relax, it will only get easier after this,' said Neena.

It didn't. For what followed next was a series of gravity-defying yoga poses that promised to stretch muscles in areas they didn't even know existed. They would have given up at the first try, but the ease with which their Woman instructor performed each asana served as an effective guilt trip, along with her declaration that all elderly and physically invalid members were exempted from this exercise if they so wished.

Mix that with the egos of three dehydrated women facing the looming shadow of menopause and you had an epic saga of determination, pain and revenge.

'I will get you for this if it's the last thing I do,' swore Renu, looking daggers at Neena.

'I'm doing this for you, you ungrateful witch,' grumbled Neena, as she twisted painfully in an attempt to grab her right ankle with her left hand.

'Do you think I would be eligible for a refund if my kidney burst halfway through?' asked Anupama.

'So, he actually told his mother about you, huh?' Neena asked her, gasping in her pose.

'We are not discussing that.'

'Yes, we are. I need a distraction,' she croaked. 'What are you going to do now?'

'What can I do? If I back out now, it will only make things worse.'

'It's a strategy,' said Renu, bending forward as sweat beads dripped off her forehead onto the floor.

'What do you mean?' said Anupama, attempting to follow suit as her tendons screamed in agony.

'Oldest trick in the book. His mother will see you, disapprove, and the next day, you will get a call from him that he can't go against his mother's wishes. Classic escapist ploy.'

'We don't know what she's going to feel yet,' said Neena.

''Course we do.'

'Gee, thanks, buddy,' said Anupama coldly.

'I'm just laying out the facts here. What was your first reaction when you found out Misha was seeing this older lecturer of hers?'

'It might have taken me some time, yes, but I did accept it eventually.'

'You mean after she caught you making out with Charlie?'

'We weren't making out!'

'No one goes to Bandra fort for the scenery, darling.'

Three sharp claps brought their attention back to the instructor. Her zen expression had been replaced by a rather severe one as she glowered at them.

The class progressed to the Warrior pose with the three friends in the last row wobbling on their knees.

'I think it's sweet of him. How many guys would introduce their partners to their mothers if they weren't serious about it?' said Neena. 'I, for one, didn't meet Hiten's mother until a week before the wedding.'

'They were in Namibia.'

'Wouldn't have killed them to book their tickets earlier. Can you believe they just gave us an Oven-Toaster-Grill for our wedding? What did she expect me to do with that? Open a bakery for our daily expenses?'

'Let's just focus on one issue at a time,' said Renu, raising her arms over her head with the others. 'So, what's your strategy, Anu?'

'Nothing.'

'What do you mean nothing?'

'I was just thinking I will be myself.'

'Why?'

'What do you mean "why"?'

'I mean why would you do that? I thought you wanted this to work.'

'I do!'

'Then trust me, the last thing you would want to be is yourself.'

'Wow, this pregnancy is really bringing out the best side of you.'

'I'm serious, Anu! This is going to be one of the most judgmental, nerve-racking and challenging experiences of your life. Imagine an interview where the interviewer has made up his mind that he is going to hate you before you even enter the office.'

'She has a point,' conceded Neena. 'Every mother thinks her son is the most unique piece of manhood to walk the earth. And in the case of someone like Charlie, let's just say the stakes get a bit higher. I mean, where did he get those eyes from?'

'How do you know that? You haven't even met him yet.'

'I saw the pictures Renu sent us.'

'Who's us? What pictures?'

'You're not in the group?'

'What group?'

'I think I'm going to be sick,' moaned Renu.

'Renu!'

'No seriously, I think I'm getting my first bout of morning sickness!' She raised her hand to get the trainer's attention. 'Where's the toilet?'

'Ladies—'

'Oh, fuck your "ladies", I'm about to puke!'

'Last door on the right.'

Fortunately, there happened to be a café nearby that fulfilled all of the pre-conditions that Renu had laid out for sitting in – namely, a steady supply of chocolate truffle pastries and ginger lemon tea, a complete absence of cinnamon in their menu (she had just started to abhor the smell), and a separate, readily accessible bathroom for ladies on the ground floor. The fact that the head waiter was cute and the manager a desi look-alike of Harrison Ford served as an added bonus for the trio as they sat down at a table facing the aquarium, in the hopes that the fish would have a calming effect on their flushed friend.

'Why would you have an aquarium in a café?' cried Renu irritably, glowering at the catfish snuffling innocently in the slime within the glass cage. 'It's so stupid. What if someone orders a tuna sandwich? Fucking lack of sensitivity towards our fellow creatures.'

'They are omnivorous. They eat other fish. They would probably eat the tuna if you offered it to them,' said Neena soothingly.

'Can you please stop talking about fish? I'm nauseated enough as it is,' snapped Renu.

'But you starte—' began Neena, when a quelling glance from Anupama silenced her.

Much to their relief, the chocolate truffles arrived just then, and the next few minutes of Renu's attention were spent devouring the pastries until not a crumb remained on any of the three plates. Only when she was done did she turn to look at her rather anxious friends, their ginger lemon tea untouched as yet.

'Look, I know I've been a bit of a head case lately, but this situation isn't something I was prepared for, to say the least.

So, suffice it to say that every moment that I'm not eating or pissing or puking, I'm freaking out.'

'We understand, honey,' said Anupama, patting her knee.

'You're sure you don't want to tell us who the father is, though?' asked Neena.

Renu shook her head. 'Trust me, there's no point. Neither of us had any intentions of settling down with each other, and it wouldn't be fair if I thrust this responsibility upon him.'

'But shouldn't he at least know?'

'I told you, there's no point.'

Neena was about to pursue the topic further when a well-aimed kick from Anupama's foot beneath the table deterred her. Pursing her lips, she excused herself to go to the bathroom and limped away.

'Don't mind her. She's just trying to be helpful,' said Anupama, the moment she had gone.

'He knows,' said Renu tonelessly, sipping her tea.

'Sorry?'

'The guy. He knows. I told him.'

'You did? Then why—'

'Because he's not an option. And that is why I'm asking you to be careful with Charlie.'

It took Anupama a moment to understand the correlation. 'Oh, Renu.'

'It's not that big an age difference, to be honest with you. He's thirty-one. I'd met him at a textiles conference last year in Bangalore and we've been meeting up over the months whenever he visited. He's not even from the city. And honestly, it's not like I need him in my life anyway. I'm fully capable of handling this on my own. Besides, I was honest when I said the thing with him wasn't supposed to be romantic in the first place. I'm not in love with him, and given a choice, this probably wouldn't have been my preferred course in life either. But it has happened, and now, I don't know, I feel like I want to see it through.' She placed her hand softly on her belly. 'In its own way, it feels like it was meant to be, you know.'

'So, you really don't want him to be involved?'

'I don't. I told him just so he would know. He made his stance abundantly clear to me, so I said fuck you very much and went my way. You know how men are – they always think there's a lot out there to be explored before they settle down. The only reason I haven't told Neena is because I know the moment she hears this she will take out a morcha in my name, and command him to take full responsibility. She may think it's justice, but honestly, I'd rather stay on my own happily than be with a wimp who shits bricks at the thought of this miracle.'

Anupama clasped her hand firmly. 'I'm with you.'

Renu smiled, pressing her hand back.

'And that's why you have been so wary of Charlie,' said Anupama.

'Honestly, it's you I am wary about. I know you, honey. I know you enough to know how hard you're falling for this guy. And the one thing which scares me more than the thought of this baby emerging from my body someday, is the thought of that guy breaking your heart if it doesn't work out. I'm all for you finding someone, but – don't you think it would be better if it was someone … I don't know, more…'

'Stable? Like Rajeev?' asked Anupama pointedly.

'Those were different times.'

'And we were different people. We made our decisions, and

we lived through them. So why repeat the same mistakes? I know it's a risk, but isn't it time I took one? Just for myself?'

Renu stared at her, speechless.

'Sorry I took so long!' trilled Neena, re-appearing. 'The loo was such a mess. I had them clean and disinfect it twice over before I deigned to step in. So ... another round of chocolate truffles?'

Renu and Anupama nodded, getting back to their teas with just a tiny glance of understanding at each other, as they felt their Inner Women embrace each other in a warm hug of mutual support and solidarity.

25

On Wednesday evening, between half past four and five, in a suburban, high-rise apartment building in the Nungambakkam district of Chennai, a woman was stabbed to death in a crime of passion by her next-door neighbour.

On Thursday morning, a printout of the news article reporting the crime was put up on the bulletin board of the A, B and C blocks of Atharva Hari Cooperative Housing Society. Right next to the article was a notice stating that to prevent tragedies of a similar nature, all floors of the residential blocks would now be equipped with CCTV cameras to note the comings and goings of not just the visitors but the neighbours as well, just to be on the safe side. The first floor to have this surveillance installed would be the seventh floor of the C block, whose residents included Mr (late) Rajeev Arora and family, and others. The notice included a special note of thanks from the governing body to Mrs Mehtani for coming up with this noble idea, keeping in mind the safety of her fellow residents.

On Saturday morning, Renu drove into the premises of Atharva Hari and parked her car in the residential parking slot allotted to C-703 via the permission of its owner, Mrs Anupama Arora. Upon being asked the purpose of her visit, she replied that she had just taken on the project of renovating the flat of a certain Mr Charlie, who lived in flat C-704. She was an interior designer by profession, and would require the assistance of her colleague, Anupama, in this project, which would begin every day at 9.30 a.m. and carry on until however long it took to complete it.

And thus, the universal gesture (a royal middle finger) was shown to the watchful eyes of whomsoever it may have concerned as Anupama blithely strolled in and out of Charlie's apartment for 'research purposes' as the CCTV camera sullenly recorded her walking to and fro between the two apartments day after day. The surveillance footage was there, but what good was it when you couldn't question the activities recorded? Of course, had anyone bothered to check, they would have probably found it odd that even after seven days of regular visits by Renu and Anupama, barely a curtain had changed in Charlie's place. But then, that would have required another impromptu inspection, and after the failed pest control ambush, even Mrs Mehtani had run out of excuses to make another innocent visit.

However, the Chinese whispers had begun swinging with Tarzan-like ease through the grapevine across the micro-cosmic arrangements of tea-gatherings, kitty-parties and walkers' groups. Mrs Mehtani made sure of that. Rumours began to fly of the growing friendship between the reticent Mrs Arora and her hunky neighbour next door. No one had the guts to say it out loud yet, mostly because a lot of them had as little faith in Mrs Mehtani's gossip as in the charitable causes that knocked on their doors for donations every Navratri, and also because they still owed a tiny amount of gratitude to Charlie for introducing them to the joys of a far more flattering reflection in their mirrors than they were used to. However, the idea of something so naughty and scandalous happening right under their noses was too tempting to dismiss, especially when they played over the various titillating possibilities without admitting it to anyone. Some sniggered, some sighed, and a small minority even wondered what was it that Mrs Arora had that they didn't. It's not even like she was the tallest or the thinnest or the prettiest one around. And in terms of social skills and emotional baggage – the lesser said the better. What a mismatch – a few remarked to themselves every time they saw Charlie strutting about the premises from the corners of their eyes. What an upgrade – others mused, remembering the diminutive, unsmiling Mr Arora, who always smelt of the same Amla oil brand and wore identical-looking checked cotton shirts bought in bulk discount during festival seasons. What luck, they all universally agreed without exception.

Small wonder Mrs Arora was participating in the Monsoon Goddess this year, they all concluded. Love gave you wings – wasn't that the expression? Or was it really love to begin with? It *had* been two years of abstinence, after all…

And all through these what 'if's and 'maybe's and probably's, one thing that was definitely happening was a spicing up of Anupama and Charlie's love lives in more ways than one. She hadn't even known what a 69 was, much to his surprise. And then, there were the other terms and positions he had to gently introduce her to without freaking her out, while dealing with the struggle to keep the lights on whenever they had sex. Why did Indian women have such a huge issue in admitting the virtues of nudity and pornography? Charlie wondered. Or was it only her?

Daytime was another matter, when they would retire to the bedroom while Renu sat out in the living room, waiting patiently and working on her laptop. The initial few times had been queasy, as Anupama found it discomfiting to have her friend at such close proximity during her intimate moments, but gradually, the routine set in, and so did her comfort level. Besides, beggars couldn't be choosers. She had to admire Charlie's commitment as well; he had moved to the evening shift at his salon to accommodate their daytime trysts. The curtains in his bedroom windows would be shut tight every time, not allowing the least trickle of daylight in (not that there was much, thanks to the incessantly wet and grey weather outside), almost as if she were afraid of a spy drone hovering right outside their window, waiting to transmit the first compromising visual it could capture.

'You know, you could at least remove the newspapers from your kitchen window now,' said Charlie, as they lay in bed, entwined in each other's arms. 'It would be nice to watch you as I cook. May even increase the nutritional value of the food.'

'You barely cook.'

'I was talking about the weekends, or nights. You could wear that sexy pink nightie of yours, and I could wear – well, whatever you want me to wear. We could check each other out while frying our onions and kneading our dough.'

'Mmm, you really know how to turn a woman on.'

'We could even talk on the phone to spice things up a bit, if you know what I mean,' he went on excitedly. 'I could show you something, you could show me something...'

'You know I have two kids living with me, right?'

'The best pleasures come with a certain degree of risk.'

'No, thank you. Besides, have you seen the way it's been raining? It would be impossible to see anything clearly.'

'Oh, come on,' he said, lifting the covers to give her a peek of his manhood, which was impressively ready for action again. 'You really doubt its visibility?'

'What I doubt is its life span if my son ever spots you flashing that at me. Besides, why settle for a blurry view when I can get a close up so easily?' she said, reaching down and stroking him in that way he loved.

Charlie closed his eyes, sighing. 'Man, I could stay like this the whole day.'

'Well, I can't. Have to plan for Nimit's birthday tomorrow. Plus, I have to meet with the Monsoon Goddess committee to finalize my details.'

'I thought you had already signed up.'

'I did. But there is the rest of the nitty-gritty like the outfits I wear, what I will showcase as my special skill in the talent round, and my acceptance speech in case I win.'

'That's confident.'

'We all do it. Just to make sure no one babbles or fumbles or ends up thanking their labrador in the end.'

'Will you mention me in your acceptance speech?'

'Oh, sure: "And most of all, I would like to thank my stud muffin sitting there in the back row for making me realize –

multiple times, if I may add – that I've still got what it takes. So up yours, bitches!'"

'Hear, hear!'

Anupama laughed and pressed her forehead against his, feeling the smoothness of his skin. 'What if I screw up?'

'Doesn't matter. You're already a Monsoon Goddess to me.'

'Aww,' she drawled, pulling him in for a kiss when a loud rap on the bedroom door made them both jump.

'Sorry to interrupt your coochie-cooing, but it's been three hours since we last ate, and I'm starving!' yelled Renu from outside.

'Help yourself to anything in the fridge,' Charlie hollered back.

'I checked already. There's only a wrinkled potato and a ketchup sachet there.'

Anupama sighed and got up reluctantly, ignoring Charlie's pleas to stay. It was for his own good. She didn't want him to become a casualty to one of Renu's ballistic food-deprived alter-egos.

'We really need to get you some groceries,' she said, getting up and pulling on her top. 'And stop putting potatoes in the fridge. It makes them mouldy.'

'Aye, aye, madam.'

She walked out into the living room to see Renu packed up already, her lips pursed into a tight line and arms folded. A wave of guilt rose within her for having neglected her friend's needs. It was rather ironic how the further Renu progressed in her pregnancy, the more maternal Anupama seemed to become.

'So what do you crave this time?' she asked, the moment they were out of the apartment.

'I'm not hungry.'

'But you just—'

'I wanted to get you out of there. Let's talk at your place.'

And there it was, that familiar foreboding creeping back into her soul as they crossed the hallway to her place. These few seconds before the revelation were the most excruciating for Anupama. Knowing Renu to be a rather subdued and non-dramatic figure in most moments of crises, she could tell it was serious. And personal.

Nimit was in the living room, watching TV, so they headed for her room. The moment the door shut behind them, Renu began typing away on her cell phone. Not wanting to rush her, Anupama sat down on the bed, waiting with bated breath, until she finally concluded her business and sat down facing her.

'Has Charlie ever mentioned any plans of going out to you?'

'Going out as in what – a vacation?'

The look of dread on Renu's face deepened.

'Renu, just tell me,' said Anupama.

'Did you know that he is here on a short-term lease?'

'No,' said Anupama, surprised. 'He never mentioned it, and I didn't ask. How short?'

'Three months. And if I'm not wrong, this is his third month going on, right? So, if he was planning to stay on here, he would have renewed his rental agreement by now.'

'Maybe he has.'

'I don't think so. There was nothing in his contracts folder.'

'Where did you get that?'

'What do you think I've been doing in his home for so many days? I just wanted to make sure you were investing your emotions in the right place.'

She knew she should have been angry with Renu, but right now, there was a bigger cause to worry about. Perhaps he had forgotten. Most likely it was under processing. It was probably in his bedroom cupboard. Maybe she should just ask him.

'I rang his landlord on the number given on the agreement, just to be sure. I said I was interested in the flat and asked whether the tenant had any plans of staying on. Anu, Charlie hasn't consented to a renewal, despite repeated reminders.'

'When was this?'

'Just now, before I called you over.'

The familiar stirrings of an anxiety attack rose within her. No, she couldn't be anxious. She wouldn't. Charlie wasn't a bad guy. She wasn't a bad person. Nothing bad would happen to them. The time for that was in the past. There had to be a reasonable explanation and everything would be just fine. They had been discussing the future for so long; this just didn't make any sense.

'When does the agreement end?' asked Anupama.

'The twenty-seventh of this month.'

Three weeks. Three weeks left. A lot could happen in three weeks. He would manage to do something; he always did.

Somewhere outside, the faint echoes of a distant thunder rumbled in the air.

'Anu, I'm so sorry.'

'We don't know anything yet. Let's not jump to conclusions.'

'His lease stands cancelled, honey.'

'He could take up another flat nearby.'

Renu stared at her for a long quiet moment, before nodding. 'He could,' she said gently.

'Or maybe, he is having some financial difficulties that he wants to sort out first.'

'Maybe.'

'He probably didn't want to upset me, which is why he hasn't said anything.'

Renu nodded, her eyes compassionate. Anupama wished she would stop looking at her like that. There was nothing tragic about the situation. At least, not yet.

She flipped open her phone. 'Let me just call him.'

'Anu, wait.'

'There has to be an explanation.'

'There will be. I just want to make sure you're prepared for it.'

'What's that supposed to mean? He told me he won't run away. He won't do that to me!'

'I'm not saying he was lying. But you need to stop looking at things purely from your perspective, sweetheart. He is twenty-four. He himself doesn't know what he will, or won't, do.'

'You don't know him, okay? You don't know *us*. It's different. He wouldn't hide anything from me, least of all something this big.'

She made a move to punch in his number, when Renu grabbed her hand. 'Can we at least consider a scenario where you may need to deal with your worst fears coming true? Are you ready for it? Because if you aren't, you need to be. Otherwise, you'll be broken. And I can't have that. Not again.'

'Renu, I need to know.'

'And you will. Just not like this.'

Like what? She wanted to scream. How much readier could she be? Didn't she know her? Didn't she understand? Deep inside, she had been ready the day she had begun to love him, not because she mistrusted him, but because a part of her – a fragment, rather – always knew it was too good to be true. All through her faith and hopes and self-assurances, she had kept that fragment carefully preserved inside her, like a firearm one keeps hidden in the house, trying not to think about it, hoping never to use it, yet being aware of its presence all the same – a source of anxiety, and a source of security should the need arise. How much readier could she be?

She freed her hand from Renu's and scurried out before she could stop her. She hurried past the living room, through the main door, crossed the hallway, and rang Charlie's doorbell until he answered it and let her in with a smile that quickly disappeared when he saw the expression on her face.

'What's wrong?'

'Is it true?'

'What?'

'Are you leaving?'

The momentary silence that hung between them had a weight that threatened to crush her on the spot. The silence was all the confirmation she needed. But she wouldn't cry. She had decided that.

'I am,' he said finally. 'But not for long.'

'Why didn't you tell me?'

'Because I didn't want to freak you out. You've been so tense lately and I thought you might take it the wrong way.'

'I know everything, Charlie. You're not renewing your lease.'

A look of shock crossed his face, probably at the fact that she knew. 'No, I'm not.'

'So, you're not coming back then?'

'I am. Just not here. I mean, I will be around here, I promise you—'

'I'm not here for promises. Just give me answers. Why are you leaving? Where are you going?'

'Bangalore. It's a short-term course.'

'In what?'

'Photography.'

She gawked at him, stupefied.

'Photography? Since when have you been into photography?'

'I've always had a tiny interest in it. I didn't really expect to get through to be honest. It was just a shot. I sent them some pictures that I had clicked on my DSLR and…'

But she wasn't listening anymore. She wasn't interested in the details. It was what this change symbolized as a whole that struck her with the force of a blow. She knew what it meant for him, for her. For *them*. So, it had happened, after all. His passion had changed yet again. And with that, so had his journey.

'It's only for three months. I'll get another place around here again when I'm back.'

'You had promised me … you assured me you were happy…'

'But I am! It's just a course. What's the big deal?'

'Isn't this how it always starts with you? You try something new and then you stick with it, forgetting the past and moving on into that new life. Is that why you didn't tell me? Because you knew I would try to stop you … except that you wouldn't. You wouldn't stop. You never have.'

'Anu—' He moved forward to touch her, but she recoiled. Hate such as she had never known coursed through her, and it was aimed right at him. She felt cheated and scorned. At that moment, it honestly didn't matter to her whether he would come back or not. The fact that he was leaving was in itself such a disappointment, such a heart-breaking betrayal … Nothing really mattered anymore, did it? It was all an illusion, just like everything important in her life had been.

'Go on, then. Leave. I won't stop you. Just get lost!'

He called out to her and reached for her arm, but she was already out. Charlie ran out into the hallway after her and desperately tried to hold her back; but Anupama yanked her arm free and pushed him away.

At that moment, neither he nor she, and not even the watchman engrossed in a re-reading of *The Trial* at his post, was aware of the CCTV camera recording their squabble on screen number five, the black-and-white grainy footage capturing every second of the tussle, tug, push and pull between the duo, the nail-raking, the pleas, the punches – and finally, the reluctant submission of Anupama as Charlie wrapped her into a tight embrace, kissing the top of her head as she ineffectually tried to break free one last time, before giving in. Its lens unblinking, the little oblong device dispassionately observed the sobbing woman and the young man comforting her from its dark corner overhead, where it had been unobtrusively and strategically positioned as a mute witness.

And mute it was. For now.

26

The next morning, Anupama knew something was off the moment she woke up. It was a rather peculiar, nagging feeling in her gut, almost like a presentiment. Like when your subconscious seems to know something more than your conscious mind does, but won't tell you exactly what it is, much to your annoyance.

Her suspicions were strengthened when she stepped out to get some groceries after her children had left. For one, the young watchman didn't seem as uninterested as he usually was, but actually *gazed* at her for all of two seconds before returning to his book. In contrast, the three ladies she met on the way refused to look her in the eye, each murmuring a quick good morning before scuttling away. Weird as it was, she didn't have much time to dwell on these incidents. She had wished Nimit a very happy birthday this morning and had given him his much-admired iPod Shuffle as a gift, delighting him in a way that only a sixteen-year-old could be delighted by a three-inch over-glorified walkman player with a half-eaten apple as its logo. Yet, the real surprise was waiting for him tonight, when his friends would welcome him home after he returned from his tuitions. Renu was in charge of the invites, and Neena was going to take care of the refreshments, leaving her at home to manage the rest of the arrangements. Easy-peasy. She smiled at the thought of the look on his face. It was his sixteenth birthday. It had to be special. She would make sure of that.

It was only after she returned home that she saw the two messages and six missed calls on her cell phone (Misha had often chided her for this: 'it's called "mobile" for a reason, Mamma!'). The missed calls were all from Mrs Govindikar, a fact that set off the alarm bells in her head, while the two messages were from Mrs Chatterjee, asking her how she was and to get in touch if she needed help. Needed help with what? What on earth was going on? Before she could ponder any further, her phone buzzed with an incoming call from Mrs Govindikar. With an anxious heart, she answered it.

'Where are you, Mrs Arora?' she asked in a clipped voice – no pleasantries, nothing.

'Home. Why?'

'I need to see you right away. Stay there.'

And the call was cut.

Her heart was beginning to pound now. Something was terribly, terribly wrong. But what? She reviewed the previous day's turmoil and the rather amorphous half-resolution in the end. They had been a bit reckless in the hallway, no doubt, but at that moment, discretion and public opinion had been the last things on her mind. Besides, no one had seen them. No one had been around. That much she was sure of. The only ones in the hallway were her, Charlie and no one el—

Her breath caught in her throat.

The camera. The damn CCTV!

How could she have forgotten?

An icy numbness spread to the tips of her toes, making her legs go wobbly. She sat down gingerly on the sofa, mouth agape, as the implications and repercussions of yesterday began to dawn upon her. The surveillance system must have recorded *everything*. There was no turning back now, was there? Not even if she wanted to. No more second chances. It was all irreversibly out.

Mrs Govindikar arrived at her door, looking livid.

'What in God's name were you thinking?' she snarled. 'I trusted you, Anupama. I trusted you to know what was good for yourself! How foolish could you be?'

Her first instinct was to apologize, but apologize for what? Getting caught? Lying? Risking her heart and dignity for a man who may not even be here by the end of the month? Even in the stress of the moment, she couldn't help but feel the bitterness return, threatening to choke her.

'Who all know?' she asked instead.

'Does it even matter? D'you think this can actually remain a secret anymore? You had a chance, my dear, and you blew it! I can't protect you anymore. And why should I? You don't value my opinion anyway. I should have known. I knew that boy was bad news right from the start...'

She wanted her to be quiet. She wanted some time alone to think. She wanted that painful, throbbing headache at the base of her temples to stop.

'Honestly, you should be ashamed of yourself, Mrs Arora. You have disappointed me. And more than anything, you have disappointed yourself, your family, your—'

'Shut up.'

She never got the full list of whom she had disappointed, for the rest of the list was choked in Mrs Govindikar's throat. Her eyes bulged. She looked comical, with her reddened ears and that bulging vein running through the centre of her forehead like an obscene, fleshy worm.

'What ... did ... you ... say?'

'Something you ought to have been told a long time ago. *Shut up.*'

Mrs Govindikar drew back aghast.

'How dare you—'

'Did anybody ever tell you that you resemble a dolphin when you're annoyed?'

Mrs Govindikar stared at her flabbergasted. It took her a moment to find her words. 'Have you ... lost your mind?'

'Finally, a relevant point of discussion. And the answer to that is: yes, I have, Mrs Govindikar. I have officially lost my mind, because I think it's about time I did. All my life, I have struggled and slogged and killed myself to stay in control of things that probably never needed my control to begin with. And to what end? What major milestone has any one of us achieved with our control and decorum? What bloody difference has it made?'

Mrs Govindikar's mouth opened and closed wordlessly, like a dying halibut. 'This is because of that boy, isn't it?' she spluttered finally. 'What has he done to you?'

'Do me a favour, Mrs Govindikar, and please open your ears and eyes. This isn't about him. This is about you. You and me. You think I don't know what's going on? The CCTV footage is supposed to get checked every weekend as per the rules set by you in the notice board. Today is Wednesday. So how, pray, did you get the report of our "indiscretion" so early in the morning?'

For the first time since she had known her, she found Mrs Govindikar to be at a loss for words.

'Of course, my first assumption was that it was Mrs Mehtani, because I know that all the other occupants in this block actually have a life,' continued Anupama. 'But then, she would obviously need your permission to access those records, right?'

'I—'

'Which in turn leads me to believe that I have been singled out and discriminated against by you two for quite some time now. Now it's your turn to answer my questions, Mrs Govindikar. What exactly is your problem?'

'My problem?'

'What difference does it make to you whether I'm seeing him or not? Which facet of your universe does it affect?'

'This isn't right, Mrs Arora! I'm just trying to protect you!'

'Protect me from what? Being human, for a change? How about asking me the real questions, Mrs Govindikar, the ones that actually matter? Is he an adult? Yes. Am I an adult? Yes. Was it consensual? Yes. Did we hurt or cheat anyone? No. Is it anyone's goddamn business what we do in our personal lives? No. And most importantly, did I ever volunteer to become the holy centre of virginal morality for this entire goddamn neighbourhood? Certainly not! *So what is the bloody problem*?!'

Mrs Govindikar's eyes narrowed. A cold smile spread across her lips. She was recovering her bearings. 'D'you really believe that the people around you are so open-minded? D'you think they care? My dear, you can rationalize it as much as you want, but the truth is, in their heads, you will be branded forever. And d'you know as what?'

'Does it matter?'

Mrs Govindikar scoffed. 'Oh, believe me, it does.'

'Didn't make much of a difference to you, though, did it?'

The frigid scorn on her face was swiftly replaced by puzzlement. 'What are you talking about?'

'D'you think we don't know about your son? With a best friend like Mrs Mehtani around, did you really imagine that you were safe?'

Mrs Govindikar's face was carefully blank, save for a slight twitch at the corner of her clamped jaw. 'I don't know what—'

'Isn't that why he went abroad in the first place? It wasn't just for his career, was it? It was to be free.'

'Free of what?'

'Free of you, Mrs Govindikar. Free of … of *this*,' she said, waving her arms around. 'Free to be him. Isn't that why your plans to visit him keep getting cancelled? How can you expect him to accept you in his life when you haven't even accepted his basic identity?'

Abandoning her sanctimonious stance, Mrs Govindikar struggled for words, her face turning shades of puce by degrees. 'I—don't know what you have heard … Mrs Arora … but—'

'My daughter is still friends with him on Facebook, Mrs Govindikar. There aren't any secrets anymore. He is happy. And loved, just as he wanted to be. And maybe, it's about time you accepted it as well.'

Mrs Govindikar's voice failed her.

Anupama took a step towards her. 'I've wasted a lot of time envying you, you know. Often, I have wondered what it would be like to be the way you are – strong, certain, unrelenting. But now, now I understand … just how exhausting it must be to be you.'

She locked eyes with the old, suddenly frail-looking lady in front of her. 'Aren't you tired, Mrs Govindikar? I know I am. Isn't it about time we just … lived?'

It might have sounded a bit dramatic, but the truth was that in the silence that followed, one could hear the ticking of the clock on the wall, marking each second that passed in that minute of that hour that neither of them would ever forget. To give the devil his due, Mrs Govindikar's eyes remained steady, with nary a hint of moisture in them, but the rest of her seemed to be on the verge of collapse. Something within her was struggling for release – a feeling Anupama was very familiar with by now. Something long-repressed and denied. The part that made her a human just like the rest of them. The part that would crack the shell she had built around her forever, if only she would let it. They were so close…

And then, it was gone. The jaws slackened, the rigidity of the shoulders eased and the tightness over Mrs Govindikar's face receded, until all that remained was an emptiness, incapable of giving or receiving anything.

'I should go,' she murmured.

Anupama allowed her to pass. Her steps were slow although her back and shoulders ramrod straight. Not that it mattered anymore. The only thing Anupama now felt for the woman was pity. She would never be free.

Mrs Govindikar paused at the door for a moment. Without turning around, she said, 'The confirmation day for the pageant participants is Saturday. Make sure your costumes are ready and talent duly recorded. Mrs Mehtani and Mrs Kaushik will coordinate the event management. I'll send a notice around in the evening.'

'I won't be participating, Mrs Govindikar. Besides, I am not eligible.'

'There is no rule barring widows—'

'I don't consider myself a widow anymore.'

Mrs Govindikar's brows raised for a fraction of an instant. 'As you wish.'

And with that, just like that, she was gone.

———

It took Anupama quite some time to get over what had just happened. It was one of those moments, the impact of which struck you in slow, broken tremors of varying intensity, rather than all at once. Had she said too much? What was to be done now? Was everyone aware of her perfidy by now? What about Nimit? When should she tell him? Would Charlie help and how? She couldn't remember whether she had had breakfast yet.

It was Nimit's birthday today!

She pulled herself together. There was a lot to be done. She had wanted it to be a very special day. Now, she just prayed for it to be normal. *No more surprises, please.*

With trembling hands, she picked up the phone and called Neena, clearing her throat to make sure her voice stayed steady. She would need her and Renu's help to tide over this new crisis, no doubt, but not today. Today was all about Nimit and everything had to be perfect.

———

It was all she could do to not break down. Everything was going wrong. Despite her specific instructions to avoid cartoon characters, Neena had chosen to drop by with some Mickey Mouse balloons; and for the sake of variety, they had Daisy Duck thrown in for good measure. Nimit was never going to forgive her for this.

As if that wasn't enough, seven people had cancelled already, four from her own block citing miscellaneous lame excuses (had the word got to them so fast?). The cable connection had given up the ghost, which meant no TV for the younger guests, and the cake was running an hour late because the delivery man's bike had stalled – something that spelled disaster in this weather. Renu, who had volunteered to get the food and drinks in spite of Anu and Neena's attempts to dissuade her, had a nasty bout of morning sickness that had continued into the afternoon. She was asleep now and would hopefully make a full recovery by the evening. However, there was a strong possibility that she would not be able to make it, in which case there would be a mad scramble to arrange for catering at the last minute.

By 5.00 p.m., most of the setbacks had been sorted. The balloons replaced, as were the kindergarten cutlery and plates. The nearest branch of MacDonald's had been contacted as a contingency measure. However, shortly after that, Renu confirmed that she would be arriving after all, as were the rest of the guests. Nimit had decided to treat his friends to a movie after school and would be back around seven. By then, all the guests would be neatly assembled for the main event.

It seemed like the evening would go just as she had planned, after all.

And then came the telephone call from Nimit's school, asking her to come immediately. There had been an emergency.

27

Anupama quickened her pace, with Neena in tow, as they headed to the principal's office at the end of the rather dank, grey corridor flanked by intimidating pillars, walls at the far end embossed with sharp stone edges. The hard tiles underfoot emitted a sharp staccato sound with their every step.

She knew it was bad the moment she spotted the back of Mrs Mehtani's all-too-recognizable head in the principal's cabin. The tiny flickers of doubt in her head were dispelled at the sight of her son and Sahil's (Mrs Mehtani's son, Nimit's classmate) bruised faces. Nimit had a deep gash across his cheek and Sahil's lower lip was badly swollen. Their clothes were filthy and ripped. Although first-aid had been administered haphazardly to the pugilists, the band-aids weren't doing a very good job of hiding the nastiness of the wounds, which could not have been the result of a simple fall.

They were all seated in front of the principal, Mr Sharma, who looked like he wanted to be anywhere but here. Feeling like she was witnessing the scene rather than experiencing it, Anupama asked what the matter was in the calmest voice she could manage. Mr Sharma, reddening at the ears, politely asked Neena to wait outside as the matter was of a personal nature.

As Neena exited, Anupama sat down between her son and the livid Mrs Mehtani, who was absently patting Sahil's head.

'So, what happened?'

'What does it look like? Your son attacked Sahil in the football ground,' lashed out Mrs Mehtani.

'Why?' asked Anupama, keeping her eyes fixed on Mr Sharma.

'Ask him yourself. Shouldn't be much of a surprise though, considering the company he keeps—'

'Mrs Mehtani and Mrs Arora,' interrupted Mr Sharma gravely, 'the reason why I have called you both here is because the matter seems to be rather delicate. Apparently, as per the witness accounts, Sahil and Nimit had first gotten into a verbal argument which quickly escalated to physical violence. At one point, Saahil even got knocked out of his senses for a while—'

Mrs Mehtani gasped in horror.

'—but there is no cause for worry as, after a thorough medical check-up, we have confirmed that neither of them have sustained any serious injuries or concussions. However, there is the issue of the cause.'

He paused darkly, the acute discomfort back on his face. 'Now, neither of them have told us what triggered the argument, but we got some bits that were overheard by some by-standers, and ... well ... I think it would be best if you talked to your children yourselves. Of course, if you wish, we could always arrange for counselling.'

From the corner of her eyes, Anupama spotted the look of comprehension slowly dawning across Mrs Mehtani's face too.

Both the boys were sitting with their eyes downcast. Nimit's face was puce with rage.

'Thank you. Can we … can we take them home now?' asked Anupama.

'Of course. We just wanted to make sure you personally escort them home. And as I said, please do have a talk with them. They are nice kids, and obviously, can't be expected to understand everything at this age. So…'

Nodding silently, both Anupama and Mrs Mehtani bundled their boys out; none of them making eye-contact. Neena, who was waiting outside, glanced at the expression on Anupama's face, and nodded in understanding.

Not a word was uttered until they were halfway home, with Neena driving and Anupama beside her, while Nimit sat sullenly in the rear, staring outside.

'Is it true?' he croaked.

'What?'

'The thing they are saying. About you. Is it true?'

'Nimit—'

'Beta, you need to rest first. We can always talk later,' suggested Neena.

'Tell me, Mom.'

'What exactly are you talking about?'

Nimit winced, shaking his head. 'I can't even say it.'

'Say it.'

'That assho—Sahil … was saying some pretty, crappy bullshit about you. You and … Charlie … obviously, it's not true, right?'

Anupama sat still in her seat.

'Right?' asked Nimit.

She could lie. That would be easy. It wouldn't matter to him what he heard from anyone else as long as she denied it. It wouldn't even matter what he actually did believe, as long as he had her false assurance to fall back on. She knew that more than anything, it was her denial he was seeking right now. It would make him happy – and relieved. But for how long? And to what end? How many more fights would he get into to defend his version of the truth? How many more times would he scream out his truth against that of the others? She remembered her confrontation with Mrs Govindikar this morning, the brief glimpse she had had of the person when her mask was down, and the utter hopelessness of her entrapment.

Her heart sank. It was his sixteenth birthday. She had wanted it to be special.

'I wish you hadn't found out this way,' she said slowly.

There was no sound, but she could feel the weight of Nimit's horror behind her. She swivelled in her seat to see him sitting frozen.

'W—What are you saying?'

'It's true.'

His mouth fell open. His eyes darted to and fro. 'Shit…'

'Nimit—'

'Stop the car.'

'Beta, listen—'

'Stop the car. I'm going to be sick!'

He swung his door open and hurled, heaving the contents of his stomach onto the concrete below. Neena swerved the car to the side, narrowly missing the bus behind them by inches, and came to a halt. Anupama undid her seatbelt, got out and rushed to the rear door, only to have him shrink away from her.

'Don't touch me,' he moaned.

Tears welled up in her eyes as she saw the disgust on his face. 'Nimit…'

'Just – stay away, okay? Just…'

He slid across his seat, opened the door on the other side and got out.

'NIMIT!' screamed Anupama.

Like one possessed, he dashed across the road – ignoring her and Neena's cries – and vaulted over the lane divider fence and landed right in the path of an oncoming cab from the opposite direction. It slammed hard into him and flung him forward like a rag doll. He tumbled a few feet forward before lying still.

The next few seconds were a blur for Anupama as she and Neena ran across to Nimit; he lay bloodied and bruised, a small crowd already gathering, his white uniform shirt speckled with blood and dirt, his arms skinned so badly in places that it made her nauseous. The world around her was a fog of chaos and confusion. Neena was on the phone, someone was giving her instructions, people were staring, clicking pictures, passing bottles of water, pointing, murmuring … and a dull, tinning sound was echoing in the back of her ears, getting louder with every passing second until she felt she could bear it no longer…

And then, she was in the hospital. The minutes (or hours) that had passed in between hadn't quite registered in her muddled mind. All she could tell for sure was that she was seated in this hospital corridor, and her son was inside the ward, still unconscious, still being tended to. She looked at the clock at the far end of the corridor. Nine twenty. Was it night already? What had happened to the party? The surprise birthday party back home that she had planned for her son. Here came her friends with Misha, walking down the bleached white corridor – Renu carrying a paper cup of what she was sure was tea – when had she arrived? Did they have cream biscuits by any chance? Vanilla preferably. Cream biscuits – wasn't that how it had all started on an innocent rainy day?

'How are you feeling now?'

She turned around. Charlie.

He was still wearing his black T-shirt with the salon logo on it, so she guessed he must have come directly from work. How long had he been sitting there?

'How is he?' she asked.

'Some of the bruises will take time to heal, but thankfully, nothing serious. The doctor said he should rest for now, though.'

She felt like laughing. '*Nothing serious*'? Had they any idea?

'I'm really sorry, Anu. I had no idea things would get this bad.'

'He asked me whether what people were saying was true, and I said yes.'

'I know.'

'I didn't even ask him what he had heard, what the nature of the rumours was that I was accepting … I should have asked him … I should have been more patient, more sensitive, but I just said yes. I wanted to be brave. I wanted so badly to be brave that it made me selfish. Selfish and stupid.'

'It wasn't your fault.'

'He could have died. I could have lost him.'

Her vision blurred as her eyes brimmed over with tears. Her throat imploded. Charlie pulled her close, kissing the side of her forehead. She didn't want sympathy, but the warmth felt nice, and she was too weak to disengage.

'Mamma …' Misha came over and hugged her tight, her arms brushing over the space that Charlie's had just left, the shoulder of her top getting wet with her tears. The touch of her daughter was like a soothing balm. 'It's okay … everything will be fine…'

Although they both knew that the assurance was a mere formality, it felt good to hear it all the same. She opened her eyes. Renu and Neena were standing right behind Misha, their expressions just the right balance of consolation and encouragement. She wasn't alone, she realized, and for now, that was enough. It had to be.

28

The next morning, she woke up with a start. It took her a moment to realize she was still in the hospital waiting room, having obstinately refused to go home in case Nimit woke up. It took her another, to realize there were voices raised in anger in her vicinity.

'You have some nerve to show up here!'

It was Misha, an overladen coffee tray balanced precariously in one hand, the other, truculently on her hip as she glowered at Mrs Govindikar and Mrs Mehtani.

'Now, my dear, I know you are tense, but what happened was nobody's fault—'

'Oh, I beg to disagree!'

'What's going on?' asked Anupama, rising from her seat. Her neck had cramped terribly.

'We just came to see how Nimit was doing and to check if you needed any help,' said Mrs Govindikar.

'Well, we don't!' cried Misha.

'Misha,' said Anupama, silencing her just as Mrs Govindikar passed Mrs Mehtani a laden look.

'And I wanted to apologize for Sahil, as well,' she said. 'Obviously, what he did was wrong, and—'

'Don't.'

'Sorry?'

'Don't apologize for your son. What he did was what any immature juvenile in his position would do. It's what *you* did that amazes me. Who shares such things with a fifteen-year-old? How stupid or hateful do you have to be to do such a thing?'

'Now, Mrs Arora—' began Mrs Govindikar.

'It was his birthday yesterday, Mrs Mehtani. He was happy, and that was how I wanted him to remember it. But, thanks to you, he almost got killed, and that's not even the worst part. He hates me now. My son is lying unconscious and hurt inside that medical ward, and he hates me. So, be my guest and gossip all you want. No matter what you do, you cannot damage me any more than this.'

Mrs Mehtani looked at her numbly, her eyes wide. 'I—look, Mrs Arora, what happened—'

Without warning, Anupama gripped her by the shoulders, startling her. Her face inches from the alarmed woman's face, she grinned, although her eyes were welling up again. 'You won, my dear. You won!'

'Mrs Arora, please!'

'Go into that ward. Look at my son. Remember it forever because that's the greatest token of victory that you will ever carry!'

Mrs Mehtani struggled to free herself, almost in tears now, as Mrs Govindikar tried to pry her loose. 'Mrs Arora, please calm down…'

'Mamma,' said Misha, gently loosening her grip.

'I am … I am sorry,' sniffed Mrs Mehtani, her lip trembling. 'I didn't mean to…'

'Go away,' said Misha coldly, as she guided her tired mother back into the chair. After lingering uncertainly for a few more seconds, the two ladies retreated.

It was nearly noon before Nimit regained consciousness. Charlie, Renu and Neena, who had been in constant touch with Anupama, were delighted to hear the news. He was still quite weak though, which was why Anupama and Misha had to wait on tenterhooks for a few more minutes while the doctor examined him. The doctor emerged from the room with the rather grim announcement that Nimit wished to only see his sister and no one else. Pain lanced through Anupama's heart.

No, she would not crumble. She had promised herself that. Thanking the doctor, she marched into Nimit's ward, with Misha in tow. She opened the door to see her son having soup, not an easy feat, considering that three fingers on his right hand were tightly bandaged. He froze seeing her.

'I said I only wanted to see Di.'

'How are you feeling now?'

He ignored her. Anupama pulled up a stool next to his bed, taking the soup bowl and spoon from his hands. It was tomato soup, his favourite. Too hot, she observed, blowing into the spoonful before offering it to him. Nimit obstinately kept his mouth shut.

'She has been here all night, Nimit,' said Misha. 'We were worried as hell about you.'

'I don't want to talk to her.'

'Don't talk then. Just eat,' said Anupama.

She kept the spoon hovering by his lips. A second passed, then two, before he finally opened his mouth and took a reluctant sip. She offered him another spoonful, which he accepted. Within a matter of minutes, the bowl was empty.

'Do you want to drink something? Milk? Juice?'

Nimit shook his head. She felt like he was five again, sulking after a scolding. Except that this time, she was at the receiving end. It pained her to see him so aloof.

'How can I show my face in school again?' he asked Misha. 'Everyone will know by tomorrow.'

'You don't have to tell them it's true. After a point, everyone will forget. It will just be a stupid topic over which you guys had a fight,' replied Misha.

'But if Sahil keeps saying it—'

'He won't,' said Anupama.

'No one can tell that.'

'I can. I spoke to his mother. He won't.'

After a second's pause, Nimit turned his eyes towards her. 'But you did do it, didn't you?'

'Do what?'

Scowling, he turned his face away, sinking into his pillow.

'Do what?' asked Anupama.

'You …' the words choked in his mouth, as he struggled with his revulsion. 'You … slept with him?'

'I love him, Nimit. We are in a relationship.'

'So you did sleep with him.'

'Nimit!' said Misha.

'Yes, just like I slept with your father when I was married to him,' said Anupama.

'Ugh! Please, Mom!'

'Which is how your sister and you were born in the first place,' she went on sternly. 'I'm assuming it's a little too late to be having the birds and the bees talk with you, but you must be familiar with the basics by now.'

The agony on his face was brutal. It was like he was being subjected to third-degree torture with no place to run.

'I know that at your age sex is all that seems to matter. It might seem like something plainly vulgar or titillating to you right now. But you need to know that when you mature into an adult, the meaning of a relationship goes far beyond the physical aspect of it. What I had with Charlie wasn't a fling, or an affair, it was a completion of myself. There was nothing dirty or embarrassing about it.'

'Then why did you hide it from us?'

'Because I didn't think you were ready to know. And now, I am sure you can understand where I was coming from.'

'But ... he's so *young...*'

'So?'

'So how do you know what he's thinking? What if it is just a fling for him?'

'You will have to trust my judgment on that.'

Looking unassuaged, Nimit glanced at Misha. 'You knew about this?'

'I did. And I think it's great.'

'Oh, you do, do you?'

'Open your eyes, dumbass. I know you spend most of your time in your room these days, but even you couldn't have missed how happy she's been for the past month or so. Wouldn't you rather she stayed like that all the time?'

'Wait, what do you mean "all the time"?' he said, panicking. 'Holy shit, are you guys engaged or something?'

'No! She's just being hypothetical.'

'So, hypothetically, if tomorrow you two, what, get married or something, I'll have to call him – Dad?'

'You don't have to call him anything you don't want to. And it's too soon to think about such things.'

'This is so weird,' said Nimit, shaking his head. 'This is so, so weird.'

'You can take as much time as you want. Just know that this doesn't have to change anything between us.'

'Easy for you to say. I used to think of him as an older brother.'

'You've barely met him half a dozen times,' said Misha.

'We were Facebook buddies! I had added him to all my WhatsApp groups too. We used to share all sorts of non-veg jokes with each other, for God's sake. Oh God, now I will have to re-look at his jokes too…'

'Okay, now you are over-thinking it,' said Anupama, just as the nurse came in with a bath sponge and announced that it was time to clean him up.

Feeling somewhat lighter at heart, Anupama left him with the nurse and stepped out with Misha. She needed some fresh air. A walk, maybe. And some tea. Lots of tea. And a shower, of course, urgently. But for that, she would have to go home.

She didn't like the idea of leaving Nimit alone here for the three hours that she would be gone. Furthermore, she didn't want Misha to miss college either. Suddenly, she had a brainwave, she could go to Neena's place, which was only a twenty-minute ride from the hospital. A quick phone call to inform her, and Anupama was on her way.

After spending a night in the stuffy, sterilized ambience of a hospital, it was sheer joy to walk out into the crisp morning air. The sun had emerged at long last with only a spattering of clouds in the sky. The monsoons were receding, she observed. Just a matter of days now.

———

Neena's place was exactly the way she remembered it – a mix of ethnic and contemporary, with just the right balance of space and furnishing. Not a spot was too cramped or too empty, and the figurines, vases, pots, rugs and authentic Rajasthani paintings that adorned the walls and shelves gave one an earthy, grounded feeling of welcome. Happy family photos were stacked against each other in the overhanging glass cabinets, bearing mute witness to their moments of achievements, vacations and childhood memories.

She had often envied Neena for her impeccable domesticity, the way she had effortlessly slipped into the role of a wife and consequently a mother. There had never been any complaints, queries, or doubts from her side. No internal conflicts plagued her. Even now, as she stepped in carrying a tea tray with Good Day biscuits and chaklis, she seemed so much in control, so poised, almost like she had been preparing for this moment her entire life.

After pouring tea into both the ceramic matte finish cups, Neena sat down, legs crossed at the ankles just as they were taught in school. 'Glad to know Nimit's better. How is he taking it?'

'It will take some time, obviously, but doesn't look so bad for now. Could have been better, of course.'

'Of course.'

Nodding gently, they both sipped their tea. A few seconds passed by in a surprisingly awkward period of silence.

'I really like what you have done with your bathroom,' said Anupama.

'Thank you. We had it redone three months back. I'd have asked Renu, but we both weren't talking at the time so...'

'Of course. So, how's Deven?'

'He's good. Just busy with his pre-boards, you know.'

'I'm sure he will do well.'

'Thank you.'

'And Hiten?'

'Oh, well, you know Hiten. He's the same.'

She turned her attention back to her tea. Following her cue, Anupama took another sip.

'Do you want me to turn on the TV or...?'

'No, it's fine,' said Anupama, feeling more and more out of place by the instant. What was happening here? 'I hope I'm not interrupting anything?'

'No, no! I'm glad you're here. Usually, it's just Hiten's friends who come over every now and then. Otherwise, I am just free.'

'How do you pass your time then?'

'Just, you know, doing stuff. I tried a pottery class last week.'

'Oh?'

'It was nice. We made little clay mugs and learnt how to decorate them. Quite satisfying.'

'That's nice.'

'I learnt origami too. There was a workshop in Colaba last month.'

'Okay.'

'I hope you're not getting bored.'

'Not at all.'

'It has been such a long time since you've been here.'

'I know.'

Anupama looked closely at Neena; the feeling of something being off getting stronger by the minute.

'Neena?'

'Hm?'

'Is everything okay?'

'Yes, of course. Why do you ask?'

'I don't know. You just seem a little different.'

'Do I? Oh, it must be the weather.'

What weather? Anupama wanted to ask, but decided to let it go.

'If you want, I could stop by the hospital for some time,' suggested Neena. 'You must be exhausted.'

'Thanks, I'll let you know. And, of course, I am really grateful to you and Renu for being there for me. God alone knows what I would have done without you.'

'Please, what are friends for?'

'Although, I have to admit, I was a little surprised at how wholeheartedly you supported me when I told you about Charlie. Not that I wasn't counting on it, but … I don't know … I was expecting a little more resistance.'

'I can understand.'

Anupama waited for more, and when it didn't come, she

quietly got back to her tea and sipped the remaining few dregs. 'Well, I should be on my way now.'

'You're not doing anything wrong, I hope you know that,' said Neena in a somewhat hurried voice.

'Huh?'

'It's just – with all this happening – I was worried you might reconsider … You shouldn't. I'm really happy for you, Anu. You deserve this.'

'Er, thanks …'

'I mean it. Why should you live your whole life from others' points of view? Why shouldn't you get a chance?'

'Again, thanks, Neena, but I'm really past all that. Now, I am just taking things as they come.'

'And I hope it works out. I really do.'

'Okay, what's going on here? Is there something you want to tell me?'

'No, I'm just being supportive.'

'Yes, maybe a little *too* supportive. I already have a lot of complications in my life right now, Neena, so a little frankness from your side would be very helpful indeed.'

Neena chewed on her lip thoughtfully. A long moment passed before she let out a sigh and said, 'I don't really care for pottery, you know.'

Anupama nodded, still waiting.

'I don't even like getting my hands dirty. I don't know why I took that stupid course.'

'Maybe you just wanted to try something different.'

'Or maybe I just don't know what I want anymore. I mean, look at this house. It's supposed to be me, or at least a part of me, and that's what I thought all along. But it's not, actually. Or maybe, it is. You see, I'm not even sure of that.'

'Neena, I'm sorry … I don't understand. Don't you want this?'

'I don't know. I like to think I do. Otherwise what would the point be, right?'

'What else do you want then?'

'I don't *know*, Anu. That is the whole problem! I never got a chance,' she cried. 'And you know what the worst part is? It was nobody's fault but my own. I don't even have anyone to blame! I screwed myself.'

'But you love your family.'

'I do! I just … I just wish there was more, you know. Is that so wrong?'

'No, no, not at all,' said Anupama, clasping Neena's hand warmly, for she was on the brink of tears.

'I don't even know what I'm complaining about. Most people would consider themselves blessed to have what I have. A perfect life with a happy family, no wants, no needs, no serious problems. But see, that's the thing, Anu. I envy the broken ones, the ones with issues, because at least, they have something to look forward to. They have a journey. I'm already at my destination, and I've been here for some time now. Do you understand?'

'I do.'

'I know. I know you do. Because you have been there too. Which is why I was so, so happy to hear about you and Charlie. I saw an adventure for you, Anu, a chance to be something … something special, and different. And, I don't know, maybe,

I wanted to live that adventure through you. I guess it was selfish of me. But what choice do I have? I'm taking pottery and origami classes, for God's sake!'

She reached for a tissue and dabbed at the corners of her eyes. Watching her, Anupama was reminded of a version of herself that she had long forgotten. The seemingly perfect wife with the seemingly perfect life. And a dark, turbulent maelstrom brewing just beneath the surface. Now here she was, with a son in hospital, a scandal in the neighbourhood, a relationship with an uncertain future, and a personal and social struggle waiting to greet her at home. And here sat Neena in her impeccable home, envious of her, desirous of all the challenges, twists and turns that lay in her path. Where exactly did happiness lie on this scale? Or was it simply a utopian myth, lacking an absolute definition? Or perhaps, at the end of the day, being happy was simply a matter of acknowledging that someone somewhere had a pottery class to match your cream biscuits.

29

The next afternoon, Nimit was deemed fit to go home by the hospital. Persuading him to come home, of course, was a whole other matter. It was only after his two stipulations – that (a) Charlie wouldn't be permitted to enter the house, and (b) any further snide remarks from Sahil regarding this controversy would be dealt with legally – were conceded that he finally deigned to give in.

It was a quiet block that they returned to. A few complimentary messages had popped up on Anupama's mobile from Mrs Govindikar and her troupe, wishing Nimit a speedy recovery, while Mrs Chatterjee and a few other tenants from the neighbouring blocks made sure to send over some packed lunch boxes to save her the trouble of cooking. However, there was one conspicuous change that she noticed immediately upon arrival, and that was the absence of those dreadful CCTV cameras on her, or for that matter, on any floor in the building. It seemed that the rules had changed quite significantly while she was away.

Now that her son was ensconced safely in his room with his usual distractions to fall back upon, Anupama found herself at leisure to dwell upon her other worries – chief amongst them, the issue of Charlie's departure. She had been mostly avoiding his calls and messages for some time now, keeping her replies as brief and formal as she could. She was still upset over his covert exit strategy and the social and familial chaos that had built up around their relationship did not help matters. It seemed as though, however inadvertently, he was throwing her to the wolves and leaving her in the lurch to deal with all the sanctimony and condemnation while he toured around and studied composition and lenses in some idyllic retreat. Didn't he understand that she needed his support now more than ever? And what if he met someone over there? Wouldn't be the most incredible thing to happen. What a joy it would be to wake up one morning and behold a picture of him smooching a bikini babe on Facebook, as she pined away like a lovesick teenager awaiting his return.

What we have is real. What we have can't be put in a box and sealed away.

But why not? Everything else in his life had been, including his family photos. They didn't even have any pictures together, she realized. It had just seemed too unsafe, too unnecessary. Of course, that was when she had assumed that they were going to be together forever. She had planned to get some pictures taken at Nimit's birthday party, where they could have been together without raising comment, but that was not to be either. What if he deactivated his FB profile tomorrow? She wouldn't have a single picture or record of him to remember him by. How long would it be before his features turned hazy in her memory? She made a mental note to download some of his profile pictures into a private folder that very day, creepy though it may have sounded. It would be a souvenir. Something to show her grandchildren when they became teenagers.

See that, kids? This was at forty-two. That's the kind of standard you should aim for...

Her rational mind came into play, snapping her back to reality. What was wrong with her? Besides, the way things were going, she wasn't even sure whether her future self would be permitted to visit her grandkids...

She wanted to go out, but the monsoons were doing their annual swansong and it was bucketing down. After the nerve-racking hell of the past few days, she just wanted to rest. Perhaps take a nap. Yes, some shuteye would give her the energy and clarity she needed. Just ten minutes, at the most.

After what felt to her like ten minutes, she woke up to see that her room and the surroundings outside had turned dark. She was appalled to see that it was after 7.00 p.m. How could anyone sleep for seven hours straight during the day? Why didn't anyone wake her up? And why was she still feeling like crap? Fumbling around in the darkness, she flicked on the bedroom lights before walking down the corridor to see Misha curled up in the living room with a Coke, watching TV.

'Heyy.'

'Why didn't you wake me?' croaked Anupama.

'You needed the rest, Mamma.'

'How's your brother?'

'Good. He's gone out.'

'What? Why didn't you tell me? What if he bumps into Charlie on the way?'

'I don't think that's going to be an issue.'

'Why?'

'Because it's Charlie he has gone out with.'

She thought she had misheard. And then the moment passed, and her heart contracted, pumping spasms of cold terror through her arteries. So this was how it was going to end, after all. Her son murdering her lover, or vice versa. Who would have guessed that one day her life would have all the makings of a Greek tragedy? She marvelled at her daughter's casual callousness, plugged into the idiot box while those two arch-nemeses were out somewhere doing God knows what.

'Before you freak out, let me just tell you that they both seemed to be pretty cool with it,' said Misha.

'W—When did you see them?'

'About an hour ago. They were on their way out as I walked in.'

'Charlie was here?'

'Yep. I thought you knew.'

What was going on? Had she just stepped into an alternate reality? Or had the past few days only been a figment of her imagination? Why weren't the cops here yet?

Her head felt light. She had just collapsed in a heap on the nearest couch when she heard the door being unlocked from outside. Nimit entered, jingling the house keys, followed by Charlie, looking dapper in a shirt, jeans and a sling bag over his shoulder. Anupama hurried over to them, scanning her son and then Charlie for battle scars. Both of them appeared unscathed, well, as unscathed as they were to begin with.

'Where were you two?'

'Oh, we had just gone out shopping for a bit,' replied Nimit.

'Shopping?'

'I owed this big boy a birthday gift,' said Charlie, reaching into his bag and taking out a pair of what appeared to be a humongous pair of fancy sunglasses with straps that went all the way around.

'Check it out! My first pair of Virtual Reality glasses!' cried Nimit excitedly.

'Nice,' exclaimed Misha from the settee.

'So … you are okay?'

'Yeah. I mean, we had a long talk, and yeah, I guess, things are fine for now,' said Nimit.

Anupama threw Charlie an awed glance. It was all she could do to not hail him as the new Messiah on the spot. Was there anything he couldn't do?

'You got a minute?' he asked, gesturing her to come aside.

Anupama hesitated, glancing at Nimit, who was busy scrutinising his new toy.

'Going in for a talk, buddy,' Charlie said to him.

'Sure, sure. Just leave the door open.'

Rolling his eyes, Charlie strolled into her room, followed by Anupama. It was only when they were inside that she was able to articulate her stupefaction, 'What just happened?'

'You're welcome.'

'What did you do? How…?'

'I'm a guy, Anu, and so is he. Let's just say that when I put myself in his shoes, it became pretty clear what the right course of action was. Although, let me just add here that your birds-and-bees talk left him quite traumatized. Next time, try keeping those graphic details to yourself.'

'What graphic details? I just said that we slept with each other.'

'Eugh.'

'Seriously? "Eugh"?'

'I mean, "eugh" from his point of view. Why would you say that?'

'I just wanted to be frank and honest with him for once.'

'Anu, he is a sixteen-year-old guy with the hormones and sexual curiosity of a sixteen-year-old guy who has just discovered that his mother is seeing the bhaiya next door. The last thing he needs is frankness! Trust me. It's a miracle he didn't jump out the window.'

'So, what did *you* tell him?'

'I just figured out what his worst fears were, and then tackled them accordingly. He didn't have a problem with me. He had a problem with what people would say about us, especially you. And of course, the whole thought of you, you know, doing it with anyone.'

'He knows I'm human too, right?'

'Again, speaking as a guy, let me just tell you that there are a couple of years of maturity to go before he can accept that. He is just learning to swim, Anu. At least let him paddle in the shallows for a while before shoving him into the deep end.'

'So, what *did* you say?'

'I told him just how pissed off I was with Sahil and how I had almost bashed him up to an inch of his life.'

Her breath caught in her throat. 'You did what?'

Charlie held up his hand. 'Let me finish. I also told him that I had warned Sahil that he would spend the rest of his life in a wheelchair unless he stayed mum about the issue or perhaps deny it claiming it was his dumb idea of a joke.'

More than anything, it was the sheer pride on Charlie's face as he narrated all this that alarmed Anupama. What kind of psycho had she introduced into their lives?

'Obviously, it's all fictional, Anu,' he said, as if reading her thoughts. 'I just said that to assuage his biggest fear of social stigma. And Sahil is in on it with me. Apparently, Mrs Mehtani gave him quite the dressing down as soon as they got back. He was genuinely remorseful and had to agree that this was the best course.'

'But ... it's a lie.'

'Which will ensure that the rest of your son's school days pass in serenity.'

She shook her head, trying to absorb it all, and failing miserably. 'And – what about us?'

'That was tricky again – thanks to your birds-and-bees talk. But in the end, he admitted he had no problem with me as a person. And when I assured him that I had absolutely no intention of taking his father's place, he was ready to give me a chance as a close friend, at least. The only condition being that in the meantime, we don't indulge in any hanky-panky without his consent.'

'Are you kidding me?'

'Well, it's not like he stays home the whole day, you know. I'm just trying to give the chap the peace of mind he needs right now. What he doesn't know won't hurt him. That's all.'

Anupama sat down on her bed, breathing deeply. 'This isn't right.'

'I know it's not ideal. I'm just trying to buy some time.'

'But that's the thing, Charlie. We don't have time. You are leaving in a couple of days. And then what?'

Charlie grinned, his eyes lighting up. 'I guess I've got something to tell you too.'

He pulled out a sheaf of papers from his bag and handed it to Anupama. It was a stamped and signed rent agreement contract for Charlie's apartment with the renewal period mentioned as:

'One year,' she said.

'I got it extended.'

She looked up at him in disbelief. 'But … your photography course—'

'I could always apply next year. If I'm still into it, that is.' He sat down beside her, clasping her hand. 'You didn't really think I was going to abandon you in all this, did you?'

Eyes moistened with relief and love, Anupama reached for him and hugged him tight. He was a marvel at eradicating one's worst fears. Charlie kissed her on the cheek warmly, burying his nose in her hair and breathing in deeply.

'God, I missed this,' he sighed.

Slowly, they parted to face each other. Their eyes had just locked for what appeared to be a deliciously suggestive moment, when Nimit materialized in the corridor outside the bedroom door. He froze at the sight of them.

'Hey, let's not push it, okay?' he muttered coldly.

'It's just a friendly hug, dude.'

'Whatever!'

30

WhatsApp group: CHARLIE NEXT DOOR ;)
Participants: Renu, Kay, Neena, Anupama

Renu: Let me just start by saying what an honour it is to have a special guest with us today. Please welcome, for the very first time on WhatsApp since its inception, Anupama!!
Neena: WELCOME DEAR! ☺
Kay: Woot woot!
Anu: Thank you, everyone. It's good to be here.
Renu: Now, the objective of this group is to formulate game plans and strategies to hitch up our dear friend with her dreamboat, and of course, have fun along the way. I hereby declare the session open.
Kay: Again, why am I on this group?
Renu: Because we need to get some perspective from the other side. And you're the only male we know with enough faltu time on his hands.
Kay left the group.
Renu added Kay.

303

Renu: Kay, stop being such a drama queen. We are here to focus on Anupama. Now, as we all know, things are going swimmingly on the Charlie front. I mean, I have to say, that whole 'cancelling-the-course-to-be-with-you' thing was just rom-com saccharine sweet.

Kay: Awwwww…

Neena: ☺

Renu: However, now we are faced with the final hurdle of meeting the prospective mother-in-law who is arriving sometime today. Need an emergency brainstorming session to devise a suitable strategy.

Kay: Why not just make a nice cup of tea?

Neena: Because it's not 1971.

Renu: Plus, we have no idea what she is like. For all you know, she could be a tea hater.

Neena: Or allergic to tea.

Kay: No one's allergic to tea.

Neena: Of course, they are. It's because of the tannins.

Anupama: Why are we discussing tea?

Renu: I suggest bowling her over with your ladylike charms. She should feel like she is in the hallowed presence of Queen Victoria herself. It should be an honour to meet you.

Kay: Yeah, intimidate the Kolhapuris out of her! Make her feel like you're the one judging her.

Anupama: I want to be with her son, not take over her country.

Neena: I have a suggestion, but it could sound a bit creepy.

Renu: Go ahead.

Neena: Just don't judge me.

Renu: C'mon Neena, we don't have all day.

Neena: Momma's boy.

Anupama: Sorry?

Neena: You know, it's said that every guy looks for his mother in his wife subconsciously.

Neena: so from that logic every mother would be…

Kay: I think I just puked inside my mouth.

Neena: I TOLD YOU NOT TO JUDGE ME!

Anupama: Neena, I'm not going to play his mother to impress his mother!

Neena: It was just a shot! Okay?

Renu: Put yourself in her shoes. Would you choose another you for Deven?

Neena: I would be delighted to!

Neena: Hello?

Neena: What happened?

Neena: I can see you guys are online!

Renu: Let's just move past the awkwardness. Anu, do you have anything in mind?

Anupama: No.

Kay: Well, that's helpful.

Anupama: I'm just thinking of going with the flow.

Kay: Say what?

Anupama: Like you said, we have no idea what she is like. Although according to Charlie she is the best woman God could have ever created on this planet.

Neena: Ugh

Anupama: So what's the point of planning anything? If it goes well, great. If it doesn't, oh well. Won't be the end of the world, would it? Besides, it's not his mother I want to be with, it's him.

Renu: Wow. I have to say I'm liking this new Anu.

Neena: Seriously, babe, you are ready.

Kay: Does Charlie have a brother?

Anupama: Thanks guys! Wish me luck!

Renu: Good luck!

Neena: Hugs and best wishes dear!

Kay: You're gonna rock it!

———

It was going to be a disaster. She knew it. She could feel it in her gut. Somehow, as the time of the fateful meeting ticked closer, the bravado that she had felt this morning began to seep out and evaporate. Why, oh why, had she agreed to this? Everything was going so well…

What mother in her right mind would approve of her? How could one synopsize in a matter of minutes, and to a complete stranger, a connection that had taken her so long to understand and accept? And why meet over tea? Such a cliché. She could have invited her over for lunch and impressed her with her culinary skills, thereby setting a positive note to begin with. Or she could have arranged to take her out for shopping and bought her something special such as – what? A gift of some sort? What if she found it offensive to be treated like a mother-in-law by a woman of her own age? But isn't that what she would eventually become if this thing were to go all the way? Who would ever consent to that? Not that she was in any position to object, having accidentally called her prospective son-in-law 'sir' four times during the past couple of times that she had met him, to Misha's mortification. She wondered what kind of person Nimit would fall for, and subconsciously prayed for that soulmate to fall within the realm of social norms at least, lest it seem like she was using her whole family to prove a point. Nevertheless, she was conscience-stricken by the very thought. He had all the freedom to go for whomever he wanted. Not that she would have any leverage to disapprove.

Her eyes remained glued to the clock. Almost five. Just a minute left.

The doorbell rang stridently, startling her. Mrs Dhillon had arrived, one minute ahead of time. So, she was one of *those* people.

Taking a deep breath, Anupama straightened her kurta, adjusted her dupatta, checked her hair, and then hurried to the door (before the lady felt compelled to press the bell again), unlocking it and pulling open the door to reveal – a rather mellow, simple-looking woman (about a foot shorter than herself) with large, wide eyes that crinkled as she smiled uncertainly. She had looked so much taller in her pictures.

'Hello, I'm Mrs Dhillon. Chandr—Charlie's mother.' Her voice was sweet, low-pitched, like the last fading note of a flute symphony.

'Hello, I'm Anupama. Please come in.'

'Should I remove my shoes here or…?'

'No, no, please don't bother.'

She stood aside as the petite lady stepped in, her eyes casually glancing around the living room as she made her way to the sofa. There was an effortless grace about her that you couldn't help but notice. She seemed like the kind of woman who could fit into anyone's party – non-intrusive, unassuming. 'Nice place you have here.'

'Thank you,' said Anupama. *Smile, breathe, nod.* 'What will you have? Tea? Coffee?'

'I'm afraid my stomach is a bit too sensitive for caffeine. Anything cold will do, though.'

'Juice?'

'Perfect.'

Although her heart was beating erratically inside her ribcage as she went to fetch the juice and ice, she was glad that the meeting was going a whole lot better than she had anticipated. No sign of animosity or awkwardness so far.

Anupama: 1, Universe: 0.

Five minutes later, they were both seated facing each other, sipping orange juice, exchanging pleasantries and smiles. It was only a matter of time before they would arrive at the crux of this conversation; but for now, she wanted to enjoy the company while she could.

'I have to say. I was quite surprised – and pleased – to hear from my son that he had found someone here. This city can be quite rough, I have heard.'

'It really depends on the person,' said Anupama, barely hearing her own words. She was surprised *then*? What was her reaction now?

'I know. I believe I should thank you for taking care of him. He would often tell me how lonely he felt out here, before he met you, of course.'

Ah-ha. Things were going much better than she had foreseen. 'It's hard to think of him as lonely. He's always so upbeat and energetic.'

'For the world, yes. But as they say, no one knows a boy like his mother.'

Anupama nodded smiling, trying hard not to think of her own rather enigmatic relationship with her son. This wasn't about her. *Focus.*

'He was right about one thing. You are very pretty.'

'Thank you,' said Anupama, willing herself to keep from blushing. Bless Renu and her daytime make-up tips.

'And very brave too, I must say.'

'Brave?'

'Of course. Not many would have the courage to do what you have.'

Anupama smiled again, somewhat uncertain about the context. 'Well, I couldn't have done it without him, obviously.'

Mrs Dhillon looked at her with placid eyes. 'He said you are different.'

'Yes … he said that to me too. I don't know what exactly he means by that, though.'

'It means that he saw something in you that he didn't see in anyone else.' The statement had all the features of being a compliment, yet something about her tone was edgy.

'Oh, okay.'

'You have two children, I believe.'

'Yes, my daughter is in college, and my son is in school. He will be passing out next year.'

Mrs Dhillon nodded. 'Charlie told me. I was sorry to hear about your son's accident. That must have been hard,' she said.

'It was. Thankfully, we are on the verge of moving on now.'

'I'm glad to hear that.'

Why was there this nagging feeling in the back of her head

that there was something more to her questions? As if she was dithering on the brink of a portentous revelation.

'He must have told you about his professions by now. The various fields he tried out and moved on until he landed here,' said Mrs Dhillon.

'Yes.'

'Did he mention his relationships?'

'No, he didn't.'

Mrs Dhillon placed her glass down on the coaster with the same deliberation that she chose her words. 'I know this is his personal matter, but I also feel that as a woman who can understand your position, I have a responsibility to tell you exactly what it is that you are getting into.'

Anupama stared at her, curious.

'His first serious relationship was with a girl who had just joined his class, back when he was in the eleventh grade,' said Mrs Dhillon, with a reminiscent twinkle in her eye. 'The odd thing about this new girl was that she never talked to anyone, even though she wasn't really mute. She had the ability to speak, she just chose not to. No amount of punishment or threats or cajoling could get her to open up. She had no friends, well at least not until Charlie came along. You know how charming he can be. The very fact that nobody wanted to be with her was what attracted him to her. She fascinated him. It wasn't long before she began responding to him too. They wouldn't talk, yet somehow, they always managed to communicate. People would make fun of them and mock them, but it didn't matter to him. Knowing that this girl – this girl who wouldn't speak to anyone, not even her parents – knowing that this girl had chosen him ... it just brought him the biggest joy. She was the soulmate he had been seeking all his life, he claimed. Things got so serious that at one point the teachers began to warn me, asking me to keep an eye on him. Perhaps even they didn't know what exactly it was that scared them, but they just felt that something was horribly wrong. I have to say I had my doubts too. My biggest fear was the day that I would have to tell him to break it off, because honestly, I didn't see a future there.'

Anupama nodded wordlessly, wondering where this was going.

'As it turned out, I didn't need to. Because one day, that girl did something that broke his heart and their relationship forever. She *talked*. She talked to Charlie because she felt he was the only person she could ever trust. She told him everything – about how she had initially begun to stay mute for attention, until it became an addiction for her. She told him about all those secrets that had long been inside her, just waiting to erupt someday – secrets that I never heard, of course. She opened up to him – fully, completely. And that was the day he saw her for what she actually was – ordinary. Just a person, like you and me. The mystery was gone, and so was the allure. Everything that he had believed about her turned out to be an illusion. There was nothing left to go on.'

With a sigh, Mrs Dhillon gazed out through the window, observing the slight drizzle that persisted at the tail end of the monsoons. 'He thought she was different, and that was how it started – every time. He has been through a few relationships in his life by now, three of which I know. Each time, it has been with a person who intrigued him in some way or the other. The girl in his theatre group who cried in her sleep, the online friend who worked for a suicide helpline after having tried to kill herself thrice in secret, the ill-tempered lady in our neighbourhood who hated children and never let anyone into her garden.'

It was all Anupama could do to remain composed. What was happening here? Wasn't this supposed to be a simple matter of tea and getting to know each other? Was she bluffing, by any chance? No, she couldn't have made this stuff up even if she wanted to.

'So ... what are you saying? That he is strangely attracted to weirdos?'

'No, it's not that simple. But like I said, no one knows a boy like his mother. You know he had gone missing for a few days when he was only six years old? We nearly went mad looking for him, and just when we had begun to imagine the worst, the police found him in a dhaba, forty kilometres away, working as a waiter.'

'Really?'

Mrs Dhillon nodded. 'The dhaba owner claimed he had no knowledge of the boy's background. He had just popped up at this place one morning and had asked for work. Presuming him to be homeless, he had taken him under his wing. Everyone around us assumed that the experience must have left him traumatized. But later that night, when I was putting him to bed, Charlie confided in me that those four days had been the happiest of his life. He hadn't got lost. He had run away. Because he wanted to live a life where he could have been anybody. What six-year-old thinks like that?'

She lowered her eyes to absently gaze at the ice melting in her glass of juice, which lay forgotten on the table, perspiring onto the coaster. 'That's the thing about my son, Anupama. He is not just a wanderer, he is a seeker. And what he seeks more than anything – are stories. That is his addiction. That is the way it has always been. As long as he feels there is a story somewhere, or within someone, he stays. And when the mystery is solved, which it will be someday, he'll be gone. He doesn't do it out of malice. That's just the way he is. You don't choose the way you were made.'

Anupama had listened to each and every word with rapt attention, analysing her tone, her words, and tried to fathom her intentions. She had waited for a loophole to present itself, a crack in her tale that she could use to disintegrate her entire theory. *You missed this*, she wanted to declare. *You missed that. You don't know him as well as you think you do.* She had waited and waited until she was done. Yet somehow, everything she said, even the parts that were hard to believe, everything seemed to fit perfectly into the Charlie she knew, or rather, thought she knew. Why hadn't he ever told her this? Or was he even aware?

She had a story – that much was true. But was that all that mattered, at the end of the day?

'Please understand, I'm not trying to discourage you,' said Mrs Dhillon gently. 'Of course, I want my son to be happy. But as of now, it's not him I am worried about. It's you. If tomorrow, he chooses to leave, would you be able to deal with it? That's what you need to think about.'

If only she knew. She had been dealing with it for the past two weeks now.

'What if he doesn't?' she asked. 'What if he never gets to know my story? What if he stays?'

Mrs Dhillon smiled sadly. 'Well then, that would be just perfect, wouldn't it?'

———

'You should go,' she said to Charlie.

'Sorry?'

'Bangalore. For that photography course. You should go.'

Charlie chuckled, taking a drag of his joint. They were on the terrace now, enjoying the cool breeze, the remnants of monsoon still sticking around, for the rains had stopped some time ago. It had been a couple of hours since his mother had left. For Anupama, that was a couple of hours of deep contemplation over what would turn out to be one of the hardest decisions in her life.

'I am serious,' said Anupama.

'I've cancelled my entry.'

'You can apply again.'

'What is up with you today? I thought you wanted me to stay. Isn't that what our whole fight was about?'

'I also want you to be happy.'

'Here we go again. Arey, I am happy, baba.'

'Then why did you apply for it in the first place?'

'I told you, I just wanted to try it out. But not at the cost of us, obviously.'

'Then try it out. That's all I am saying. Don't worry about us, seriously.'

She waited for him to refute her, to say that he wasn't interested in any more changes. That he would be happier staying here with her any day. That she was all he needed.

'I can't afford to pay three months' rent here *and* the course fees,' he said, instead.

And that was it. That was the moment – when the truth became clear for what it was rather than what she wanted it to be. A prickly pang rose in her heart, threatening to rip her apart. It was a mark of her inner strength that she was able to keep a straight face right then, in front of him, even though every bit inside her had just crumbled and collapsed.

He passed her the joint, but she ignored it and gently grasped his hand instead, pulling him to face her. 'I have thought a lot about it, Charlie. And I want to do the right thing, not just for you, but also for myself.'

'What are—'

'I want to tell you everything. The whole story.'

And so she did. That very night, on that terrace marked by moonlight and shadows, she unburdened herself to him – the secrets, the regrets, the pain and disappointments, the struggle, everything that made her *her*. By the time she was done, nothing remained to be told. The irony struck her that this man, a stranger until three months ago, was now more aware of her than her children had been their whole lives. But it had been necessary. Their future had depended on it. She had left the choice to him, and asked him to think about it, but she already knew what his decision was. The darkening of his face had been more eloquent than any verbal answer could ever be.

'I don't want to hurt you,' he said slowly.

'You won't. Trust me.'

He raised his heavy gaze to look at her. 'How do I know you will wait?' he said, half-serious.

'How do I know you will come back?'

'Then why take the risk? Why mess with something that's perfect?'

'If it's perfect, then why is it a risk?'

His eyes stayed on her, peering closely, as if there were still a secret hidden behind her eyes that they could trace out. 'You have changed, Anu.'

Anupama smiled. Wasn't that the whole point?

They had stood there for a long time after that, wrapped in each other's arms. Anupama would remember every little detail of that night forever – the smell of him, the feel of his shirt, and his chest underneath, the somewhat dewy, somewhat citrusy smell in the air, the warmth of his fingers, his back, his breath, and the malleability of time, which made the world stand still for those few minutes or hours that they were up there, unmoving, almost as a final parting gift. And that instant, when she had been a woman and he, a man, and there had been nothing between them. No walls. No secrets. No pretence. Just her as her, and him as him. Just the way it should be.

Ten Months Later…

31

The monsoons this year would be particularly long and heavy according to the weather reports, something to do with a drop in oceanic temperatures on the other side of the globe. La Niña, they called this climatic phenomenon. *The girl*. Analogous to its counterpart, El Niño – *the boy*.

She had read up on both the phenomena recently, on a whim.

'La Niña often, though not always, follows an El Niño.'

How apt, thought Anupama, smiling wryly.

Perched atop one of the jagged, coppery rocks dotting the Bandstand shoreline, she could feel the mugginess of the saline, coastal air getting displaced by a subtle, tropical coolness – the kind you could inhale into your lungs and remember fondly in hotter times. The sun was beginning to dissipate into its usual plethora of colours, as the misty horizon pulled it closer and closer towards itself. Pretty soon, nothing would be left save a weak, dull explosion of reds, yellows and oranges hovering over the greyish-blue hem, like a clumsy artist's easel.

'I've been trying to call you for some time.'

The corners of her mouth split wide in a smile that was only for him.

Turning around, she saw Charlie standing with a similar grin on his face, lit by the soft amber rays of the sunset. His hair was longer, curling at the base of his neck, the stubble still intact around his cheeks. A sling bag slung over his shoulder. His camera was inside, she knew. He had been taking it to a lot of places lately, as evidenced by the vivid photos of scenery plastered across his profile gallery. She had often wished he would upload a few pictures of himself as well. Now that she was seeing him in person after so long though, she could tell there hadn't been much change, much to her relief.

'You're late,' she said.

'Sorry, shoot took much longer than expected.'

He sat down beside her, wrapping his arms around her in what could have been an awkward embrace but wasn't. He had always been a good hugger.

'You look good,' he said.

'So do you.'

'My God, how long has it been? Almost a year?'

'I think so.'

Charlie grinned. 'See, now I was hoping you would say something like, "No, it's been ten months and six days" and I'd be like, "Whoa, that's touching" and we would both smile and gaze at each other in an HBO moment. The sunset was just right too.'

It had been ten months and fourteen days, actually, thought Anupama. He had left on a Friday.

'Sorry to disappoint you,' she said, smiling.

'How's everyone back home?'

'Good. Nimit's started prepping up for his Engineering Entrance, and Misha's waiting for her NET exams results.'

'So she wants to become a lecturer too, huh?'

'Seems like it.'

'I got a lot of hate mail from Nimit for the first few days.'

'He thought you had run away. It took me quite some time to convince him otherwise. Hope everything's fine between you now?'

'Yeah, yeah, he's started following me on Instagram too.'

The sun had set halfway through. It would be dark in a matter of minutes.

'You want to go somewhere else?' asked Charlie.

'Why?'

'I don't know. We used to have so many rules earlier. Remember?'

'A lot of things have changed since then, Charlie.'

'For good, I hope. Mrs Govindikar and the others treating you okay?'

'She has been in the US with her son for the past six months now. Mrs Chatterjee is the new chairperson of our block.'

'Seriously? How did that happen?'

'After Mrs Govindikar declined from contesting in the elections, there weren't very many options left. The only prime contenders were Mrs Mehtani and Mrs Chatterjee. Wasn't much of a competition that way.'

'Wow.'

'Yes.'

'So, I guess it should be easier for me to get a flat there now?' he said mirthfully.

Anupama smiled. 'How long are you here for?'

'A couple of days. But I'm trying to get myself transferred to Mumbai soon. Let's see.'

'Good, good.' She checked her watch.

'Do you have to leave soon?'

'I'm afraid so. I promised Renu I would help her take care of the baby tonight.'

'Oh, right. Congratulate her on my behalf.'

'I will.'

An uncertainty had come over their conversation now, thanks to the looming shadow of departure.

'Are you ...' said Charlie hesitantly, 'are you seeing someone? Just generally asking.'

'No. You?'

'No. I mean, I dated one or two girls in between, but it didn't work out.'

'Sorry to hear that.'

He shrugged. 'It wasn't anything serious.'

Slowly, he turned to look at her, the casualness gone. 'I still think about you, you know.'

His hand was hovering by hers nervously. She gave it a gentle, loving squeeze. 'I think about you too. And I'm glad you came.'

'You remember that night, the first night you confronted me in the terrace over that cream biscuits packet?'

'Yes. I must have scared the hell out of you.'

'I never told you this, but that night on the terrace, before you came in, I had just made up my mind to leave this city forever.'

Anupama's eyebrows rose in surprise.

'I hated the heat, the crowds, the closed, congested spaces, the reckless pace everywhere,' said Charlie, 'and most of all, I hated the life I was living here. Every night, I felt so lonely. I had my drinking and work buddies, of course, but that wasn't the kind of bond I was looking for. This wasn't the kind of life I was looking for. And then' – he burst into a short laugh – 'and then you came in, and everything changed.'

'I stopped you from leaving?'

'You stopped me from giving up.' He gripped her hand firmly. 'I know you think I changed your life. But the truth is, you changed mine too, in more ways than I could have imagined.'

She leaned forward to kiss him tenderly, on the cheek, her lips brushing against his stubble. He still smelt the same. The sun had gone now, leaving them both in darkness. When she drew away, there was a disturbed look in his eyes.

'What's wrong?' she asked.

'It seems absurd, doesn't it? You and I. After everything we went through, how could it not work out in the end? I mean, what was the point of all that struggle and loss and victory … how could it just end so easily? Don't you think it's weird?'

The question had the gravitas of a thought that had long tortured him. Anupama had thought about it. She needed to mean what she said, now more than ever.

'I bumped into you at a time when you needed me, just like you came into my life at a time when I needed you,' she said softly. 'We didn't plan it, right? It just happened. Maybe, that's how it was supposed to be. Maybe we met each other because we needed each other without even knowing it. And maybe … maybe, we were made for each other in a way that wasn't meant to last forever. And that's okay. I'm just glad I met you.'

'So, this is it?'

She shook her head. 'I don't know. I stopped fretting over what the future holds a long time ago, Charlie. All I know is – it's a beautiful evening, and I'm glad I'm here with you. Now.'

Charlie smiled. 'I am glad I'm here with you too.'

Simultaneously, they both got up to leave.

As they were about to part ways at the bustling boulevard, Charlie turned to her. 'I know it's too soon, but suppose, if tomorrow, I get posted here on an assignment, would you … I don't know, want to go out for a coffee with me? No baggage, just talk. Or maybe, chai and upma, if you prefer that.'

The boyishness in his request was cloyingly cute. It was like they were in college, and he was speaking to the most popular girl in his class for the first time.

'I would like that,' said Anupama, smiling.

'Great. So, I guess, I'll call you.'

'Sure.'

'You take care, Anu.'

He held out his hand for a shake, just to be on the safe side. Anupama pulled him in for a hug. And thus they stood, arms around each other, surrounded by the swarm of walkers, joggers and children moving to and fro. Unnoticed, unheeded.

———

Renu was stuck in traffic, so it would be at least twenty minutes before she got home with the baby, leaving Anupama with some time to kill as she wandered about the neighbourhood. She had just navigated her way across one of the main lanes, when the thought struck her that there was another spot around there that she was familiar with, although she had only been there once. An idea popped into her head. She wondered whether they were still open. It was worth a shot.

Feeling a little giddy with excitement, she took a rickshaw and five minutes later, she was in the reception area of the same boutique salon where she had rushed to meet Charlie almost a year ago, back when he still worked there. The receptionist was the same too. Anupama wondered if she remembered her.

'Hello, is this your first visit?' she asked sweetly. Nope, no luck there.

'Not really.'

'Would you like a haircut?'

Anupama took a deep breath. 'Yes, yes, I would.'

She was escorted into the minimalist white décor interior, where a styling chair awaited her in front of a large, asymmetric mirror. She sat down and looked around. She didn't know why she felt so excited, like it was the start of another adventure. It was almost closing time at the salon so the styling area was nearly empty, and that suited her just fine, because she had wanted this moment to be private. The stylist approached – a smiling, cheerful woman in her late twenties.

'Hi, I'm Jasmine.'

'Anupama.'

Running her fingers gently through Anupama's hair, Jasmine glanced at her through the mirror. 'So, Anupama, is there anything specific you have in mind?'

Anupama shook her head, smiling. 'Surprise me.'

Acknowledgements

This work is dedicated to a few special people in my life.

To Papa, Mamma and Tinu, for being such an incredible support system. Words can't do justice to my feelings for you, so just want to say I hope to make you prouder in the future. And thanks for being there. Love you!

To my unwavering sources of friendship, love and support in the big bad city life – Anshul, Anubha, Dharam, Pushpa. Thanks for making me smile when the times were tough for us all. It's been a long and unpredictable journey, and our bond was one of the main things that helped me get through it.

To the friends who call – Dhirendra, Sarita, Karthik, Pournima, Priya, Jyoti, Sweksha, Rachita.

To the kind souls who showed more excitement about my works than myself at times –Prats, Rucha, Ritika, Ila, Nadiya, Tarang, Aradhna, Niharika and Riddhima. Muchas gracias!

To the whole Irengbam clan back in Manipur, for the memories.

To those old buddies who just don't give up on me despite my dominant anti-social behaviour – Tanmai, Prateek,

Deepak, Atiet, Adrian, Shardu, Bora and the gang of ABH and Venky (English Honours) batch 2004-2007.

And of course, to my gurus at FTII, Venky, Impulse and the film and TV industry, who have moulded me into the writer that I am today. I thank you.

Special note of thanks to Prerna, Diya and the entire team of HarperCollins *Publishers* India, for their faith, hard work and support in bringing out this book in the form that it is today. Without them, it would just be another manuscript sitting in my cupboard. Keep the good work, guys! Thanks to Manasi, for having the first look and giving it the nod that began its journey.

Due thanks to my indomitable agent-cum-sounding board, Kanishka, for being the wizard of pitches, follow-ups, and angry emoticon reminders.

And of course, a warm note of thanks to you, dear reader, for picking this book and being a part of this journey. I look forward to hearing from you. Cheers!